# CHRISTOPHER BUSH
## THE CASE OF THE FIGHTING SOLDIER

CHRISTOPHER BUSH was born Charlie Christmas Bush in Norfolk in 1885. His father was a farm labourer and his mother a milliner. In the early years of his childhood he lived with his aunt and uncle in London before returning to Norfolk aged seven, later winning a scholarship to Thetford Grammar School.

As an adult, Bush worked as a schoolmaster for 27 years, pausing only to fight in World War One, until retiring aged 46 in 1931 to be a full-time novelist. His first novel featuring the eccentric Ludovic Travers was published in 1926, and was followed by 62 additional Travers mysteries. These are all to be republished by Dean Street Press.

Christopher Bush fought again in World War Two, and was elected a member of the prestigious Detection Club. He died in 1973.

THE LUDOVIC TRAVERS MYSTERIES
*Available from Dean Street Press*

*The Plumley Inheritance*
*The Perfect Murder Case*
*Dead Man Twice*
*Murder at Fenwold*
*Dancing Death*
*Dead Man's Music*
*Cut Throat*
*The Case of the Unfortunate Village*
*The Case of the April Fools*
*The Case of the Three Strange Faces*
*The Case of the 100% Alibis*
*The Case of the Dead Shepherd*
*The Case of the Chinese Gong*
*The Case of the Monday Murders*
*The Case of the Bonfire Body*
*The Case of the Missing Minutes*
*The Case of the Hanging Rope*
*The Case of the Tudor Queen*
*The Case of the Leaning Man*
*The Case of the Green Felt Hat*
*The Case of the Flying Donkey*
*The Case of the Climbing Rat*
*The Case of the Murdered Major*
*The Case of the Kidnapped Colonel*
*The Case of the Fighting Soldier*
*The Case of the Magic Mirror*
*The Case of the Running Mouse*
*The Case of the Platinum Blonde*
*The Case of the Corporal's Leave*
*The Case of the Missing Men*

# CHRISTOPHER BUSH

# THE CASE OF THE FIGHTING SOLDIER

With an introduction
by Curtis Evans

DEAN STREET PRESS

Published by Dean Street Press 2018

Copyright © 1942 Christopher Bush

Introduction copyright © 2018 Curtis Evans

All Rights Reserved

The right of Christopher Bush to be identified as the Author of the Work has been asserted by his estate in accordance with the Copyright, Designs and Patents Act 1988.

First published in 1942 by Cassell & Co., Ltd.

Cover by DSP

ISBN 978 1 912574 15 5

www.deanstreetpress.co.uk

# INTRODUCTION

## A Mystery Writer Goes to War

### Christopher Bush and British Detective Fiction's Fight against Hitler

After the Francophile Christopher Bush completed his series sleuth Ludovic "Ludo" Travers' nostalgic little tour of France (soon to be tragically overrun and scourged by Hitler's remorseless legions) in the pair of detective novels *The Case of the Flying Donkey* (1939) and *The Case of the Climbing Rat* (1940), the author published a trilogy of Ludo Travers mysteries drawing directly on his own recent experience in British military service: *The Case of the Murdered Major* (1941), *The Case of the Kidnapped Colonel* (1942) and *The Case of the Fighting Soldier* (1942). Together this accomplished trio of novels constitutes arguably the most notable series of wartime detective fiction (as opposed to thrillers) published in Britain during the Second World War. There are, to be sure, other interesting examples of this conflict-focused crime writing by true detective novelists, such as Gladys Mitchell's *Brazen Tongue* (1940, depicting the period of the so-called "Phoney War"), G.D.H. Cole's *Murder at the Munition Works* (1940, primarily concerned with wartime labor-management relations), John Rhode's *They Watched by Night* (1941), *Night Exercise* (1942) and *The Fourth Bomb* (1942), Miles Burton's *Up the Garden Path* (1941), *Dead Stop* (1943), *Murder, M.D.* (1943) and *Four-Ply Yarn* (1944), John Dickson Carr's *Murder in the Submarine Zone* (1940) and *She Died a Lady* (1943), Belton Cobb's *Home Guard Mystery* (1941), Margaret Cole's *Knife in the Dark* (1941), Ngaio Marsh's *Colour Scheme* (1943) and *Died in the Wool* (1945) (both set in wartime New Zealand), Christianna Brand's *Green for Danger* (1944), Freeman Wills Crofts's *Enemy Unseen* (1945) and Clifford Witting's *Subject: Murder* (1945). Yet Bush's three books seem the most informed by actual martial experience.

Like his Detection Club colleague Cecil John Charles Street (who published mysteries as both John Rhode and Miles Burton), Christopher Bush was a distinguished veteran of the First World War (though unlike Street his service seems to have consisted of administration rather than fighting in the field) who returned to active service during the second, even more globally catastrophic, "show" (as Bush termed it), albeit fairly briefly. 53 years old at the time of the German invasion of Poland and Britain's resultant entry into hostilities, Bush helped administer prisoner of war and alien internment camps, initially, it appears, at Camp No 22 (Pennylands) in Ayrshire, Scotland and Camp No 9 at Southampton, at the latter location as Adjutant Quartermaster.

In February 1940, Bush, now promoted from 2nd Lieutenant to Captain, received his final, and most controversial, commission: that of Adjutant Commandant at a prisoner-of-war and alien internment camp established in the second week of the war at the recently evacuated Taunton's School in Highfield, a suburb of Southampton. Throughout the United Kingdom 27,000 refugees and immigrants from Germany, Austria and Italy (after the latter country declared war on Britain in June 1940) were interned in camps like the one in Highfield. Bournemouth refugee Fritz Engel--a Jewish Austrian dentist who in May 1940, after Winston Churchill became Prime Minister and inaugurated his infamous "Collar the lot!" internment policy, was interned at the Highfield camp--direly recalled the brief time he spent there, before he was transferred to a larger camp on the Isle of Man, for possible shipment overseas. "I was first taken into Southampton into a building belonging to Taunton's School," he wrote in a bracing unpublished memoir, "already surrounded by electrically loaded barbed wire. . . ." (See Tony Kushner and Katharine Knox, *Refugees in an Age of Genocide: Global, National and Local Perspectives during the Twentieth Century*, 1999.)

Similarly, Desider Furst, another interned refugee Austrian Jewish dentist, wrote in his autobiography, *Home is Somewhere Else*: "[Our bus] stopped in front of a large building, a school, and the bus was surrounded by young soldiers with fixed bayonets. We had become prisoners. A large hall was turned into a dormitory, and we were each issued a blanket. The room was already fairly crowded. . . . We were fed irregularly with tea and sandwiches, and nobody bothered us. We were not even counted. I had the feeling that it was a dream or bad joke that would end soon." He was wrong, however: "After two days we were each given a paper bag with some food and put onto a train [to Liverpool] under military escort. The episode was turning serious; we were regarded as potential enemies."

Soon finding its way in one of Bush's detective novels was this highly topical setting, prudently shorn by the author of the problematic matter of alien refugee internment. (Churchill's policy became unpopular in the UK and was modified after the *Arandora Star*, an internee ship bound for Canada, was torpedoed by the Germans on July 2, 1940, leading to the deaths of nearly 1000 people on board, a tragic and needless event to which Margaret Cole darkly alludes in her pro-refugee wartime mystery *Knife in the Dark*.) All of Bush's wartime Travers trilogy mysteries were favorably received in Britain (though they were not published in the U.S.), British crime fiction critics deeming their verisimilitude impressive indeed. "Great is the gain to any tale when the author is able to provide a novel and interesting environment described with evident knowledge," pronounced Bush's Detection Club colleague E.R. Punshon in his review of one of these novels, *The Case of the Murdered Major*, in the *Manchester Guardian*.

For his part Christopher Bush in August 1940 was granted, after his promotion to to the rank of Major, indefinite release from service on medical grounds, giving him time to return full throttle to the writing of detective fiction. Although only one Ludovic Travers mystery appeared in 1940, the year the author was enmeshed in administrative affairs at Highfield, Bush published seven more Travers mysteries between 1941 and 1945, as well as four war thrillers attributed to "Michael Home," the pseudonym under which he had written mainstream fiction in the 1930s. Bush was back in the saddle--the mystery writer's saddle--again.

## The Case of the Fighting Soldier (1942)

CHRISTOPHER BUSH'S *The Case of the Fighting Soldier* opens in October 1941 (about six months after the events detailed in the previous Ludovic Travers detective novel, *The Case of the Kidnapped Colonel*), with Ludo learning that the military is transferring him yet again, this time to No. 5 School for Instructors of Home Guard at rugged Peakridge in Derbyshire, where he is to serve on the lecturing staff and likely as second-in-command. For this latest turn of events in Ludo's hectic wartime life the author was able to draw on his own experience during the First World War as a bombing instructor at the Royal Naval Air Service Station at Felixstowe, Suffolk.

While the setting of *Soldier* heavily relies on Bush's previous experience at a military training station, the dramatic underpinning of the novel--the final installment in the Ludo Travers military mystery trilogy--concerns the current-day rivalries and resentments between so-called "Regular" (full-time professional soldiers) and "Not-So-Regular" members of the army. We learn that many of the surviving British volunteers in the International Brigades, which fought for the Republican, or anti-fascist, cause in the Spanish Civil War between 1936 and 1938, are employed as Home Guard instructors, "owing to their knowledge of anti-tank warfare and devices, and of guerilla tactics." Yet the Regulars--"the products of the Staff College"--condescendingly regard these "Not-So-Regular" veterans of that Spanish "sideshow" with the mere "tolerance and mild amusement that one gives to crude but enthusiastic amateurs who have the additional demerit of not being pukka [aka genuine]." Enmity predictably ensues.

At No. 5 School at Peakridge the Spanish veterans, who form their own faction of sorts, are two in number. The first man is Mr. Ferris, aka Ferrova (he claims a Spanish father and an English mother), of whom Superintendent George Wharton of Scotland

Yard, a self-professed democrat who is acquainted with Ferris, admiringly pronounces, "He was one of those who didn't spend his time hollering about liberty; he went off to Spain to fight for it." The second man is Captain Mortar, a brash mercenary who boastfully styles himself a "fighting soldier," on account of his vast experience in a variety of "shows"—the Great War, the Spanish Civil War and conflicts in Bolivia and Mexico. (He is said to have "cursed like hell because he couldn't be in South America and Abyssinia at the same time.")

When Captain Mortar winds up rather graphically dead, "practically disintegrated" by a terrible explosion in his room (a drawing of the slain man's severed arm is included in the text), there is no shortage of suspects in what proves to have been a most cunning murder, for the self-professed "fighting soldier" antagonized most of the people at No. 5 School. Superintendent Wharton arrives on the scene, after some strings are pulled at Travers' prompting, to investigate the crime, but Ludo acquits himself more impressively at detection in this outing than in his two previous ones, making a key deduction by drawing on his considerable capacity for deciphering crossword clues.

Of Wharton we learn that he is a follower of Georges Simenon's hyper-realistic tales of policeman Jules Maigret, which were then enjoying their first boomlet of popularity in England. Inspector Maigret, Travers divulges, "was the only detective of fiction about whose quiet exploits George had frankly confessed he liked to read. And no wonder. Physically the two seemed the spit of each other, and each was a product of the same hard school and imbued with what I might call the depths of domesticity." George appears at the camp in the guise of one "Captain Wharton," a new instructor (like Travers, Wharton is a veteran of the Great War), announcing that he plans "to get this school into my skin"—an ambition which prompts Ludo to liken Wharton to the fictional Maigret, who famously solves cases by absorbing atmosphere. Wharton is duly outraged that his friend would make such a comparison, when it is, he, Wharton, who first set the example for the fictional Maigret:

"Maigret, my foot!" Wharton snorted. "I was working that line and wearing out my flat feet long before Maigret was thought of. Maigret be damned!"

"Right-ho, George," I said. "We'll consider him damned."

In the years since the publication of *The Case of the Fighting Soldier*, the fame of Inspector Maigret impressively waxed, to be sure, while that of Travers and Wharton undeniably waned. Yet happily Bush's great detective duo has been issued a reprieve from sleuthing purgatory by Dean Street Press, allowing their entertaining and intriguing exploits to be enjoyed yet again by a new generation of detection devotees.

Curtis Evans

# Chapter I

ON A CERTAIN MORNING of October, 1941, I was rung up in my office by Command. A relief was coming that morning to take over the camp from me, and I was to report at the War Office two days later. The War Office, I was assured, would communicate with me direct as to the exact time.

I was not in the least surprised, for I had known for some weeks that my camp, as then constituted, was on its last legs, and that some of us were due for a change. This is a funny war for what one might call chopping and changing. All the trains are full of troops who seem to be going somewhere new, and on the roads you see convoys who are changing areas. Maybe the War Office has inveigled recruits by assuring them that if they join the Army they will see, not the world, but England. Maybe there was all this scurrying about in the Great War, though most of it was in scurrying to France and then being lucky enough to be able to scurry back again. Now there is no France to scurry to, so the bright lads at the War House have to do the best they can.

The War Office duly sent an urgent postal telegram to the effect that I was to report at Room 299 at fourteen hours on the Thursday. That gave me ample time to initiate my successor, pack my few belongings, and get into touch with my wife and George Wharton. Bernice said she could get at least one night off from the hospital, since bombing had temporarily ceased, but George was not at the Yard, so I left him a message.

Just before two o'clock on that Thursday afternoon I was once more entering the vast annexe to the War House. The last time I was there I was in a state of mild trepidation, but now I was inured to change and anticipating with a cynical indifference the fate in store for me. What was I to be this time? A Commandant again of a Prisoner of War Camp? In charge of a camp of Italian prisoners working on the land? Was I to get a sedentary job at the War House itself, and begin the slow process of fossilisation? Was I due for some wholly new job of which the rank and file had never even heard? As it turned out, I most certainly was.

The youngish major who interviewed me was not a bad fellow, though his chest was unadorned by ribbons, even of the Coronation variety. He did the usual fingering of papers and documents while he was talking, as if to dissociate himself from things and to let me tactfully know that both he and I were in the hands of some Higher and vastly Inscrutable Providence.

"We want you to take up an appointment at Peak-ridge," he said, and waited to observe my reactions.

"That's Derbyshire, isn't it?" I said.

"Oh, yes," he told me briskly.

"But I've just come from there," I protested mildly, and was quickly wondering how I could add that my orders might have been sent direct to my old camp, and the taxpayer saved a certain expense. He frowned slightly.

"Surely that's all to the good, I mean, if you know the country and all that." Then he was going hastily on with his little piece. "The official title of the place is, No. 5 School for Instructors of Home Guard. There've been only two schools in the country hitherto, but this is something quite new. It's a fortnight's Course, for one thing, as against a week at the old schools."

I'm afraid a slightly cynical smile accompanied my question.

"What do I become exactly? An administrative officer to the Home Guard?"

"Oh, no no," he hastened to reassure me. "You'll be one of the lecturing staff and probably second-in-command."

Thereupon he told me things which I knew perhaps far better than he did. The Home Guard—then the Local Defence Volunteers—had been called into being after Dunkirk to meet the imminent threat of invasion. Slowly it had become better armed and equipped, and now it actually had, in many cases, weapons superior to those of the Regular Forces. What the Home Guard now needed therefore was skilled instruction in those weapons and in the very latest methods of attack and defence, and since the paper strength of the Home Guard was in the region of two million, an enormous number of trained instructors were needed. Hence the new schools, Peakridge among them.

The camp had been specially built and sited. It was a hutted one, and would accommodate the large resident personnel and two hundred and fifty students. These would be drawn from all ranks of the Home Guard, and liberal out-of-pocket compensations would be given and the Course itself made attractive so as to ensure full and steady support. There was a magnificent central lecture and cinema hall combined, and Peakridge had been chosen because it was handy for the industrial North and Midlands, and because the very sterile and hilly nature of the land made magnificent country for bombing, detonating, and guerrilla work. The main line station was two miles from the camp, and that, he seemed to think, was the perfect distance. One Course would follow hard on the heels of another, and after every two Courses the staff would get six days' leave. I tried to appear suitably gratified when he told me that.

"But what is my exact job?" I asked him.

"You lecture on Administration," he said. "Heaps of Company and other Commanders don't seem to be able to get the hang of the administrative side, which is becoming very important."

I had had quite a lot to do with the Home Guard at my old camp; and could have made quite a pertinent comment, which was that if the paper work demanded by the War House could drive to desperation and despair an old hand like me, then no wonder the Home Guard were often at their wits' end. My new job might be summarised by saying that among the blind, I, the one-eyed, was to be king.

But I was being handed a sheaf of papers, and most of them I knew at a glance for Army Council Instructions.

"These are all the A.C.I.s that refer to the Home Guard," my major was saying. "What we want you to do, Major Travers, is to boil them down in any way you like into about two lectures of about an hour each but not more than three. That will be a matter of arrangement between you and your Commandant, Colonel Topman."

"Very good," I said. "And when do I report at the school?"

"Saturday—the day after to-morrow," he said. "I have your railway warrant and everything here."

"Good," I said. "That gives me a tiny spot of leave. I'm due for seven days, by the way."

He shook his head with a nice mixture of reproof and consolation.

"I'm afraid you won't get much leave. When you report on Saturday, you're supposed to bring with you typewritten copies in triplicate of the actual lectures you propose to give."

"I thought there must be a catch somewhere," I said with a deliberate ruefulness, but inwardly I was not in the least perturbed. I'm a pretty fast worker for one thing, and I knew where to put my hand on a super stenographer, and I was doubly damned if I was going to let the War Office hog the first hours of leave I had had for three months.

"What's the staff like?" I ventured to ask him.

"Pretty good," he said. "A mixed lot, of course. A sprinkling of Regulars, and some Not-so-Regular." He gave me a queer look as he said that, and then was hastily going on. "Of course one needs all sorts in a job like that."

"And what's my category?" I asked him, with a fine pretence at jocularity. "Regular, or Not-so-Regular?"

"You're—well, you're quite different," he said, and blushed a bit confusedly. "I mean, we have both your records—your Service and civilian ones. That's really why you were picked out for a likely second-in-command."

I don't want to be prolix about all these preliminaries to my arrival at Peakridge, so I'll say that as far as the War House was concerned, that was that. As for the remark that the staff would consist of Regular Officers and those Not-so-Regular, I knew far more about that than my young friend had imagined when he had allowed his own feelings in the matter to be clearly read from his look. Whispers, for instance, had got abroad that in Home Guard schools there had been antagonisms between the two classes he had mentioned, and I had often wondered what truth there had been behind the rumour. Volunteers in the Spanish War, for instance, had been considerably employed, owing to their knowledge of anti-tank warfare and devices, and of guerrilla tactics. It was said that the products of the Staff College regarded these with the tolerance and mild amusement that one quietly gives to crude but enthusiastic amateurs who have the additional demerit of not being pukka. You will notice that I express no personal opinion but merely acknowledge having heard the rumours.

And if you are wondering why I have brought in the subject at all, let me say at once that what I have said is very relevant to the story I have to tell. Even before I actually reached Peakridge, rumour became something more than rumour. What I have only hinted at therefore, was something which was slowly to assume alarming, and even terrifying, proportions. After the tragedy it was to lie like a mist across the path of investigation. And since I am becoming cryptic, I will leave it at that, and let the story tell itself.

Until my wife arrived at the hotel that evening, I got down to an analysis of that bundle of A.C.I.s. Owing to a shortage of hospital staff she had to get back to duty in the middle of the morning, and I thereupon settled down with the stenographer to a compilation of the proposed lectures in spite of Bernice's strict instructions that I was, in so many words, to make those lectures a War Office headache and not my own, and get out to the Park for a constitutional instead. The reason why I did not take Bernice too seriously was that I knew she was peevish at having missed the lunch which had been fixed up with George Wharton.

If you have never met George before, his personal appearance can be fixed on your mind in a very few words. He is tallish and rather bulky, but contrives to look neither. That is because of three things: the slight stoop which he affects, the vast weeping-willow moustache which he flaunts, and the patient, harried look which his eyes deceptively bear. Those are all part of his stock-in-trade. He regards it as all to the good that no man looks less like a Superintendent, and a senior one at that, of New Scotland Yard. What he loves to be taken for is a hawker of vacuum cleaners or an insurance agent, and preferably one down on his luck. Hence perhaps the aged bowler, the overcoat with the slightly frayed velvet collar, the antiquated spectacles in their disintegrating case, and the huge handkerchief with which he divests both mouth and moustache of the remnants of a meal.

As an actor, George is in the front rank, even if his showmanship is somewhat flamboyant. Flamboyant to me, that is, for I have learned through long association to see behind the repertoire of tricks and dodges. I can interpret his grunts, his derisive snortings, his affabilities, his hypocrisies and blandishments, and I can whiff his red herrings long before he has produced them from his pocket. That doesn't mean that I regard George Wharton solely as an amiable old humbug. Those are the trappings of the man, donned for specific purposes. For the man beneath them I have an enormous affection; and for his talents, his prodigious memory and tenacity I have the profoundest and most envious admiration. In that I am at one with the Yard, one of whose unofficial experts I have long been, though I have often wondered why. At the Yard they smile when George's name is mentioned, and he has never been known as anything but "the old General," but the smile is one of affection, martinet though he can be, and the nickname a comprehensive summary of what I have just told you.

George persists in regarding me, to my face at least, as the neophyte who joined him ten years ago, but somehow that never irritates me. He forces me to theorise so that he can pick what brains I have, and he bullies or wheedles me into courses of action which I loathe. He conceals information for his own purposes and assumes a tragic and mightily offended air when he considers that I have not spilled the whole of the beans. And the curious thing is that those are the things which make him so likeable. Once when he used to wax indignant, I used to be placatory; now I know he is staging something for his own or my benefit, and I enjoy the show. It is all part of a game. He knows that I see through him, but we both enjoy the pretence that he doesn't.

George was standing lunch that Friday and we met outside a quiet little restaurant just off the Strand. It was some months since we had met, and we were glad to see each other and not ashamed to show it. But that didn't last long, for he was soon trying to pull my leg.

"Still kidding yourself you're a soldier?" he said, peering at me over the tops of his antiquated spectacles, which he had donned for the purpose of reading the menu.

"That's right, George," I said. "And what particular fraud are you putting on the market at the moment?"

He said he was still at the old game of separating the goat refugees from the sheep. Hunting had been bad, but he had collared one suspected enemy agent only the previous week. Then he was asking with something of a startled air just why I was in town. Before I could tell him, he was smiling with what he doubtless believed to be cynical amusement, and supposing that I was having yet another of my numerous leaves. I told him I had a new job, at a place called Peakridge.

I saw his eyelids give a quick flicker. Then he frowned slightly. Next he shot a look at me, and I was wondering what he was going to produce from his sleeve.

"Peakridge, eh? On the staff of that new Home Guard school?"

My fingers went to my horn-rims, a trick I have when knocked off my mental perch, or when aware of a discovery.

"So you've been prying into my private affairs," I said bitterly. "You rang Bernice and wormed it out of her, and now you're trying to make out that you've achieved it by one of your comic deductions."

George was trying to look hurt. He gave me his word that until I had just mentioned Peakridge, he had had no idea that I was going there.

"How'd you know about the Home Guard school?" I challenged him.

He delayed artistically the moment of revelation. The last of his soup had just disappeared, and he spent a good few moments wiping his mouth and moustache with florid sweeps of his voluminous handkerchief.

"The fact of the matter is," he said, "I happen to know someone else who is going there."

Then he was telling me all about it. He lives, by the way, in one of the nicest of the residential suburbs, even if there is a Tube station within a minute of his front door. Jane—Mrs.—Wharton, was friendly with a neighbour who took in one paying-guest to eke out her means. In the summer before the outbreak of war she secured a treasure, a Mr. Ferris. He was supposed to be doing something connected with the Army, and when he was not away on Army business his evenings were practically always spent in the house, for he was an enthusiastic stamp collector. In appearance he was tall, dark-haired, and looked like a student, though his age was not far short of thirty.

"And where do you come in, in all this?" I had to interpose.

"You let me tell my story in my own way," George said. "My young nephew's a stamp collector too, isn't he? Well, he was only a street away so he got into the habit of going round and spending the evenings with this Mr. Ferris. The way I got called in was because Ferris was having a little bother with the local police."

"A crook?" said I, raising my eyebrows.

"Crook—my foot!" George told me contemptuously. "No, what had happened was this. Ferris's real name was Ferrova. He was one of those who didn't spend his time hollering about liberty; he went off to Spain to fight for it."

"You needn't scowl at me, George," I said. "First you as good as call me a tin soldier, and then you're grumbling because I'm not a professional gladiator."

"A guilty conscience," he said. "Still, this chap Ferrova got to be the equivalent of a Brigadier out there, and I've heard from other sources that he was a damn' brave chap, and a brainy one. He was wounded twice, and he was one of those who got away afterwards to France. The reason why our local police were after him was because he changed his name to Ferris. He thought— and he thought right—that any foreign name wouldn't be too popular when war broke out. His father was a Spaniard, by the way, and his mother English. They're both dead now. He came to see me as soon as the local police began questioning him, and that's how I came to know all the details. He's a naturalised Englishman himself, and very pleasant and all that, but he's got a look in his eye that must have scared the livers out of some of Franco's men."

"And he's going to Peakridge?"

"Didn't I tell you so?" glared George. "I happened to meet him only this morning and he told me in the course of the little chat we had. He'd talk to me where he wouldn't open his mouth to a lot, and I don't mind telling you he's told me quite a few useful things since I got to know him."

So much for that, but naturally I had to tell George in confidence about the Regular and Not-so-Regular, to which latter category Ferris would most certainly belong. George gave a preliminary snort then exploded.

"Damn all their blasted snobbery! I'm a democrat, that's what I am. This is the people's war; not made for the benefit of a few goddam brass-hats."

I had to sh! him down for people were rather staring at us. George rumbled on for a bit before he subsided, and that was only because I proclaimed myself a hundred per cent on his side. As a matter of fact I was serious enough. People of what they are pleased to call my class, have often regarded me as eccentric because I hate convention, but convention, to my mind, is only an outward and visible sign of snobbery and class distinction. In fact, as I assured George, when I got to Peakridge, my sympathies would be with my kind—the Not-so-Regular—if any sympathies were required. Perhaps all those rumoured antagonisms were after all only a myth, and we should all be pulling together.

And that is practically all that concerns this story. What we ate and what it cost is nobody's business, but I will add that I insisted on standing cigars, of which George is inordinately fond, even if a pipe is rarely out of his mouth. It was while he was puffing away and at peace again with all the world, that he added something.

"I wouldn't mind a job like yours, you know, myself."

"I don't doubt it," I told him. "And what special nostrum would you like to inflict on the students?"

"You needn't be so goddam superior," he told me, and not undeservedly. "You're not the only one who's ever been in the Army, you know. Take that time when I copped that supposed Frenchman—"

"Not again, George," I said. "You've told me that story a dozen times. I know you were a soldier and then got transferred to Intelligence, but that isn't answering my question. What would you lecture on at Peakridge?"

"Security," he said promptly, and then chuckled as my face fell. "That's a part of modern training, isn't it? Isn't there a Security Officer to every Home Guard battalion? Couldn't I tell 'em a thing or two about tricks and dodges?"

"You certainly could," I said fervently.

He basked even in that ironic approval.

"The Old Gent isn't dead yet by a long way. You'd open your eyes, wouldn't you, if he was to turn up at this school of yours one of these days?"

"I dare say I would," I told him. "And I'll add this, George. When you do turn up, I hope to be able to stand you as good a meal as you've just stood me, and in as good company."

So much for preliminaries. All you have heard is the tuning-up of the orchestra, and the overture has not begun. You have heard of three members of the cast, if you include myself, and of four if you include Wharton. You know something of the play and the setting, and all that remains is for the orchestra to strike up.

But there is something I want to do first, and because I think it may hasten the action rather than delay it. In books one often meets a host of characters in the first two chapters, and it is hard to place them easily and associate names with what I might call functions. Now in this book it is obvious that I cannot even hint at the real names of the actors, and names have therefore to be invented. In their invention I have tried an old device, of making the name suggest the man and his duties at that School for Instructors of the Home Guard.

Colonel Topman, for instance, was the top man of the lot of us. The School Adjutant is called Harness, for if ever a man is always in harness and at everyone's beck and call, it is an adjutant, as I have had in my time good reason to know. A man called Mortar will deal with trench mortars and weapons, and one called Staff will deal with the tactics he learnt at the Staff College special course. Flick will be in charge of the school cinema, which was a valuable part of training and education. Brende will be an expert on the Bren and other arms, and Store will have charge of the armoury and explosives magazine. Compress is the school medical officer, and the last man to be tabulated—Collect—is so called because of his prosy manner and the boring nature of his delivery. In fact, I could never see him without knowing that the perfect parson had been lost to the world when he first joined the Service in the dear old days. Two other characters remain—Feeder, who was Captain Mortar's batman, and Nurse Wilton, who was far too pretty to be given a tab for a name.

And now I assure you that all the preliminaries are really over. The action begins on the Saturday morning when I took my seat in the train bound ultimately for Peakridge. I am an old traveller and I was early enough to secure a corner seat. Even first-class compartments are crammed these days, but I had for travelling companions only two youngish-looking lieutenants. For myself I was at peace with all mankind and just the least bit complacent. My proposed lectures were in triplicate, and in my small attaché-case. True there had to be three of them, but I flattered myself that they were well to the point and suitably garnished with anecdote. In an hour's time the first lunch would be on, and I had booked for it, so after a quick look at the same old news in another paper, I settled in my corner seat and closed my eyes with the hope of a half-hour's sleep.

# Chapter II

THE FACT that my eyes were closed and that I was breathing regularly, probably led my fellow passengers to believe that I was definitely asleep, and that they could get off their chests those items of scandal which would have been somewhat risky, however well disguised, for the hearing of a senior officer. At first their talk was in semi-whispers, and I could almost feel the glances cast in my direction to make sure that I really was asleep. To be perfectly frank, I would much rather have been asleep. Their conversation was of no interest to me; at least it wasn't till it began to dawn on me that the two were actually discussing Peakridge.

"A hell of a fag the station being two miles away," one said. "Will there be transport, do you think?"

"They told *me* there'd be transport," the other assured him. His voice by the way, was what I would call extremely modern—a smack of what we used to call Oxford, an echo of the more precious of the B.B.C. announcers, and plenty of Service jargon. I took a cautious peep at him. About twenty-five was his age and his plumpish face was full of good living. His hair was fair with a tinge of red, and he was growing the latest thing in military moustaches. My first impression was that he had no bad opinion of himself.

"Not bad leave, six days every month," the first speaker said. "As soon as a Course is through I'll be up to town like a bat out o' hell."

He was undoubtedly Irish, and his voice, though lacking the quality of the other's, was far more attractive. Through my almost closed eyelids I took a peep at him too, and a huge fellow he was, with hands like legs of mutton. He looked as if beer, or whisky, had been no inconsiderate portion of his ration, and yet he was good-looking enough in a florid kind of way. His face was shaved so clean that it actually shone where the light caught it, and I put his age at about thirty. His name, I was soon to gather, was Flick. The other was called Staff.

"You've got to have plenty of leave in a job like ours," Staff said. "I mean, you can't keep going at full stretch—what? I mean, we're not all Mortars."

"What's that boy-o like?" asked Flick.

"Damn-great chap like a bullock. Bigger than you, Flick. You'll see him if he comes in for lunch."

"He must be a one, the same lad," Flick said.

"Damned unpopular though," drawled Staff. "Makes you wonder how he'll fit in with the rest of us. Always a remedy though. You can always keep yourself to yourself."

"Will they still be calling him Hairy?"

"Hairy?"

"Sure," said Flick. "That was the name they had on him at the other school."

"I still don't get it."

Flick laughed. "Well, he always used to reckon himself as a he-man. You know, the hairy-chested sort. A fellow called O'Brien who was there gave me the low-down on him. He used to call himself a fighting soldier, the same lad."

"You mean, Mortar did."

"Sure. That's how he used to describe himself in his lectures."

"Sheer affectation," Staff said, "We're all fighting soldiers, aren't we? Not at the moment, perhaps, because we're doing a special job of work. What I mean is, that fighting's our game. It's only outsiders like Mortar who make a song about it."

"All the same he's one hell of a lad," insisted Flick. "Cripes, what a book he could write! And what a picture it'd make! The last war, and Mexico, and Bolivia and then Spain, and they say he cursed like hell because he couldn't be in South America and Abyssinia at the same time. Some boy-o that!"

"Oh, he's picturesque enough," granted Staff. "And he does sound a bit like the films. But it's a bit unreal, don't you think, this mercenary stuff? And if he was really all that good, why didn't he stay in the Service after the last war?"

"I did hear some yarn from this chap O'Brien about his mother and sister being wiped out in an air raid on London in the last war," Flick said. "That's why he's been looking for scraps ever since."

"Well, I suppose the Home Guard will simply lap him up. They're a very mixed lot, you know."

"They're some good lads all the same," Flick said. "But won't those boy-os love a fellow like Mortar, who sprouts barbed wire on his chest."

"My idea," said Staff, "is that there'll be a pretty strong conservative element at Peakridge that'll keep men like Mortar toeing the line. I liked Topman, didn't you?"

Flick hesitated, and I wondered why. Then he dodged the question by saying that it'd be hard going to make men like Mortar toe a line.

"Well, if you come to think of it," Staff said, "what *was* this ruddy Spanish war they all keep harping on?"

"Just a good back-yard scrap."

"Exactly. That's what Mortar and a lot of those so-called Spanish instructors won't realise. And that's what they've got to be made to realise. I don't mean openly, of course, but by—well, by force of example, if you know what I mean. I think the Colonel thinks that way, and I know Major Collect does."

I decided that the time had come to lend more realism to my supposed sleep, so with a gentle movement of the knees I made my paper slither to the floor. Evidently the touch was not a bad one, for Staff was producing from his pocket the list which I had also been given, of the Peakridge staff.

"Collect's a sound man," Staff said, eyes evidently on the list. "He was at Sandhurst the same year as my father. A personal friend of Topman, too, I believe. What's this Major Travers like? Heard anything about him?"

What happened then I can only surmise, but it was really amusing. Probably the eye of one of them caught again the crown on my British warm, and immediately there was a hush and a wonder. On the attaché-case at my side were the letters L. T., and I could imagine the two interchanging glances and raising eyebrows. What they thought of my six-foot three of lamppost leanness and my huge horn-rims, I can't say, but the voices became an inaudible whisper, though they still persisted. I am vain enough to say that I would at that moment have given the whole of the overheard conversation for only an inkling of what they might have said about myself.

The whispering continued for another quarter of an hour, and then the voice of the restaurant attendant was heard coming nearer. His head was popped into our compartment.

"Take your seats for the first lunch, please."

On he went, and I made what I hoped was an artistic awakening.

"I don't know if you've ordered lunch, sir," Staff was saying in his best Guardee manner, "but it's ready now."

"Thank you very much," I said graciously, and followed the two to the corridor. They soon out-distanced me, but there were plenty of vacant pews, and I secured one at the far end, with a strategic view of the restaurant car entrance. I was looking out for the Fighting Soldier, and in less than a minute I saw him coming in. He hesitated a moment near the table where Staff and Flick were sitting, then made straight for a table just in front of my own. During his brief progress I had a first-class front view of him.

He reminded me somewhat of Victor McLaglen, with a toughness that still showed plenty of what we are accustomed to call breeding. His eyes were held level and both his look and his movements had an assurance that were inoffensive, but part of the massive strength of the man himself. His face, curiously enough, was rather sallow, for the whole man was an embodiment of action. He had an M.C. ribbon and a double row after it, and as our eyes met for a casual moment when he turned to take his seat, I saw that his were either grey or a cold blue. His voice when I first heard it as he spoke to the waiter, was a pleasant surprise, for it was a resonant baritone and definitely attractive.

My table filled soon after that and I could see little but the broad shoulders and bull neck of Captain Mortar. When the car began gradually clearing after the meal, I saw a shortish, very plump major standing by the table of Staff and Flick. Staff was doing the talking and being most deferential. Flick was smirking a good deal and standing stiffly to attention, but all I could really see of the major was a perfect tonsure of a bald spot at the back of his head. When he moved off, both Staff and Flick gave incipient salutes, and I guessed, and rightly, that there went Major Collect, who had been at Sandhurst with Staff's father in the dear, dim, distant post-Boer-war days when Sandhurst was Sandhurst and soldiering was—well, you doubtless have your own ideas.

Mortar went out almost at once, but I stayed on over coffee and a pipe. If those two young officers had guessed who I was, and precious few brains were required for the purpose, then my presence in the compartment might make things rather awkward. The attendant told me we were only twenty minutes off Derby, so I lingered out a few minutes in a lavatory, and the brakes of the train were actually grinding when I went in to collect my gear. When the train for Peakridge drew in after a few minutes' wait, I avoided the pair and was lucky enough to get a compartment to myself.

At Peakridge station I had my first sight of Colonel Topman. He was a six-footer and as thin as myself. If you ever saw those caricatures of British Army officers that used to abound in the foreign comics, then you can visualise Topman, for he had a hooked beak, slightly protruding teeth, a red-pink complexion and a white moustache with brushed-up ends. His lips, when they closed over the teeth, made a thin, fretful kind of mouth, and his manner struck me at once as fussy, and I was having considerable apprehensions. After being my own master, as it were, for best part of a couple of years, I had every reason to wonder if this man, under whom I was about to work, was one with whom I *could* work without friction.

He had a big car by which he was standing. Collect and he greeted each other like old friends. My salute was met with a wintry smile, I was introduced to Collect, and we two were asked to get in. The rest of the staff I should see later, Topman said. Then as the car moved off he began talking about the school, and his remarks were directed at me. Collect, I gathered, already knew all there was to know; and while the Colonel spoke of this and that, put leading questions to find out my experience and capabilities, or paused to wave at some essential part of the landscape, I was aware that a most unpleasant idea was creeping into the back of my mind. George Wharton has made bitter remarks about my theorising, but if a man is right once in four times, then I claim that the fourth time is worth all. What I was now deducing was this. The Colonel was not talking to me as if I were his veritable second-in-command. It was as if he were trying to let me down gently by hinting that perhaps there was a better man for the job, none other than Major Collect, who sat nodding in assent to his superior officer's remarks, and occasionally reinforcing them with some experience or theory of his own.

As that short ride progressed, I began to be rather amused. Collect amused me, with his precise little voice; placid, parochial, and vicarial, as if indeed he had done nothing all his life but minister soothingly to some peaceful and accepting hamlet. Thank God, I am not cursed with intellectual arrogance; men, not brains, birth, and breeding, are the things that matter more than ever, but I can only present old Collect as I saw him. As for a subtle ousting of myself, well, I love a good scrap. There might be quite a lot of fun, I thought, in making sure of my ground, and standing it.

"A magnificent site for a school of this kind, don't you think?" Collect was asking me.

The camp was now in sight, and I agreed. It was certainly very open, very spacious, and all beautifully new. Behind it towered enormous hills and country that looked lovely in the late autumn sun. The actual hutments formed a rough crescent in the immediate front of which was a parade ground, large enough to be used for small demonstrations. The very large building was the lecture room, Collect said. The other large one, on the right, was the dining-room where we all fed together, building on the left, by the Adjutant's office, was the hospital.

"Must have a hospital in a show like this," the Colonel said as he got out of the car. "You never know what might happen."

An ambulance car drew in behind us, and I saw it had been used to transport some more of the staff from the station. Behind was a truck with our luggage. Orderlies appeared under a corporal, like railway porters on the platform of an incoming train. Then I noticed Ferris getting down from the ambulance. Wharton's description had been a good one, for Ferris certainly looked an intellectual. But he also looked decidedly foreign, and at once he was reminding me of someone. Almost at once I knew who that someone was—a rather better-looking De Valera, as a young man. Then I had to smile. Ferris was a Spaniard and was so De Valera, so there wasn't anything very remarkable in the resemblance after all.

It turned out that the Colonel had met the whole of his staff except myself, so Harness, who appeared from nowhere, did the introductions all round as soon as the Colonel disappeared inside the Staff Mess. Harness, a tubby, but extremely imposing little man with waxed moustaches, was obviously a Warrant Officer who had been commissioned for this new job of Adjutant to the school. He struck me as highly competent and a disciplinarian. Of such, as far as the Army is concerned, are the Kingdom of Heaven.

"Where do you want this, Captain?"

It was a Cockney voice and came from a soldier in a brand new suit of battle-dress, standing by a tin trunk that had come from the luggage truck.

"Leave it where it is, you bloody fool," Mortar told him, but not in the least annoyedly. Then he turned amiably to Harness. "That's my batman. He's a bit of a tough, but he's quite a good chap."

Harness's eyes had goggled and his face had purpled. I thought it was because of the decidedly unorthodox conversation between master and man, but there was more to it than that, as I was to learn later. But Harness said nothing then and merely handed us over to our orderlies. I found I was sharing a man with Collect.

The living-quarters were very comfortable, and except that the Colonel's room was larger than the rest, we were all housed

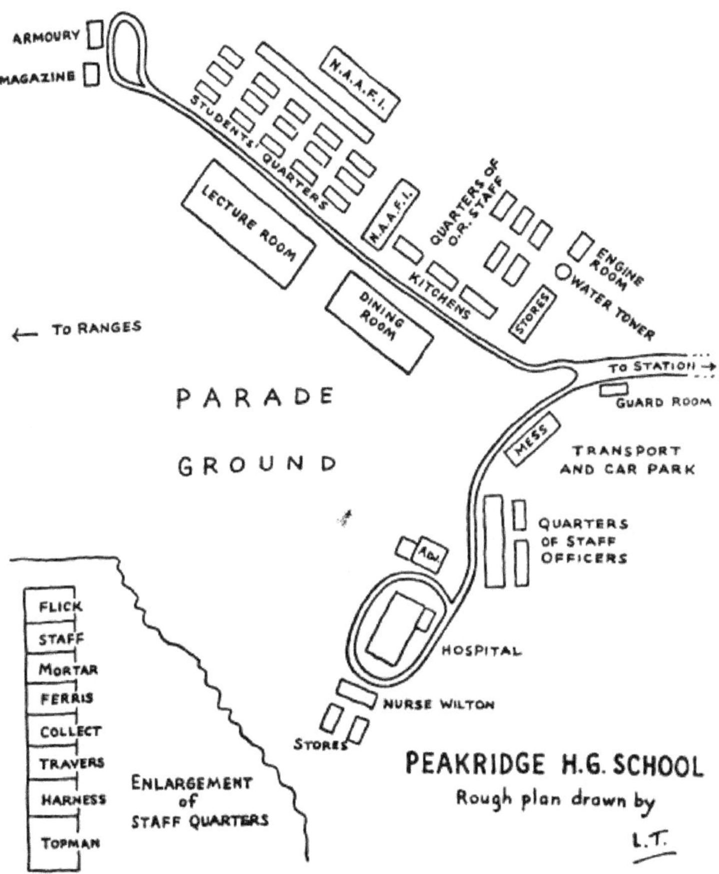

ARMOURY
MAGAZINE
STUDENTS' QUARTERS
N.A.A.F.I.
QUARTERS OF O.R. STAFF
N.A.A.F.I.
LECTURE ROOM
ENGINE ROOM
WATER TOWER
KITCHENS
STORES
DINING ROOM
← TO RANGES
TO STATION →
GUARD ROOM
PARADE
GROUND
MESS
TRANSPORT AND CAR PARK
QUARTERS OF STAFF OFFICERS
ADM
FLICK
STAFF
MORTAR
FERRIS
COLLECT
TRAVERS
HARNESS
TOPMAN
ENLARGEMENT of STAFF QUARTERS
HOSPITAL
NURSE WILTON
STORES
PEAKRIDGE H.G. SCHOOL
Rough plan drawn by
L.T.

in similar rooms partitioned off in one very long hutment. Lavatories, baths and showers lay immediately behind, while just off to the right was the Mess, as it was called, which was a large lounge and a bar for the use of the officers of the staff. After I'd had a clean up and unpacked my frugal gear, I saw that pinned on the notice-board of my room was an announcement that there was tea at four o'clock to be followed immediately by a conference in the Mess.

There was half an hour to go, so I thought I'd get my camp bearings. As I stepped out on the parade ground, Harness joined me.

"I'm sorry I didn't mention the fact to the officers just now, sir," he said. "I mean that you're the second-in-command."

"I expect they'll soon pick up the fact," I told him, but I don't mind saying I was a bit relieved, and even gratified, for an Adjutant wouldn't be wrong in his facts.

"A very fine camp you've got here," I told him, and at once he said he'd show me round. As we strolled along we got somehow to telling each other all about ourselves and we actually found that in the Great War we'd been wounded in the same engagement. I was to have quite a good friend in Harness.

As for the camp—by which term one means the material layout, as it were—if you consult the map, you should have it well in your mind, though an additional note or two might be helpful. The Magazine and the Armoury were built into the sheer walls of the rocky hills which towered round the camp and made a vast amphitheatre to its west side. N.A.A.F.I., for the benefit of the uninitiated, is a canteen and recreation hut combined of the Navy, Army, and Air Force Institutes, and the two huts of the camp were for other rank staff and students respectively. The Home Guard is a democratic institution, and the officers and N.C.O.s who comprised the students would naturally expect to share the same recreation room and bar.

Perhaps, too, when I refer to the staff, you will understand that I mean the officer, or lecturing staff. When I say general staff, I mean the hundred or so men employed in the school as assistant lecturers and instructors, sappers, gunners, general utility men, orderlies, cooks, clerical workers, and what not. Compress, who was an R.A.M.C. lieutenant, slept in the hospital. In the centre of the levelled parade ground you must imagine a flagstaff, and from it all sorts of paths led to the wide area used as ranges. There was also a drying-room for wet clothes, and I should have told you that the Staff Mess had a reading-and-writing room in addition to its bar and smoking lounge.

By the time Harness and I were strolling back across the parade ground, we were very definitely old friends. That may explain why he spoke so openly.

"What did you think about that man Feeder, sir?"

"Feeder?" I said.

"Captain Mortar's batman."

"I thought he certainly looked very much of a tough," I said. "And I wondered why a man of his age and ribbons should address his officer as Captain."

"The whole thing's very irregular," Harness said, frowning. "There's a rule that none of the officers bring their own batmen, and when I spoke to Captain Mortar just now he said he thought that applied only to the student officers. Then it turned out that Feeder had no right to wear uniform. He's not a re-enlisted man."

"What did Captain Mortar say about that?"

"He said he had permission to use Feeder at the last school, and for him to wear battle-dress. He said Feeder had been with him all over the world for the last twenty years, and that was good enough. If we wanted to fight the matter out with anybody, 'I'm a fighting man, Harness, and so's Feeder.' That's what he said."

I couldn't help smiling. Feeder had looked even more of a fighting man than his master. He looked rather like a gorilla somewhat the worse for wear, and the kind who is always spoiling for a scrap.

"I hate to have trouble just when we are starting this show," Harness was going on. "Between you and me, sir, the Colonel doesn't cotton to officers like Captain Mortar, though he's just the right sort for a school like this."

"Was he a Regular?"

"Oh, yes," said Harness promptly. "He was a Gunner and he was one of those who got fed up with things after the last war, so he sent in his papers and started out on his own, so to speak."

There was no more talk about Mortar because Harness glanced at his watch and remarked that it was after four o'clock, so we hurried to the Mess. I noticed that Mortar and Ferris had already got well acquainted, for they were sharing some joke or reminiscence with each other. My old friends Staff and Flick gave me a quick look, but I hope my face was as impassive as it had been at the moment of our first official introduction. Then the Colonel called me over to where he was sitting with Collect.

"I thought of making tea very much of a scratch meal, Travers," he said, "and we'd have it here. We ought to get away from the dining-room sometimes."

Then he was showing me an almost final draft of the syllabus for the Course, and saying what he proposed to do in the week before the first class assembled. As the same ground was gone over at the conference which followed, I shall go into no details. In fact I shall bother you with nothing about the conference either, but give you a very short summary in my own words. I preface it with the remark that Topman rose very much in my estimation after I had grasped those preliminary ideas of his. I was always to regard him as curiously prim, secretive, in many ways biased, and as one who took himself too seriously and was inclined to fuss in an emergency. But the man was no fool. And I was to gather that he was much more under the thumb of Collect than the other way about. Out of Collect's company I found in him much that was genuinely likeable.

This then was Topman's scheme as announced to the conference. Beginning on the following—Sunday—morning, we were to cram into six days a fortnight's Course. It could be done because several things could be taken for granted. Each lecturer would give his lecture in the lecture-room in the sequence as laid down in the tentative syllabus, but his audience would be his fellow lecturers. Demonstrations—though much abridged—would follow in the open air or at the ranges just as if the students were assembled, and each evening there would be an hour's conference to discuss the lectures that had been given, and to amend if necessary. Within the bounds of discipline, talk was to be frank, though the only criticism allowed was the constructive kind. On the Saturday the Colonel and I, with Collect, perhaps, would finally settle the syllabus in line with the week's happenings. The rest of the staff would have local leave, and on the Sunday the first Course of two hundred and fifty students would be arriving.

To them the Colonel would give an introductory and general lecture in the early evening, and Flick, who was to be Mess President in addition to O.C. Cinema, would explain all messing arrangements. Then on the Monday morning, at eight-thirty, the Course would fall in on the parade ground, where Harness would smarten them up in company drill. At five minutes to nine they would march to the lecture-room, and Harness would go to his office. Those lecturers not actually at work would be free, unless the Colonel needed them for any special duties.

Now that struck me as an uncommonly good scheme. It was a magnificent rehearsal for those unaccustomed to public speaking, and it would dissipate the first nervousness. Each man's lecture would be appraised by experts, and liaison between lectures and demonstrators could be made to run as smoothly as if on ball bearings. So there I leave things till after my first night's sleep. By then I had gathered a few more details about the staff. Collect, for instance, was the lecturer on Camouflage and Concealment. Ferris had been given a special commission as lieutenant. Feeder was already throwing his weight about, but was reported on as highly popular. Captain Mortar was a hard drinker, whose Mess bills were likely to outrun his pay, and curiously enough, for one of his toughness and experience, he didn't carry his liquor any too well.

# Chapter III

WHAT I MUST try to do now is to cram into a few pages the whole of that week's rehearsal. I do not think you will be bored, unless you already know all there is to know about modern weapons and tactics, and I once more assure you that all you will be told is what is absolutely essential to the story.

Something, however, must be left to your imagination, and the highlights only will be given. It might be better, too, to give the summary according to lecturers and their subjects, rather than to make you live through the week lecture by lecture and day after day. We begin then with Staff, whose subject was Tactics.

By tactics one means the correct use and application of weapons, but Staff's first lecture preceded those on weapons because it merely showed the relation of the Home Guard to modern warfare, and how the Home Guard have become the defenders of those Defences in Depth which are the latest answer to break-throughs by Panzer Divisions. Staff had his material pat, but was too academic. A little humour might have helped.

At the first conference that Sunday evening, Mortar bluntly brought the matter up.

"I don't see what you mean," Staff said rather frigidly. "Well," said Mortar, "you mentioned that when the Home Guard can't hold a defensive position any longer, they break up and become guerrillas and harry the Hun. You might add this story, which I'll give you for nothing." Thereupon he related the story of the semi-inebriated gentleman in the lounge of a commercial hotel who looked up to observe the entry of someone in uniform, and wanted to know what branch of the Service the newcomer was in. He was told, the Salvation Army.

"Who are you fighting for?" demanded the maudlin one, and he was told that the enemy was the devil. "Where're you fighting?" was the next question. "Well, last week I was in Cornwall," the other said. "Then I went to South Wales, and then up to Aberdeen, and here I am in Suffolk."

The tight gentleman regarded him with admiration. "You mayn't be winning," he said, "but, by God, you're keeping the swine on the run."

All of us, including the Colonel, laughed at that and thought it very apposite. Staff was not amused. He said it might offend the susceptibilities of any friend of the Salvation Army. Mortar said, "My foot!" or words to that effect. Staff spluttered angrily, the Colonel interposed, and there was the beginning of the feud.

Weapons can be divided for our purpose into three classes—bombs and anti-tank devices; weapons, like mortars, projectors, and bombards, that propel bombs; and finally, sub-machine and machine-guns. Mr. Brende, a first-class Warrant Officer from the staff of a famous Weapons School, lectured on what I might call the guts of weapons, that is, how they work, and how to handle them, strip them, and clean them. He was a tallish, wiry chap, with lantern jaws and a thin line of moustache, and he knew his stuff. I was sitting quite near when Mortar tried to correct him during the course of one of his lectures, and I noticed the flush on his face. Before that week had gone, it was clear that Brende and Mortar were not working together any too harmoniously. Brende resented the interferences of one who, though his immediate superior officer, was a mere dabbler compared with a super-expert like himself. Mortar's view was that as a fighting soldier he had used under war conditions many of the weapons which Brende had handled only at demonstrations. In any case, he didn't give a hoot for what Brende or anyone else thought. His method was to say what he thought, stick to his own opinions, and then go straight ahead.

On the theoretical side, Mortar dealt with the tactics of the weapons Brende had analysed, and he was in charge of demonstrations, with Brende and Ferris as right-hand men. He also lectured on what I might call official explosives—the kind of thing that one associates with the Sappers. These were, for instance, various demolitions, as the blowing up of houses and bridges; the methods and varieties of fuses, and discharge by electricity. Finally, he combined everything in one of the two lectures on

Guerrilla Tactics, showing how the Home Guard could harry the Hun. Ferris did the second guerrilla lecture.

As a lecturer Mortar was not first-class. He was none too sure of his sequences and apt to get a bit muddled, though that didn't stop him from barging on. At the evening conference, which happened to discuss his final lecture, Staff got something of his own back, though not much. Mortar had mentioned guerrilla warfare in which he had taken part, and Staff's objections related to a certain incident.

"Just read the whole paragraph from your script, Captain Mortar will you?" the Colonel said. "Then we can see what it is that Mr. Staff doesn't like."

Mortar read it:

"I'll illustrate what I mean by something that happened to me some years ago, in a certain country where there happened to be a spot of bother. We'd been trying to locate the headquarters of some other guerrillas, and we did so by sheer luck, because we had to make a detour one night on account of floods. I remember we went along a narrow stretch of water, and then we barged clean into a house right against a lock. Someone challenged us and we sheered off. That's the point I want to emphasise. The fact that there *was* a sentry told us that there was something important inside the house. That sentry ought to have kept his mouth shut, and kept flat on his belly. He could have let someone know inside the house and we might have been followed up past the lock and wiped out with a bit of resolute bombing."

I had been imagining the scene—a dark night, the stealthy movement along the banks of the canal, the house by the lock, the challenge, the hoarse whispers and the silent sheering off into the night. Staff's voice came in. "That isn't what I meant, sir. It's the next bit."

"Oh, that," Mortar said airily. "How we came back the following night and blew up the whole show with explosives. What would you have done?"

"You're referring to the unfortunate fact that there happened to be civilians in the house as well as the guerrillas, isn't that it?" the Colonel asked Staff.

"Yes, sir," He tittered slightly. "And the—well, the luscious way Captain Mortar said they'd all been wiped clean out."

"But Captain Mortar did add that that was the fortune of war," I cut in. "War is war and you've got to be ruthless."

"All the same, sir," Staff told me doggedly, "I do think a story like that creates a bad impression. If anyone did kill women and children, he needn't advertise the fact."

"Hm!" went the Colonel. "Would it make any difference to you, Mortar, if you left out that experience and substituted another?"

"Not in the least, sir," Mortar said. "I'll find something really gory. A certain other happening in Mexico."

The Colonel shot him a look. "You'd better submit it to me first. I know a certain amount of goriness, as you call it, is—well, it's essential, but we've got to be reasonably careful."

Ferris, who was already Mortar's bosom pal, lectured on Bombs and Anti-tank Devices, and he was head and shoulders above any man in the school. He never threw his weight about, or made his illustrations personal, yet you felt that he was the man who had known the things he so vividly described, and often his eyes would seem to burn and the whole man would shake with the intensity of his passion for the one great object—the killing of Germans. Like Mortar, he had fought on the side of the Spanish Republicans, and he made no bones about being as passionately now on the side of Russia, the greater backer of the Spanish Reds.

As for the remaining lectures, Staff talked about the tactical handling of regular weapons in action, the use of smoke, the defence of towns and villages, and the tackling of parachute or air-borne enemy troops, applying the latest lessons straight from Crete. It might be said that he, Brende, Mortar, and Ferris did the brunt of the lecturing work. Before the week had gone I could see the four as two: Staff and Brende, the latest thing in theory, as opposed to Mortar and Ferris, almost the latest thing in the hellish school of practice. Discipline might keep the difference beneath the surface; Mortar and Ferris, secure in experience, might ignore the attitude of the other camp or treat it with a humorous tolerance, which is far more infuriating, and yet beneath that surface there was already smouldering a pretty considerable hate.

Dear old Collect prosed away to us in two lectures on Camouflage, and even the Colonel nodded on the verge of sleep. Mortar once gave a prodigious and audible yawn, but Collect droned on unperturbed. He also gave a lecture on what he called Scoutcraft, and all I could wish was that the same talk could have been given to Ferris, who would have made it live and pulsate. Happily, he and Mortar both covered again much of the same ground, and by a little manoeuvring, and a certain shameless collaboration on my part with Mortar and Ferris, we got the Colonel to see that Collect's effort was redundant. Collect was quite peevish about its removal from the syllabus and a talk by Compress, on elementary first-aid, substituted. Mortar and Ferris were very friendly with me after that; respectful, mind you, but markedly friendly, as if counting me in on their side.

Flick ran the cinema, which operated in the huge lecture-room. He was an expert and he guaranteed to have a half-dozen experts trained by the time the first Course assembled. I regarded his work as some of the most valuable. The shows were after dinner when men need recreation. The movie—and talkie—show gave it, together with first-class instruction that supplemented both lectures and demonstrations. The captured German war films were marvellous, as were the Russian ones, and there were enough of them and similar material to last out the fortnight's course with an hour's show every night.

As for my own three lectures, I was the luckiest man on the staff. No one in that first week had a glimmering of knowledge of Administration as affecting the Home Guard, so I could blether on unchecked. Prattling is my forte, and everybody seemed to be interested and amused, especially at the sallies against our mutual enemy the dear old War House. So much then for the theory. Now for the demonstration and practice.

The vast amphitheatre which I have mentioned was nowhere more than half a mile from the centre of the camp, and its answering crescent was half a mile across, so that there was ample room for explosives work. Also it was country strictly barred from the civilian, which was a great load off our minds. Naturally precautions had to be taken, however. Men were posted on look-out. Any unexploded bombs had to be located and detonated, and a most rigid account was kept of issues and expenditures.

The bombs included the Mills—officially the No. 36—the Sticky, the big Anti-tank, and the various phosphorus bottles that flame on bursting. That with the coloured top is used in the famous Northover Projector, of which more later. The mortars included both homemade and official issues, including the famous Blacker Bombard, which is death to tanks. There were also antitank mines and traps, and fougasse. One also fired the various machine-guns, including the well-known weapon of the gangsters—the tommy-gun, or Thompson sub-machine-gun.

I should like you to imagine a road running between banks. In the side of one bank are buried drums of tar, with a propellant charge behind them, and a device to make them burn. The fuses of the charges are connected to a plunger which operates electrically from a convenient distance. Along comes your tank. At the right moment, press down the plunger, pop goes the charge, out one tar drum is blown to the road, and the rest when you want them where they make that road a real river of fire. Simple, isn't it? And most effective. Tank drivers wouldn't like it a bit.

Then there is the Northover Projector, usually known simply as the Northover. It fires the coloured bottles, as I said. We had tank models, indestructible ones, at various heights and distances, and there was some wonderful shooting. Through the air hurtled the bottles, and generally smack on the target. At once that target was concealed in the dense smoke and flame from the burning contents of the bottle. Tank drivers and crews would think even less of that than the Devil is said to think of holy water. And the Northover can also fire smoke bombs, or Mills grenades.

The Mills we also saw fired on an improved method from that which some of us used in the Great War. Now there is a cup discharger fitted to the end of the rifle, which is held for firing, and with a special cartridge, at an angle of forty-five degrees. As for the numerous mortars, they ranged from the vest-pocket type, as it were, to the huge Blacker. That fires a pretty big bomb, and where it hits there is a pretty considerable racket. A tank driver wouldn't mind that, for he'd never know what had struck him. He'd merely cease to exist, and there wouldn't be much left of his tank either. I must say I enjoyed those cold, dry half-days on the ranges, for it was healthy, hungry, and interesting work. Not only did I fire guns that I had previously only seen, but I saw in action the latest things in weapons of which I had never before heard. Everything was intensely realistic. Compress was always present in case of accident, an ambulance stood by, and Nurse Wilton was there too, watching the displays with as keen an interest as the rest of us.

I think I have hinted that she was a pretty woman. She was, in fact, a highly attractive one, and looking even younger than the twenty-six which I discovered was her age. She was of the jolly type, always ready for a joke, but according to Compress she was absolutely first-class at her particular job. Flick, whom I had suspected of being a lady-killer, seemed to me to be with her on every possible occasion, and on most evenings she was at the cinema shows.

But there was nothing even remotely resembling an accident during that week, and only one happening was really important as far as concerns this story. First of all, before telling you what actually happened, I should make one point perfectly clear. Mortar, Ferris, and Brende did not work with each other when weapons were fired or bombs thrown. Each had a class of bomb or a certain weapon, and he was assisted, if necessary, by a team drawn from the general staff. When the Blacker Bombard was fired, Brende was in charge, and he had a team of three other men.

That bombard is squat, like a toad, and into its mouth goes that winged bomb weighing twenty pounds. Details of mechanism are not necessary, and all you need know is that Brende lay behind the steel-plate that acted as guard, and aimed the bombard and fired it. The rest of us, and the team, had to lie flat, for an accident would have been a nasty business.

With my usual curiosity I was taking a surreptitious peep at the moment of firing. Off hurtled the shell, but it was aimed low. I saw a spatter of earth where it struck, and then it ricochetted off to the left. We still waited for the roar of the explosion, but nothing happened. A minute, and we were getting sheepishly to our feet. The Colonel was in a dither, and perhaps he had reason. A twenty-pound bomb was lying there somewhere, and it had to be found and rendered harmless.

Now I don't know what actually happened, for we were told to stay put while Mortar, Ferris, and Brende went off with a score of men to locate the bomb. I saw the actual country later for myself, and could verify that the search was difficult and highly dangerous, for the rocky ground was covered with briars and low growths under which that bomb might be cunningly concealed. It might even have buried itself in some softer patch of ground. At any rate, after a long wait we were told to disperse. The whole likely area was red-flagged as dangerous, and the Regular Sappers were to be informed.

Mind you, there were other outdoor demonstrations besides these on the ranges: anti-tank operations with mines and flame-throwers, for instance; smoke attacks, attacks on parachutists and supposed air-borne troops, and various guerrilla exercises. The students would also have three long spells of night operations, but those we were spared. All I can repeat is that as far as I was concerned it was a marvellous week, and invaluable as a rehearsal. As for the Home Guard personnel who would go through the full Course, I couldn't help thinking they were exceedingly lucky people.

That week also had made us of the staff well acquainted with each other. The Colonel was rarely in the Mess, and Collect was not a gregarious soul either, but the rest of us spent most of our leisure there. I did a lot of my work in the inner reading-and writing room, and Staff was often in there too. Ferris, Mortar, Flick, and less often Compress and Harness kept the bar going, though it hardly seemed worth while our having a separate bar. The idea, however, in the Colonel's mind was that the staff ought not to make themselves too familiar in the N.A.A.F.I. of the Home Guard, which was out of bounds for us as far as drinking was concerned.

One evening before dinner I was doing some writing when I heard voices raised in the bar. You may have gathered that I am the Nosiest of Parkers; at any rate I put away my writing and went to investigate. At the bar were Ferris, Mortar, and Staff, and I was in time for the following words from Mortar.

"Young feller-me-lad, what you don't keep on remembering is that I was a fighting soldier when the cradle-marks were still on your backside."

The tone was suave and condescending. Mortar was one of those people who could tell the filthiest of stories in a voice of such charm and good breeding that only afterwards did you realise how unspeakable a yarn it had been. Ferris, by the way, was holding a glass in his right hand, and his left elbow was resting on the bar counter, while a smile of quiet amusement transformed him into something avuncular and genial.

"What's all this?" I said. "A spot of leg-pulling?"

Mortar beamed at me. I've told you that he and Ferris regarded me as definitely on their side.

"Hallo, sir. Have a drink."

"Thanks," I said. "I will. I'll have a sherry, and I'll pay for it myself."

He stared. I smiled.

"You know the regulations. No standing treat. That won't stop me from drinking your very good health."

"Dammit all, sir, the Colonel stands a drink," he told me.

"So shall I when I'm a Colonel," I told him. It wasn't a particularly amusing remark, but we laughed. Staff didn't. He was standing just a little aloof, rather flushed and very much on his dignity. He wished me a good-health as I drank to all, then finished his drink and said he had a job to do. When he'd gone I shook my head at Mortar.

"You really mustn't keep baiting Staff," I said. "The last thing we want in a show like this is bad blood. We've all got to live together."

Mortar shrugged his shoulders. "I know, sir, but he's so damn' conceited. He's a bloody young whipper-snapper."

"Honestly, sir, he's devilish offensive," Ferris said.

"You listen to an old man for once," I said. "First of all, though, damn the regulations and you two have a drink with me."

When we'd said, "Here's how," and Mortar had added his private toast of: "May the skin of your bottom never cover a banjo," I talked to the two like a Dutch uncle.

"You two are fighting soldiers," I said. "Everybody grants it, but there's no need to keep harping on it. The Colonel was a fighting soldier, unless he's not entitled to his ribbons. I've been one myself."

"We know that, Major," cut in Mortar.

"Maybe," I said. "But the point's this. Staff may be what you call a fighting soldier, too, even if he hasn't had the chance to prove it. There's not so much wrong with this generation, you know. So you, and you, Ferris, pipe down on the fighting business. If the time comes when young Staff definitely shows a yellow streak, then you can reopen the subject, and I'll be with you. Meanwhile, live and let live."

That was the gist of what I told the two fire-eaters. That same night, just when I was turning in to bed, there was a tap at my door and Staff came in. In less than no time he was unburdening his soul to me. Captain Mortar was making his life hell, he said. He could stand up for himself in argument and he didn't mind being contradicted in private, but Mortar was treating him like dirt in front of N.C.O.s and men, and Staff said he was damned if he was going to stand for that.

I was rather sorry for Staff, in a way, and I talked to him, too, like a Dutch uncle. I told him to pipe down a bit on the theory business, and to try going out of his way to be friendly to Mortar and Ferris his satellite.

"Wipe out all your preconceived notions," I said. "If you'd been under heavy fire and gone through the things those two have gone through, you'd see their point of view."

Placating Mortar, he said, would be about as effective as placating a rhinoceros, but when he left my room I think I had knocked some sense into him, and I was hoping there'd be an end of unpleasantness, even if I had to confess to myself that Staff was far from a likeable person. But I did like Mortar. I should say he was as brave a thing as ever stood on two feet, and he never bragged by giving evidence to prove it. If I had still to pick a man to be alongside me in a tight corner, I would go no farther than Mortar.

I liked Ferris, too, though for me there was always something more menacing about him, for all Mortar's airy talk of gore. I still recall his lecture on guerrilla tactics by night, and the murderous knife he suddenly produced from his leg, and how his eyes gleamed as he demonstrated the quick upward thrust in the dark, and the twist of the knife before the withdrawing. It made my blood freeze as he did it, and yet in what I might call ordinary life Ferris was the mildest man alive. It was he who bought a kitten for the Mess, and looked after it. And, of course, there was his hobby of stamp-collecting.

One evening he took me round to his room, where I saw a couple of albums that represented, so he said, the pick of his collection. He was engaged in re-cataloguing, and I had to own that I was as ignorant about stamps as could be. He soon made it interesting, especially when we were looking at certain Spanish War stamps, which were certainly rare already and likely to become very valuable indeed.

"Isn't it rather dangerous leaving them in a place like this?" I said, for they were in the drawer of a flimsy chest against the partition that separated his room from Mortar's. He merely smiled quietly in that likeable way he had and said his batman was reliable, and, after all, the drawer was kept locked. I don't really know why, but I never mentioned to him that I knew George Wharton. Perhaps I said nothing because George and I, and he and George, had been talking confidentially.

Well, the week came to an end, and I was in many ways sorry. The Colonel and I, with Collect more than once thrusting himself upon us to help, reviewed results and agreed finally on the new syllabus. Everything was typed out by the Sunday morning and notices suitably posted. The afternoon was one of activity, particularly for Harness and his office, and for transport, for the latest hour of arrival for the students was five o'clock.

The whole two hundred and fifty vacancies were taken up, and when we assembled for dinner that night the huge dining-room was filled. We of the elect sat at the high table, and I could run my eye along the assembled Course. They were a fine body of men, ranging in Home Guard rank from Major down to Lance-Corporal. Many had pretty high rank in the Service, and there was one retired General who was now a Second Lieutenant. One heard all sorts of accents from the broadly provincial to the pukka and even the refained, but there was no doubt about the patriotic leaven in the lump. I felt something of a thrill at the prospect ahead, and I could think myself also a lucky man.

After the meal and the loyal toast the Colonel made his somewhat lengthy speech from the high table, and I had the suspicion that he must have practised it for the devil of a long time before the glass. But it was a good speech on the whole, especially where he said that Peakridge, new and without tradition, was in the hands of every Course that assembled there. His voice lowered rather too dramatically when he mentioned the always present possibility of accidents, and the consequent need for rigid discipline and prompt obedience to orders.

After the Colonel had sat down, Flick gave messing details, and Harness announced general routine. Then the staff filed off down the gangway between the standing students, and the immediate preliminaries were over, that night I waited for sleep with too impatient an anticipation, and I lay awake long after my usual time. Had I known what that Course was going to produce, I doubt if I'd have slept at all.

# Chapter IV

ON THE MONDAY MORNING the dry bones stirred and the camp was bustling with life. That previous week of rehearsals, much as I had enjoyed it, seemed by comparison something forced and childishly elementary. The whole atmosphere of the place had changed.

The Colonel was anxiously and fussily keen on making the school more than a success, and it was he who wanted the stamp of the pukka to be imprinted from the very start. I turned out at eight-thirty to watch the first fall-in on the parade ground, where Harness was in charge, and in his best regimental voice. Over and over again he put that double company through its paces, and made no bones about making the scathing remarks associated with the training of raw recruits. Just before nine hours the double company marched off, and for a first effort it made a brave show.

I felt something of a thrill as I saw the men swing away. There, I thought, went a visible witness to the virtues of democracy. Those two hundred and fifty men, of ages from under twenty to anything up to seventy, drawn from every trade and profession and represented by every social class, showed what free people were prepared to do in their own defence. Those two hundred and fifty were the representatives of two hundred and fifty towns, villages, and hamlets, in each of which was a Home Guard battalion or company or humble platoon, ready for Hider if ever he came.

As for the two hundred and fifty who formed the Course, they looked fit and keen, and the smartness of their movements was a revelation to me, in spite of Harness's upbraidings and exhortations. But it was in the lecture-room that one really became aware of the keenness. I found it disconcerting at first talking to men whose eyes were on their notebooks and then on myself, with faces disappearing as others bent down to write. But the real test was at the end, when I asked for questions. My first request produced a barrage, and there wasn't one that wasn't pertinent. When my lecture was over and I was making my way through the room, I was still besieged by students who wanted to know this and that. As a result of that and similar reports by others of the staff, the Colonel instituted a special half-hour from six o'clock to six-thirty when the staff assembled in the N.A.A.F.I., which was closed for other purposes, and became a kind of Advice Bureau.

Just one other word about myself, for you'll probably be thinking that with only three lectures of an hour each to be delivered in a fortnight, I was about to have a remarkably easy time. But there was more to it than that. The Colonel and I took alternate half-days of general supervision, so as to keep a constant finger on the pulse of things. Then at the end of the second week there were all the notebooks to examine and to assess the passing-out standards of students according to the instructors' reports. That would mean at least two days off my supposed week's leave at the end of two complete Courses. That supervision, taking me as it did to lectures and demonstrations, and all over the camp, was to be invaluable at the investigation into the first of the tragedies that happened. What I propose to do, therefore, is once more to give you the highlights. You may regard them as a series of apparently disconnected happenings. I prefer to say that I am making you wise *before* the event. You will see only the pertinent happenings before the tragedy when I came to look back I had to sort out the pertinent ones from a score of other happenings.

One other little thing. I am a student of human nature, and you may not see things through my eyes, hard as I may try to make you do so. Mind you, I am not boasting. To be a student is to be patently ignorant, but perhaps you will allow me to explain for your own benefit just what the statement means. My wife used to accuse me of staring at the contents of any new room into which I was shown. That was my collector's instinct, appraising other people's pictures, furniture, and china. That became less of a passion when I began years ago working with George Wharton. Then I had to transfer my instincts of curiosity to people. I got in the habit of trying to place strangers, and of assessing the motives of acquaintances, and generally of trying to get clean into the skins of the people who mattered. That's all that I mean by being a student of my fellow men.

The Home Guard simply loved Mortar and Ferris. They knew what their own role was in defeating Hitler's attempts at invasion, and they liked to be taught by practical men. The lectures on guerrilla warfare were the most popular of all, and no wonder.

"You know there's a sentry or a watcher just ahead of you in the black night," Mortar might say. "What would you do? You freeze into immobility like a cat. Ever watch a cat hunting? Have a look at it next time and watch what it does. Watch it move forward inch by inch. You wouldn't hear a sound if you were half an inch off it. Then it springs, like a marble from a catapult, and God help the mouse or the bird. Now one of you come here. Not you—that big fellow."

Up would come some strapping fellow to the platform. Mortar would say all lights were going out, and he himself was to be the stalker and the student the sentry. Off would go Mortar's boots and out would go the lights. In about a couple of minutes there would be a shout of "Lights on!" There would be Mortar with that sentry's throat in his grip.

"No weapons, gentlemen. Not even Mr. Ferris's little knife. Just get your hands like this, and your legs like this and then hold on. Try it in your dormitory hut to-night. Try it in your drill halls when you get home. If you're the bigger man, don't wait for him to collapse. Just give a little jerk like this. Wait for the crack of the bones, then that little job's over."

One thing I should relate which struck me as rather amusing at the time. I was going by Flick's room one evening when I heard the very deuce of a clatter going on inside. So astounding was it that I tapped at the door and peeped inside. Two startled and very sheepish people regarded me—Harness and Flick. They had been practising that thuggery business, and I had to laugh as I apologised for the intrusion, for their faces were red and the sweat shining on their foreheads.

"Boys will be boys," I said. "And who was the winner?"

"Look at his fists," Harness told me indignantly. "Just like a pair of hams. I reckon I ought to be handicapped."

"Look at the shoulders on him," Flick told me, with a brogue which I have never attempted to convey. "He's the one who should have the handicapping. And what about yourself, Major?" he told me. "What about you and me having a try?"

"God forbid," I told him, and hastily backed out of the door.

Then there was Ferris, a fanatic when it came to killing Germans, anywhere and anyhow. That twist of his knife still curdled my blood, and the menacing voice was as bloodcurdling too. The greatest tribute I can pay to Ferris is to say that during his guerrilla lectures there were few notes taken. Men were so eager not to miss a word or a gesture that their eyes rarely left the speaker's face.

One thing did strike me as peculiar about Ferris's illustrations, and yet I suppose there was no real reason to think them so. He was talking to a British audience, and yet he never based his own hatred of the Hun on such things as indiscriminate bombing, which should have had a sure appeal. What he told his hearers was the record of murder, massacre, and duplicity in Spain. Nothing peculiar about that, you may say, for his sole experience had been in Spain, and the man himself was a Spaniard, incredible though it was to take him for other than English.

To sum up Mortar and Ferris—who, by the way, was to me also so essentially British that I never thought of him as Ferrova—I will say that about Brende and Staff, excellent lecturers though they were, there was always something a bit too academic. Each knew his subjects pat, but there was the one thing lacking. Each lacked the fervour of killing. Don't think I'm aping the fire-eater, but I knew, as the Home Guard knew, that in this war you either kill or get killed. And the Home Guard were at Peakridge to learn how to achieve the one and avoid the other. From Brende and Staff they learned things; from Mortar and Ferris they not only learned but they experienced.

Between Mortar and Ferris there was never the faintest suspicion of jealousy. Each quoted the other, and they dovetailed perfectly. Each praised the other to me behind that other's back. Mortar said his greatest ambition in this war was to spend a few dark nights in France in Ferris's company. Ferris spoke of Mortar as of a superior officer in whom one had unlimited confidence. I thought even more of Ferris after that, for in Spain it had been the younger man who had held far the higher rank and had made the greater reputation. And so much for what I might call things in the open. Behind the scenes; behind the stirring, pulsating life of the school and its colour and movement and noise, other things were quietly and dangerously stirring.

Mortar had a genius for making enemies. Harness never really liked him, but he was the only one on the borderline. The rest made no secret of their dislike or loathing. Staff and he were no longer on speaking terms, so I was a failure as a peacemaker. Slowly we began to form up into two definite camps, with myself as a kind of liaison officer. Mortar, Ferris, and Flick—though less definitely—were one camp, at least at first, and the Colonel, Collect, and Staff the other. Brende, as a Warrant Officer, had only courtesy access to the Mess, and rarely availed himself of it, but he was very definitely an anti-Mortarite.

By the way, there was rather a peculiar happening one morning. I was off duty so I strolled round for a breather. The regular Sappers were due the following day to recover that unexploded bomb, and I made my way in that direction. It was bad walking country, and what with the rocks and undergrowth and red flags everywhere.

I soon decided it was no spot for a constitutional. Then as I was turning back I caught a movement. Someone was well ahead of me and searching for that bomb, and who should that someone be but old Collect!

Why should I be so startled? Well, there was a tubby, academic cove like Collect grubbing about in country where at any moment some contact with that twenty-pound bomb might send him sky-high, and if he was not looking for the bomb, then what on earth was he doing there? Moreover, he must have known himself to be doing something suspicious, for no sooner did he catch sight of me than he was out of sight like a shot, for there was plenty of handy cover for concealment, let alone pockets of dead ground.

As for Collect's reasons for loathing Mortar, there was of course a very deep jealousy of the success of the man as a lecturer and his popularity with the Course and general staff. Collect had no use for me, if it comes to that, even if he covered that particular jealousy by effusiveness. And he had never forgiven that loss of his own lecture on Scoutcraft, and the plain speaking there had been at the particular conference which sat in judgment on it. Collect, I knew, was a bad hater, and when I came to theorise to myself I thought he was trying to locate the bomb so as in some way to discredit either Mortar or Ferris, even if Brende had been responsible for aiming and firing the bombard.

I said that Flick was at first one of the Not-so-Regular gang. That lasted for about a week, and then he transferred to the other camp. One night I was taking my usual ten minutes' stroll before turning in, when I barged almost full into a couple strolling towards the hospital. I sheered off at once, but I knew that one of the promenaders was Nurse Wilton, and the other I guessed was Flick. Then, as I came to the door of my room, I actually saw Flick, for he came round my end of the hut to get to his own room at the north end.

The following evening I was doing some writing in the Mess. I had gone in as usual to finish a job just before dinner, and when I came out to the bar, Ferris and Mortar were having a drink. I gathered that as far as Mortar was concerned it was one of a series, for he was carrying almost his full load.

The wireless was in full blast just inside the room. It was a new set and we had asked to have it there so that we could listen to the news.

"Turn the damn' thing off, Major, will you?" Mortar said airily. "You can't hear your ruddy self speak."

It was a bit raucous, for a noisy variety show was on.

"If there's one thing I loathe it's the B.B.C. comedians trying to be Irish," Ferris said. "How a regular boy-o like Flick can stand it beats me."

"You've got a bit of an Irish accent at times," I said, and so he had, though it was only when he was excited that I had thought I recognised it.

He looked surprised and even startled. Then he smiled. "Sure I have," he said, and with none too good a try at the real thing. "Plenty of Irishmen in Spain, weren't there, old-timer?"

Mortar nodded, being engaged at the time in finishing his drink.

"I generally worked with the Irish in my Brigade," Ferris said.

"Good at a scrap—the Irish," Mortar said.

"My God, yes," Ferris said, and gave a reminiscent kind of nod.

"What you might call fighting soldiers," I added maliciously.

Ferris grinned a bit sheepishly, then asked me to have a drink. I did a glance round. "Well, seeing we're in good company, I don't know that I won't," I said.

Ferris ordered three drinks, then changed his mind and made it two.

"None for you, old-timer," he told Mortar. "What about that job of work you had to do?"

"My God, yes!" said Mortar. He lifted his glass to make sure there was definitely nothing more in it, gave me a cheerful and rather tottery salute, and went off.

"Where's Flick?" I asked. "Isn't he a regular caller at about this time?"

Ferris shrugged his shoulders.

"Come on," I said. "Out with it. What's in the wind now?"

Ferris frowned with a kind of secrecy. "I rather think Mortar's pinched Flick's girl."

I raised my eyebrows.

"Mortar's a bit of a lady's man," Ferris went on. "He had a narrow escape from a rather peeved husband in Spain."

I had to frown. "Why don't you keep him a bit more in check? Never knew such a pair as you are for stirring up trouble. Well, not you," I added, at the surprise in his face. "And look at things from the lady's point of view. These things get around and her name oughtn't to be bandied about. She's here on a serious job, not for fooling around with members of the staff."

"I think you've got the wrong angle, sir," Ferris told me, and rather amusedly. "It's the lady who's a bit flighty."

"The devil she is!" I said ruefully, and then had to bolt the rest of my drink, for there was the sound of the second bugle. I was not too pleased with myself either, as I made my way to the dining hut. I ought to have known that, since the man I saw with Nurse Wilton wasn't Flick, then it must have been Mortar, for the two were exactly alike in build.

Beneath the surface, then, there was an atmosphere of strain that made the communal life of the staff more than uncomfortable for a lover of peace like myself. By the end of the first week it had become more than a perceptible undercurrent. For one thing, the seats at the high table had been rearranged. Staff had sat at first alongside Ferris, but suddenly they were changed till, as you looked along the table from left to right, they ran— Ferris, Compress, Mortar, Travers, Topman, Collect, Harness, Flick, and Staff. Flick must have been responsible for the changes, in his capacity of Messing Officer, but undoubtedly Collect had also had a hand in it. Baulked of his supposed prize of the appointment of second-in-command, he had transferred his interference to Flick's department, and Flick, I had gathered, was only too willing for the Reverend—as Mortar and Ferris aptly nicknamed him—to get on with the job.

Then there were all sorts of furtive whisperings and nods and undoubted intrigues. Staff was clinging to Collect's cassock, and I became aware of surreptitious visits and approaches to the Colonel. Altogether, as I said, there was little communal life that wasn't sham, and for the life of me I couldn't see how to remedy matters. What I actually began to hope was that there might be a real explosion of some sort, which would give me the chance to do some plain speaking, and somehow get the air a bit clear.

Then something did happen. The Colonel asked me one night after dinner to come to his room.

"Make yourself comfortable, Travers," he said, and that wasn't difficult, for there were a couple of easy-chairs in the room, and a better electric stove than most. I was not particularly keen on a drink, but he was having a whisky and soda so I had one, too. Then we talked about the Russians and the ups and downs of the war, and all the time I was wondering when he was coming to the real point, and what that point was.

"And how do you think things are going here?" he asked at last.

I told him I thought they were going magnificently. The Course was keen as mustard, and the way they marched off the parade ground that morning would have made a regular battalion envious.

"Yes, yes," he said, just a bit impatiently and as if he had expected me to give him an opening. Then he took a positive header, and before I was hardly ready.

"What's your opinion of Captain Mortar?"

"Captain Mortar, sir?" I echoed rather feebly. "Well, I think he's a first-class man and an asset to the school. Mind you, sir, I know he has his faults."

"Ah!" went the Colonel, and I knew he had what he wanted. From then on I knew, too, though the voice was of the commandant, the words were the words of Collect.

"That's something I wanted to talk over with you in confidence," he went on. "You're the sort of fellow who gives everybody credit. Don't deny it, Travers. I know, and it's a fine spirit to have. All the same, we've got to think of wider—er—implications. My own information, and my own ideas, of course, are that Captain Mortar is having not so good an influence as you'd think." He cleared his throat noisily, then produced the bombshell. "In fact, I don't know that I'm not of the opinion that we oughtn't to get him transferred."

I did some quick and hard thinking. "Suppose such action struck you as essential, sir, wouldn't it be difficult? Doesn't Mortar hold an appointment direct from War Office? I mean, there'd have to be a confidential report. Later on he'd have to see it, and he'd have the right of appeal."

"I know, I know," he told me impatiently. "I thought you were pretty astute, and you might suggest a way round."

Now if there's one thing that can get my back up, it's to be called astute.

"There's the regulations, sir," I said laconically, and brought the subject nearer home. "But do you mind telling me the precise charges against Captain Mortar? The charges that would form the basis of your confidential report?"

That had him. Mortar was a heavy drinker, he said, and it wasn't thinkable that he should be obviously under the influence of drink at the high table where the whole Course could see him. I said I thought that a slight exaggeration, and that what mattered was that Mortar was always cold sober when about the jobs that mattered. Then the Colonel said Mortar was cantankerous, and lacking in discipline.

"His manner's always perfect towards me," I said.

"I mean general discipline," he said, and snorted. "What's the man been these last few years? Nothing but a kind of pirate. There's that man of his too—Feeder. He's here in defiance of regulations. A horrible fellow, and looks like a savage."

"His ribbons show a first-class fighting record," I pointed out.

"What are those other two ribbons he wears?"

"One's the Croix de Guerre—I admit it's a bit dirty and I believe the other's a French decoration too. Something to do with the Foreign Legion."

"Ah!" said the Colonel. "Has he permission to wear it?"

"That's a matter for Harness, sir," I pointed out.

"Exactly, exactly," he said, and frowned. "The trouble about the whole thing is that I think Mortar has influence."

"Of what sort, sir?"

"Well, between ourselves, Government influence. This Labour element, you know. Lacking in discipline, and full of intrigue."

What could one say to a man like that? A war on, and his rule of measurement was still the dear old Conservative Party. I did make some further protests, and, in fact, I think I induced him to refrain from all action till after the completion of the first two Courses. If the faults of Mortar became more heinous, then by that time there might be an unanswerable case to put forward, influence or no influence. If Mortar could be cured of some of his faults then the situation would not arise.

But the whole business infuriated me. That the Colonel had been nobbled, there was no doubt. There he was, professing to have nothing at heart but the success of the school, and yet lending himself to subterranean intrigues. One could make excuses, but it was still a bad business. The way I ended the whole thing was by suggesting that I might have a word with Feeder, after a brief inquiry into the eccentricities that were apparently making him, according to the Colonel, as notorious as his master.

The Colonel and I parted the best of friends, at least on the surface. He told me he had been and was still very worried because the Sappers had not found that bomb. He had written a snorter of a letter about it and insisted on a larger search-party. I agreed that it was certainly disconcerting to have that bomb somewhere around, and did venture to point out that it wasn't a danger.

The following morning, which was a Saturday, Mortar was lecturing, so I made my way to his room, where I knew Feeder was having the usual clean out. Who should be there but Ferris, sitting at his ease and yarning with Feeder while he worked. I gave a private signal for Ferris to clear off.

"Mr. Ferris is a rare nice gentleman," Feeder told me. "Him and me often have a yarn about old times."

"You were in Spain?" I asked.

"In Spain!" He snorted contemptuously. "Was I bloody well not! The Captain and me have been together since '19."

It was an interesting story he told me. He had been down and out and had tried singing from street to street. Mortar had come up and questioned him and had then taken him straight into his employ, and the two had been together ever since, except for a spell of five years, when Feeder himself had got fed up with the absence of a fighting job and had joined the Foreign Legion after a first-rate row with Mortar. Mortar had bought him out again, for the express purpose of taking him to Spain. His fifth ribbon, he told me, was a French Colonial one, and, in his own words, "For something I and another couple of blokes done after some of our gang had been scuppered out at El Aglish." It was dirty, as was the Croix de Guerre, because he kept those two original pieces of ribbon as souvenirs.

I think he rather liked me, for he allowed me to talk to him like a father, though doubtless he had his tongue well in his cheek. I liked him too, even if his free and easy discipline was somewhat disconcerting, for once he actually addressed me as "chum," and he more than once assured me that the Captain thought a lot of me.

Well, that was that. I hadn't done all I had outlined to the Colonel, but I hoped I had put oil and not sand in the general works. Mortar said to me later in the day, "I hear you've been doing a bit of spit and polish with Feeder, sir. That'll do the swine good." I knew the term was one of affection, and I could deduce that between master and man there were precious few secrets.

And now you know as much as I do about all those things which were later discovered to be essential clues. On the following Monday was to be the first of the queer accidents that culminated in the appalling tragedy.

# Chapter V

I WAS ON DUTY on the Monday morning, and at ten-thirty hours I made my way to the ranges where firing was to take place. By the way, this seems a good moment to set some settled policy about the use of the Army twenty-four hour clock. From now on, then, we shall use the time as used at the school, and it isn't so difficult to get accustomed to recognising, say, eighteen hours as being six o'clock in the early evening.

Firing was actually to take place at eleven hours, and was to be with the rifle and the Northover each firing Mills bombs. Mortar and Ferris and Brende each took a third of the students for the actual firing of the rifles, and then the whole Course gathered round while Mortar fired the Northover projector. They made a crescent, standing a good forty yards back, for, as Mortar and others had already explained, there was just the faint danger of an accident.

For the benefit of those who are not acquainted with the most famous of all bombs—the Mills—let me give a brief description, and then you will appreciate what Mortar meant when he assured the spectators that an accident was an improbable thing. Once more I must pause to do a little explaining. No official secrets are being given away to the Germans by calling the Mills by its correct name or by printing this diagram. They must have captured many thousands of them in the last war, and they know as much about the Mills as we do.

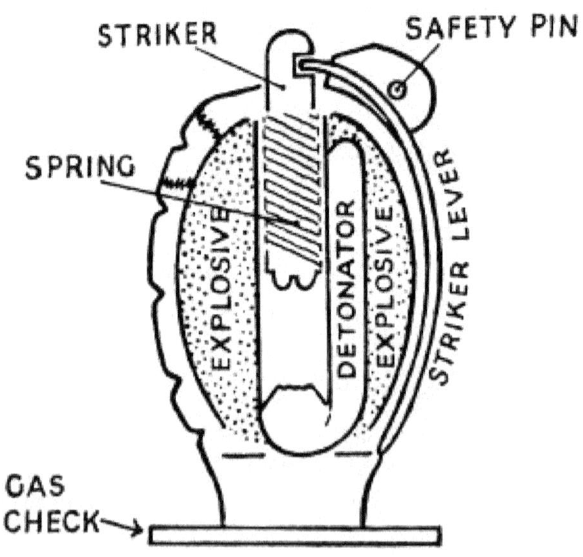

A Mills bomb is roughly the shape and size of a good lemon. Inside is the high explosive, and a detonator with a fuse attached. The fuse, which may be a four seconds' one, is set off by the action of the striking hammer, and this is held in place by a lever which retains the spring. The lever arm is outside the bomb and kept secure by a pin. When your fingers close round the bomb, and therefore round the lever, the lever is held in place even if you pull out the pin. When you throw the bomb, the lever flies up, the spring is released, down goes the hammer, the fuse begins to burn, and in four seconds the bomb explodes.

Now it so happens that the barrel of the Northover is just large enough to admit the Mills bomb, so that you can fire a Mills from it by exactly the same method as the phosphorus bottle. But the point I wish to make clear is that when you put the Mills in the barrel, with the pin out, the lever cannot move since the bomb nestles in comfortably. When you put in the charge and fire, if some obstacle in the barrel stops the bomb from coming out, there can't be an accident, for until the bomb actually leaves the barrel, the lever can't spring off.

But suppose the obstacle in the barrel, and it may be some slight roughness, is sufficient to check the speed of the bomb after the firing of the charge but still not enough to stop it emerging from the barrel, then it is clear that the bomb may fall anywhere between the end of the barrel and the target it should have reached. If the obstacle has been rather serious, then the bomb may fall only a foot or so away from the front of the projector. In that case the gun crew have four seconds, or just under, in which to spring back and drop flat.

Mortar was acting as second man, that is to say, he was aiming and firing the projector, and a sergeant of the general staff was his number three, or loader. Number one was unnecessary, for his job is to look out for targets and warn of enemy approach. We all stood with our eyes on the target at which Mortar was firing, for we were familiar with the working of the simple mechanism, and in any case Mortar's bulk hid the front of the projector.

The breach slammed to, the cap was put on, Mortar crouched and almost at once there was the plop! of the cordite charge. But no Mills came hurtling out. Two seconds must have passed in the wonder of what had happened, then came the roar of Mortar's voice.

"Get down, you bloody fool!"

He had leapt round and had grabbed the sergeant by the collar, and as the two went flat to the ground, the bomb went off, and about a yard from the front of the projector. Flying debris was in the air and spattered down on our steel helmets, but I was running forward. Mortar was on his feet again as I got to him, and he was shouting to the others to stay put.

"Nothing to get the wind up about," he shouted. "Just a little mistake that couldn't happen again if we tried."

"Get the other gun," he told the sergeant, who was looking a bit shaky; and then *sotto voce* to me, "We'd better carry right on with the other gun. It won't do to let those men think there's any risk."

I didn't ask any questions because that might have given the impression that danger was in the air. But it certainly had been. Even if both men had gone to ground at once, either might have been hit by shrapnel flying sideways. As it was, the sergeant had stood like a stoat-scared rabbit for two valuable seconds, and if Mortar hadn't yanked him over, heaven knows what might have happened.

Well, the second gun was brought, for the first had a nasty dent or two in the end of its barrel. Mortar took infinite pains in squinting down the barrel of the second gun, and he took a Mills with the pin in and let it slide down from the top to the breach. Then he waved the men to come forward.

"This gun is going to fire all right," he told them. "What happened with the other one was that a tiny piece of something was in the barrel and we didn't spot it. Even so, the Mills came out, as you saw, and we had tons of time to get clear. But you don't want that happening too often, especially when it puts a gun out of action. And it won't happen if you use elementary care. This is the first time I've ever known it happen. Now get back again and you'll see this gun fire perfectly."

And it did fire perfectly. When the men gathered round again afterwards, Mortar explained things by saying a leaf must have blown down the barrel and lodged there after he had looked down it. That was a plausible explanation, for it was a gusty day and leaves were scurrying everywhere.

"Just the most elementary care," he said in his final summary. "That's all you need. If the barrel's clear, the gun must fire right. What you saw happen this morning couldn't happen again in a million years."

That firing was the concluding item of the morning, and when the men dispersed, Brende and Ferris came across. "What'd you do wrong, sir?" Brende asked.

Mortar's eyes narrowed. "Wrong be damned! When I looked down the barrel, it was clear."

"You think it really was a leaf?"

"You heard me," Mortar told him curtly.

"The trouble is," I said, "that you can't examine the actual bomb to see if anything did adhere to it. The bomb's in a million pieces."

"But you can examine the barrel, sir," Brende said. "I'll take it and have a real good look."

"No, you don't," Mortar said. "I'm the one who's going to have the real good look."

As I moved off I saw Mortar and Ferris interchange glances. What I had to do was to report the matter to the Colonel, and at once. He was in a high state of perturbation. The worst possible thing that could have happened, he said. Nothing like accidents for giving a school a bad name. I quietened him down considerably, and I took advantage of the opportunity to tell him that Mortar's conduct had been more than admirable, and that many a man had got a medal for less than he had done. The only person to criticise was the sergeant, who had momentarily lost his nerve, and he ought to be dropped from the squad.

But the gun had to go back to Ordnance, and a report with it, so we held a local Court of Inquiry. Nothing emerged beyond what you already know, and the cause of the stoppage in the barrel was given just as Mortar had explained it. Nothing whatever had been found in the barrel when he and Ferris had examined it, so whatever had caused the obstruction had come out with the bomb.

That was satisfactory enough, but what I didn't like was the satisfaction I detected in the Colonel's manner. Brende or someone must have got at him privately and put in more than a hint of carelessness on Mortar's part. In a dozen ways I could tell that one more accident, however trivial, when Mortar was in charge, would give the Colonel just the final pretext he wanted to rid the school of one whom he had been induced to consider undesirable.

I was on duty on the Tuesday afternoon, and then off again on the Wednesday morning. I listened to the last part of Ferris's final lecture on bombing, and then went out with the Course to the practice bombing ground, where, with Mortar as principal judge and three staff sergeants as assessors, the dummy-throwing was to take place on which the merits of the throwers would be noted, and their fitness as bombing instructors when they got back to their units.

The men had already been weeded out, and there were about a hundred of them left. They were lined up in two very open lines facing each other with a distance of a hundred yards between. The sergeants and Mortar stood on the flanks of each line, so as to watch the actions of the particular thrower, and Ferris conducted operations from the middle of the dead ground into which the dummy bombs would be thrown.

He had a voice that carried none too well, and again it was a blustering, cold day, so he moved along the centre of that dead ground, turning each way to make his voice carry. What happened was so sudden and astounding that it is impossible to give any preliminary account. All we knew was that there was a crashing roar of something exploding, turf and dirt went flying in the air, and there was Ferris on the ground.

He was on his feet at once, for instinct had sent him down at the first sound. Then he was calling to everyone to stay put, but I made for him, and Mortar was moving too. As I put on my glasses again, for in the excitement of what had happened I had been up to my old nervous trick of polishing them without being aware of the fact, I saw Ferris stoop and put something in his pocket.

"What on earth's happened?" I said, when I'd got close enough.

"A live Mills, wasn't it?" asked Mortar.

"A Mills all right," Ferris told him grimly.

"But how the devil did it get there?" I wanted to know.

"Do you mind if I speak to the men, sir?" Ferris said.

"By all means," I told him, and wondered what on earth he was going to say.

He didn't let them join up over that dead ground, in case there might be another live bomb, but marched one line round the flank and then closed both lines in.

"This is a very bad business," he told the men. "You see what happened. A Mills went off and it happened to go off about five yards from me or I wouldn't be here now. There's only one explanation of how it got there. Some man or men must have been practising throwing, and some bloody fool used live stuff instead of dummies! One of the live bombs was left behind and it didn't go off although the pin was out, perhaps because the lever stuck in some curious way and then got wedged into the ground. Then just the movement of the ground by my feet was enough to set it off." He paused and looked over the lines. "Now then, who did it? What men have been out here practising?"

Men looked at each other and then blankly forward.

"Come on," said Ferris impatiently. "If there was more than one man responsible, everything's bound to come out. If it was only one man, let him be a man and own up."

Not a soul stirred. Ferris whispered with me and then I made the announcement. The bomb-throwing would continue on a piece of suitable ground about two hundred yards away, and instead of the usual parade at thirteen-thirty hours, all students would fall in inside the lecture-room.

Then I had to hurry to make yet another report to the Colonel. To my relief he attempted to cast no blame on Ferris, and he didn't even mention Mortar's name. At thirteen-thirty hours he harangued the two hundred and fifty men from the platform, but the culprit or culprits made no move. When he had finished, a Home Guard major asked to be allowed to say something, which was that he would personally guarantee that every man there, other than the culprit, would at once do everything in his power to find out who had been responsible for what might have been a terrible accident. If the man were his own brother, he said, he'd hand him over, and he was confident every man there felt the same.

There were "Hear, hears," followed by tremendous applause. The Colonel was obviously surprised and almost overwhelmed by that spontaneous display of the school and team spirit which had been the basis of his opening speech on the Sunday. He was content to leave things like that, he said, and there would be no need for a Court of Inquiry. He and I also agreed in private that no report on the occurrence should be made to the War House. Two accidents, however explicable, might be enough to damn the school, and its staff.

I drew into the Mess that evening for a quick one before dinner, and Ferris was there alone. As a matter of fact he was just going out, and we did our talking by the door.

"Do you ever go into the town, sir?" he asked me.

I told him I had been in twice. It was a nice little country town of about four thousand people, and out of bounds to the students except on Sundays.

"Then you know the Greyhound," he said. "Like to join Mortar and me there after dinner?"

"I'll walk down with you," I said.

"You meet us there, sir," he said. "The private bar at about twenty-one hours."

"What's the idea?" I said. "Something confidential?"

In the semi-darkness I could just see his grin. "Only what the lawyers say, sir. You might hear something to your advantage."

After dinner I took good care to dodge the Colonel, and I was in the private bar of the Greyhound well on time. Mortar and Ferris were already there, and but for a couple of *habitués* in the other cosy corner, we had the room to ourselves. Mortar insisted on standing the first round.

He drank our healths in amusing but unprintable terms, and then I asked point-blank what was in the wind.

"You do the talking, Ferry," Mortar ordered.

"It's like this," Ferris began. "When we two examined the barrel of that Northover we discovered traces of what we thought was chewing-gum."

My eyes goggled and my fingers were already at my glasses. "Good God! You mean, some student tried a practical joke!"

Ferris smiled grimly. "Joke—hell!" said Mortar.

"You see, you've got to take things in conjunction with what happened to-day," Ferris said.

"Just a minute," I told him. "I'm gathering that you two have been throwing dust in everybody's eyes, and in mine in particular."

"Why not?" asked Mortar, with his usual amiable indifference.

"You shut up, old-timer," Ferris told him with the same amiability. "You see, it's like this, sir. We've been putting our heads together, and we don't like the look of things a bit." Then he was producing something from his pocket and handing it to me. "This takes a bit of explaining, for instance."

*This* was a length of stout twine attached to a peg. The base of the peg was dirty, as if it had been in the ground. My fingers went to my horn-rims again.

"This is what I saw you pick up this morning?"

"I wondered if you'd spotted me," he said. "But you see the idea. That peg was in the ground and the other end of it was attached to the lever of a live Mills. The Mills must have been in a carefully prepared hole, with the pin out and the lever just held. I was supposed to kick against the string, which I did, and as I'd been walking *towards the Mills*, it'd go off just as I got to it."

I couldn't say a word for a moment. The whole thing was so simple, and yet so diabolical, that I could only snap my bat eyes. Then I thought of something. "Who knew you would be doing exactly as you did this morning?"

"Everybody," he said simply. "I'd done the same thing before, and in the same place, when we had elementary throwing. The lines were flagged out. All someone had to do last night was to plant the bomb."

"Just a minute, Ferry," cut in Mortar. "You didn't tell the Major that all this is to be kept under his hat."

"I get you," I said. "If you hadn't said so, I'd have told you the same thing. What we're handling is dynamite."

"We looked at it like this," Ferris said. "The old-timer here and I have got in the way of settling our own grievances without any outside interference, and we're proposing to deal with this in our own way."

I stared. "You're not—"

Ferris smiled. "Oh, no. We're not going to bump anyone off. We're only going to let him know where he gets off."

"Yes, but who?"

"That's the question," he told me. "That's why we decided to put things up to you. Take the Northover. Who put the chewing-gum in the barrel? It was the gun that Brende was demonstrating with."

I nodded warily.

"And he's always chewing gum," went on Ferris. "Just a simple thing, wouldn't it be, sir, to press down a little wedge along the inside end of the barrel. Anything to discredit Mortar."

"There's something else you've left out," Mortar said. "Brende swears blind that the gun was the one Ferry had, but I happen to know he's a bloody liar."

"That's right," Ferris said. "But there's something more serious to come yet. Last night at the Mothers' Meeting"—the half-hour Advice Bureau, he meant—"a man asked Mortar what he'd do if a Mills fell outside the barrel, and Mortar, like the bloody fool he is, said he'd have time to chuck the bomb clear, but he wouldn't ever advise the bloke to do the same thing. Brende was listening, and he brought the matter up with you later, didn't he, old-timer?"

"That's right," Mortar said. "Threw his ruddy weight about and talked about the Colonel not liking it. I said he could ruddy well lump it."

"Let's get down to brass tacks," I said. "What's being suggested is that Brende stuck the chewing-gum in, and handed over the gun as clear. He hoped the bomb would fall where it did, and he knew you'd try that damn-silly stunt, Mortar. To put it bluntly, there was a deliberate attempt at murder."

"I wouldn't go as far as that," Mortar said. "All the same, I might have got a tidy shaking up."

"And the implication is," I said to Ferris, "that the same person fixed this morning's Mills where it would give you a nasty shaking up. I prefer not to say, where it would have blown you to blazes."

"There's something in that, sir," Ferris said, as if the idea had only just struck him. "The trouble is that grenades are common enough. They're an issue to the Home Guard. I don't mean that the students were fools enough to bring any live stuff with them, but the local Home Guard have 'em. If someone didn't get pally with them and lift a bomb, then the same somebody was pally enough with old Store to lift one from the magazine. Store swears every one of his is accounted for, but you never know."

"He and Brende are friendly?"

Ferris shrugged his shoulders. "They're the only two Warrant Officers here, and they mess together, so to speak."

Another round of drinks came along and I thought things over for a bit. Then I had to put a pertinent question and insist on an answer. If the two discovered the culprit—a better term than murderer—then just what action did they propose to take?

The two hemmed and hawed for a minute, then Ferris spoke for both. "All we'd do, sir, would be to tell him we knew what we knew. Then we'd give him the tip to resign his job and clear out. If he didn't, we'd warn him privately that two could play at accidents."

I did some more hard thinking. "Look here," I said at last. "This is an ultimatum on my part. You two are to promise to take no further step at all without my knowledge and sanction.

Either you promise me that or I'll spill all the beans to the Colonel, and we'll thresh everything out at a Court of Inquiry."

Well, to cut the story short, they promised, and we had another round to seal the bargain. When I started back to the school alone, with the other two to follow later, I was none too happy about my part in that argument, though it seemed the best thing I could have done. While I did not resent being manoeuvred into a false position, I had no doubt that I was in that position. I was acting behind the Colonel's back, and yet even then I could see good reasons for keeping my mouth shut. The Colonel was biased, there was no doubt about that, and in many ways Mortar and Ferris could not be blamed for playing a lone, unorthodox hand against those responsible for that bias.

As for the actual attempts to get rid of Mortar and Ferris, I had no doubt that each should be bluntly classed as an attempt at murder, and dastardly, underhand attempts they were. It was a poor consolation, too, to think that the two would in future be on guard against any new attempts of the kind. Excuses of flying leaves and over-keen students couldn't always be found, and if there were any third accident I made up my mind that I would withdraw my pledge and insist on an exhaustive inquiry, even if it meant going over the Colonel's head and appealing, as was my right, to the War Office.

On the Thursday afternoon the notebooks began to come in and I was extremely busy, even if my three lectures had been given. It was now our idea to rush those notebooks through so that the students could get them back before leaving, and save work and postage. Everybody was then to lend a hand in drawing up the brief report that would be sent to the unit of each student. That meant a lot of work for the staff, with a new Course arriving on the Sunday afternoon.

I saw little of Mortar and Ferris, and neither sent me a word about those disclosures made at the Greyhound. Friday night came, and the last dinner, and then Saturday morning with all its bustle. A special train would be leaving Peakridge at twelve-fifteen hours, so there was a rush to get the students off.

At ten-thirty hours the Colonel gave his final talk, and he wanted me on the platform in support. I must say he spoke exceedingly well. He was not going to hold it against the Course, he said, that one of their number had endangered a valuable life and had not been man enough to come forward and confess. He preferred to think of that first Course as a kind of first-born, and he would always remember them with affection.

At the end of the talk the same major rose and expressed the gratitude of the Course. There was not a man, he said, who would not think of Peakridge with the same affection, because, as far as the acquiring of vital knowledge was concerned, it had been both father and mother. Then three cheers were given for the staff, and a minute later there was a wild scramble of students to get to their huts and die transport that would take them to the station.

It was curious at lunch that day, with only the staff in solitary state at the high table; far worse, indeed, than one's own house after guests have gone away. Mortar was not there, and as we came out to the parade ground I asked Ferris what had happened to him.

"He's got a binge on," he said. "It's his birthday."

"It's a real birthday," he said as he caught my look. Some of the students, it appeared, had come to Peakridge by car and so were independent of the train. Mortar was meeting a gang of them at the Greyhound, where they had ordered a special lunch. He had promised to be back by fifteen hours at the latest.

"You be a good fellow," I said, "and keep an eye on him when he does get back. If he's under the weather, keep him out of the Colonel's way, and other people's."

"I'll see to that, sir," he said. "I'll be on the look-out for him and I'll get him to work in my room where I can keep an eye on him."

I worked on steadily that afternoon and had my batman bring me tea. Just before eighteen hours I felt the need of a breather, so I walked as far as the lecture-room. A new batch of German and other films had arrived, and I had had an idea that Flick was running them through. But Flick was not there, and one of his trainees told me he was not running the new films off till after dinner. He had become something of an expert himself, so he ran one short one through for my benefit. The whole batch, he said, would take about two hours, so something would be going on if I looked in at any time between twenty and twenty-two hours.

I had a cold bath and a change to clear away my feeling of frowstiness, and went to the Mess for a quick one. Only Harness was there, and we yarned till the bugle went. Neither Mortar nor Ferris was at table, and Staff told me, with something of a thin little sneer, that they were working in Ferris's room. His own share of the work was finished, he said, and he hinted that mutton-fisted fighting men were none too good when it came to administrative work.

It was a gloomy meal, with the huge room full of echoes in its emptiness, and I was glad when it was over. Half an hour later my share of the clerical work was completed and deposited in Harness's office.

"And now if I stay in my room," I told myself, "it's ten to one on someone fetching me to the Colonel to give him a hand. I know what I'll do. I mayn't get time in the morning, so I'll dig myself in in the writing-room and get off my letter to Bernice."

I was still feeling somewhat jaded, so I got Shorty, the resident barman, to mix me a long tonic, and with the door to the bar closed behind me, I settled down on my job. It was at twenty hours forty-five that I actually finished the long letter—I am an uxorious sort of cove in the best sense, of course—and I remember glancing at my wrist-watch as I fixed the stamp on. Just then I became aware that the dim voices I had just heard in the bar were becoming more loud, and even obstreperous. Then there was a tap at the door and it opened. Ferris nipped in.

"Shorty, you've got to have a drink."

"Sorry, sir, but it's against orders."

"Come on, Shorty, be a sport. It's my birthday—"

That was what I heard as Ferris opened the door and nipped through. The voice, of course, was Mortar's, and had a thickness which I have not tried to convey.

"Will you come in a minute, sir?" Ferris said urgently. "He's tight as a lord and I can't make him go to his room."

I gave a sigh as I got to my feet. Mortar was still leaning against the bar maintaining the same maudlin, repetitive arguments with Shorty. Tucked under his left arm was the little white kitten.

"Here's Major Travers," Shorty said warningly.

"Ah! the Major," Mortar said, with a somewhat incoherent enthusiasm. I frowned at Shorty, who sheered off from behind the tiny bar.

"I'm talking to you straight, and officially," I said to Mortar as I grasped his arm, and Ferris gently removed the kitten. "You apparently haven't sense enough to be your own friend, so I'll be a friend to you. Into your room you go, and stay there. Get that? If not I'll have you up before the Colonel in the morning as sure as my name's Travers."

He glared at me, snapped his eyes, then swayed back. Ferris had him by the other arm.

"That's a sensible chap," I said soothingly, while we steered him towards the door. "If the Colonel or anyone saw you like this, there'd be hell to pay."

It was a cold night, and clear, though there was no moon. Mortar's legs gave way as the air struck him, but we got him along. As we drew him warily to the shadow of the long hut, Ferris gave a sudden 'Sh!' and we halted.

"Flick!" whispered Ferris. "What the devil's he doing there?"

I strained my eyes to see what was happening, then Ferris gave a sigh of relief. "All right, sir. He's gone now. A narrow squeak, that."

We came to the door of Mortar's room.

"Better get him in before we turn on the light," Ferris said.

So we got him in, switched on the light, and saw the black-out was in order. Mortar had flopped down in the easy-chair just inside the door.

"How're you feeling?" Ferris whispered.

"Bloody awful," Mortar told him drearily.

"Shall we put you to bed?"

"I'll be all right."

"You'll give me your word you won't leave this room again to-night?" I asked him bluntly. He was smelling like a brewery on wheels.

He smiled. "You're a good old sport, Major—"

"You answer my question," I told him. "You won't leave this room again to-night?"

"I'll be all right," he said. "Good chap, Ferris. Good sort is old Ferry."

Ferris had been undoing his shoes, and now he was tying the laces in intricate knots. If Mortar wanted to put those shoes on again, he'd have the devil of a job.

"Going to bed now," Mortar drawled sleepily. "One little thing to do and then going beddy-byes."

Ferris glanced at me and I nodded. "Cheerio, old-timer. Mind you sleep," he said.

"Don't forget you've given me your word," I added, and out we went. Very gently Ferris turned the key in the door, and there was a good job done.

"You keep the key," I told Ferris.

"I thought I'd slip back in a few minutes and turn off the light," he said. "He'll be bound to leave it on and someone might see a crack."

We had been moving in the direction of the Mess, and for a long minute neither of us spoke.

"I left my letter behind," I said at last. "Where are you bound for?"

"I'd better see Shorty," he said. "He's got to keep his mouth shut about all this. Perhaps you'd like a word with him, too, Major."

I suddenly went hot and cold all over at the thought of the news flying round that I had helped put Captain Mortar to bed. The Colonel would be furious, and naturally enough, at my failure to report the matter.

"I think I will have a word," I said.

But I was never to have that word, at least as I was planning. What happened I can't quite say, but just as the last word left my lips, there was the most shattering roar I have ever heard in my life, and I have been fairly close to a bomb or two in my time. In the same split second I was on my back, and my head got the devil of a crack. My ear-drums seemed to burst, and then as I snapped my eyes and began trying to get up, something crashed on the roof of the Mess behind me. Then in front of me, where there had been darkness, flames began to curl, and as I began struggling to my feet again, I saw that where Mortar's room had been was a queer sort of nothing. Nothing, that is, except the mounting flames.

# Chapter VI

A DOZEN THINGS were happening at once. Only the tricks of a cinema camera could give you the faintest idea, with split-second changes and super-exposures, and a wild whirling of this and that. You must bear with me if I fail to convey the impression of speed and confusion, and also I want you to get certain happenings clearly in your mind.

The reason why I was not able to get up at once was that a length of weather-boarding, blown from the hut by the terrific explosion, had fallen across my middle. As I did struggle to my feet, I heard Ferris, but as if at a far distance, for my ears were humming. As a matter of fact he was actually standing over me.

"My God! What's happened? You all right, sir?"

"I'm all right," I began, and then he was suddenly gone. The mounting flames made a fine light, and I saw him hold his arm before his face to protect it from the heat, and then he disappeared round the north end of the burning hut. In the same moment, as I moved off that way myself, I was aware that the camp was astir. Distant voices were nearing, and were becoming shouts.

As I came round in the comparative darkness by the north end, Staff was suddenly on me.

"It's you, sir," he said excitedly, and as if he'd been looking for someone else. "Do you know what's happened, sir?"

I shook my head and hurried on. It was queer that I should have noticed that he was wearing a gun, but the light caught the butt of the Colt where it protruded from the holster.

Once round the corner I could see clearly to well beyond the hospital. But everything was still confused, with sparks flying from the burning building, and the heat already so intense that I had to shield my head as I circled warily round. I could hear the Colonel shouting orders. Men were removing furniture from the undamaged rooms, and then suddenly I heard the hiss as the first of the hoses got to work, and the water sizzled on the flames.

"Come out of that, sir!"

There was a shout on my left, and I could see Ferris and Brende struggling within a few yards of the flames. Ferris had evidently determined to get into that flaming room to see if Mortar were still alive, which was about as mad a thing as could ever enter a man's brain, for I could see now that nothing was left of Mortar's room but the floor. Compress came running over, and he and Brende dragged Ferris back. I didn't see what happened then because a swirl of smoke and sparks came my way, and I sheered off to where the Colonel had been. There was no sign of him when I got there, and then I heard him shouting for the hoses to be played on the unharmed rooms.

As the smoke cleared again I could see that Staff's room was well alight, as was Ferris's, but that Flick's and Collect's were practically intact, though windows had been shattered. I think it was just at that moment that I realised what had happened, and a cold sweat was all at once on my forehead. That terrific explosion must have killed Mortar before he had known a thing, and it had probably blown him to smithereens. Curious, wasn't it, that I should stand there and be regarding the whole thing so impersonally, but even at that moment, with Mortar's room virtually gone, everything seemed so unreal. Then as I stood there, suddenly shivering in the cold wind, I saw everything in a different way. Mortar was dead. Mortar, and I had seen him and talked to him only a few minutes before. Mortar dead! It was incredible somehow, and all at once I found myself polishing my glasses and blinking away at the flames and the darkness beyond.

"That you, Travers?"

The Colonel was dashing up, and Collect puffing at his heels. Compress appeared and the Colonel was on him like a flash.

"You're sure there was nobody in his room?"

"Pretty sure, sir," Compress said. "Mortar wasn't likely to go to bed at nine o'clock."

Another cold perspiration came over my forehead. The singing in my ears had almost gone, but my voice sounded queer to me as I spoke.

"Were you asking about Captain Mortar, sir?"

"Yes. Why?"

"I'm afraid he *was* in his room, sir."

"My God! You sure, Travers?"

"Dead sure, sir. I happened to see him in the Mess and he'd had just about as many drinks as he could carry. It was his birthday—"

"Get on with it, man!"

"Well, Mr. Ferris and I induced him to go to his room, and so that he shouldn't get out to the Mess again, I saw the door locked and Mr. Ferris took the key."

"Why'd he do that?"

I explained, and somewhat tersely. The Colonel is one of those annoying people who are always wise after an event. He could always inform you afterwards what you should have done, and he would do it with an air of conveying that that was what he would have done in the same circumstances.

"If I *had* left the key and told him not to leave the room, I'd no guarantee he'd have obeyed me," I said. "If you're suggesting, sir, that he'd have still been alive, I say most emphatically that the force of the explosion must have killed him at once. It blew me off my feet and I was near the Mess."

"No point in argument," the Colonel told me testily.

"One fact does remain," Collect put in suavely. "Undoubtedly he had explosives in his room, and he was doing something with them. It's possible that he knew there was going to be an explosion, but he couldn't get out of the door."

"Are you suggesting I was responsible for his death?" I asked him quietly, but I was taking a step or two nearer. "Not at all. Not at all."

"Then stop chattering," I told him angrily. "There'll be a time for talking and you can do it then."

"That will do, gentlemen," the Colonel said, and stepped in between us. "Things are bad enough as they are, without all this argument and—and talk."

Then, happily, Nurse Wilton's voice was heard and we could see her coming across.

"Get her away, Compress," the Colonel snapped. "Tell her to go to her office and be ready to treat any men who get burnt. Collect, you tell those men to put everything back again in the rooms. The fire's practically over." It *was* practically over, and I was suddenly aware of the gloom and depression now the light from the flames had gone. Somehow I couldn't help thinking of the difference there would have been if it had been Collect, say, who had died in that gap between the blackened, sodden wrecks of rooms that flanked the space where Mortar's room had been. "Poor old Collect," it would have been, and, "How terrible!" and all the rest of it. But it was Mortar who had died, and not Collect, and neither the Colonel nor a soul had uttered a single expression of what one calls grief. Then as I looked round I saw the Colonel had moved away again, so I moved off too.

Round the north end of the hut I came on Ferris, at least I had to stoop to make sure it was he, for he was sitting on a box or something that had been left there, elbows on knees and head in his hands.

"Feeling a bit knocked over?" I asked him gently.

"Just a bit, sir," he said, and got to his feet. He shook his head as if to rouse himself, and then he was coming quite close to me. "What killed him, sir?"

It was my turn to do the head shaking. "God knows," I said. "But most undoubtedly he had some explosives in his room and he was fooling around with them after we'd gone."

"Wait a minute," he said. "Do you remember what he said to us? He said he had something to do first and then he was going to bed."

"That's right," I said, and I saw the room as clearly as if I was still in it. Mortar lolling in that low chair and making as if to rise. "One little thing to do and then going beddy-byes." Behind his back Ferris had been gently removing the key from the lock.

"Feeder will tell us, sir," Ferris was saying. "I bet he knew everything that was in that room. He'll know if Mortar had any explosives there."

"Where is Feeder?" I said. "I've forgotten all about him. Why hasn't he turned up here?"

"I got him out of the way," Ferris said. "Mortar had promised him a half-day in the town to celebrate the birthday, and then when Mortar came back from that lunch he told Feeder to stay, after all. I knew he'd be working in his room and probably having Feeder bring him relays of drinks, so I got him to change his mind again, and made him come to my room instead."

"I remember now," I said. "And very wise of you it was. Still, as soon as Feeder gets back he'll have to be questioned."

Then Ferris was shaking his head in a queer way, and I saw his lip droop.

"I don't think we'll get much from Feeder."

"What do you mean?"

"Oh, nothing, sir," he told me. "All I was thinking was that the third time pays for all."

"What the hell are you talking about?" I said, and then ended with a lame, "Oh."

"You see it then, sir?" he said, and the lip curled again.

"I'm seeing nothing," I told him, "and I advise you to do the same. When the time comes to talk, that's when to do the talking."

"Major Travers! Major Travers!"

Someone was calling me, and it turned out to be Compress. The Colonel wanted me in his room at once. The explosion had dislocated the electric light system, he told me as we hurried along, but a temporary wire had just been rigged up. The men were just about to rig up another over the floor of Mortar's room and he was then going to search for what remained of the body.

Collect was there, and I'm afraid my eyebrows lifted at the sight of him.

"Ah! come in, Travers," the Colonel said, and quite mildly. "We've got to talk this business over and decide on a line of action."

I nodded as I took the chair he was pointing to.

"It's hellish, you know," he went on. "Perfectly hellish. Whatever Mortar was, there he is—blown up and—well, it doesn't bear thinking about. And the school. Is there a curse on the place, or what?"

"Just bad luck, sir, that's all," I told him. "What we've got to think about is that it might have been far worse."

He stared.

"It happened when the Course had dispersed," I explained. "True, a new Course assembles to-morrow, but all they'll see will be the results of the fire. The staff should keep what they know to themselves, and—if I may venture to suggest it—we should encourage the impression that it was due to the electric lighting. That one of the staff officers was unlucky enough to get trapped in the fire and burnt to death, would follow as a matter of course."

"Now that's a capital suggestion," the Colonel said. "I was telling Collect here that I knew you'd be of considerable help."

"And by the way," said Collect leaning forward, "I'm sorry, Travers, if I offended you just now. I assure you it wasn't intended."

"Forget it," I said. "Perhaps I spoke a bit too freely too."

The Colonel cut in quickly. "Well, you've taken a load off my mind, Travers. And now the point is, what ought we to do and how ought we to do it. Undoubtedly there'll have to be a report to the War Office."

I thought the time had at last come to throw my weight about.

"Do you mind if I tell you something personal, sir?"

"By all means," he told me, but was looking a bit wary again.

So I told him that inquiries were right up my street, for they had been a part of my civil occupation. I also said I'd had trouble at the camp where I'd been Commandant, and much the same situation had arisen.

"Really?" he said, and with quite a changed tone. "And what are you proposing we should do in this case?"

"I think we should hold our hands for an hour or two," I said. "If Compress finds the body and sufficient of it for identification, that will alter the whole report. If we can't prove that Mortar was in that room, then whoever answers the 'phone from the War Office end will be bound to ask if we're sure Mortar was there, and was killed. We'd look fools if we had to say we didn't know."

"He's right. He's dead right," the Colonel told Collect.

"And I think we should interrogate the man Feeder," I went on. "He would be bound to know if there were explosives in the room. He and Captain Mortar hadn't any secrets."

"We'll get him at once," the Colonel said, and went over to the 'phone that communicated with Harness's office. It was working all right, but Harness wasn't there. The Orderly Sergeant said that he was in the Mess writing-room, supervising the issue of bedding and furniture so that Staff and Ferris could sleep there that night.

"Handle it yourself," the Colonel told him testily. "You don't want to leave everything to Mr. Harness, do you? Get Feeder sent to me at once." Then he caught my frantic waving, and handed over the 'phone to me.

"This is Major Travers," I said. "If Feeder isn't in camp, then he may be in town. If he isn't back in a minute or two you might get in touch with the Peakridge police."

"What's he doing in town?" the Colonel demanded.

"I believe Captain Mortar gave him permission. A special half-holiday as it was the Captain's birthday."

"But the town's out of bounds till to-morrow morning," Collect said.

I shrugged my shoulders. "Those are the facts as I've learned them."

There was a tap at the door, and at the Colonel's shout, an R.A.M.C. sergeant came in. "Mr. Compress's compliments, sir, and he says there's no doubt about Captain Mortar being there."

The Colonel grunted and rubbed his chin. "What's he doing now?"

"Still searching the site, sir."

"Right," the Colonel said, by way of dismissal. Once more I had to butt in.

"Don't you think, sir, that sentries ought to be posted round the site at once? You know what men are like for scrounging souvenirs. The Sappers will have to go over all that wreckage to try to find the cause of the explosion, and some vital thing may get taken away."

"Heavens, yes," the Colonel said. "You see to it at once, Major Collect, will you? Get Brende to take it in hand."

No sooner were we alone than the Colonel was making for the cupboard where he kept his whisky and siphon.

"I don't know about you, Travers, but I feel as though I could do with a good stiff drink."

I knew that was his way of showing some sort of gratitude for the suggestions I'd made, obvious though they seemed to me. As soon as we'd taken the first swig he was assuring me that we were well on top of the job, and he was pretty sure everything would be all right. I couldn't help wondering if some of the satisfaction were prompted by the realisation that Mortar had gone. At the same moment he was giving some confirmation of the suspicion.

"Well, Mortar might have his faults but he had his good points," he said, and nodded at his tumbler. "When you and I have to go, Travers, I'd think we'd like to go as quick and painlessly."

I winced at the thought, and then fortunately, before I had to reply, there was another tap at the door and Harness came in.

"I've got Mr. Staff outside, sir, and I think you ought to hear what he's got to say."

Staff had a most amazing story to tell. When he went to his room after dinner he found a note that had been pushed under the door, for he always kept his room locked when he was out, and the batman had a duplicate key. The note, as far as he remembered, read like this—

*Keep an eye on your room to-night. Mortar's going to rag you.*

By that he had gathered that at any time Mortar might appear and play up hell in the room. Mortar, as the far bigger man, might also try some game like de-bagging if he found Staff there.

"Where is the note now?" I asked.

"Destroyed, I expect, sir," Staff said. "I laid it down somewhere and now of course it's gone."

"Any envelope?"

"No, sir."

"Type-written?

"Yes, sir. Type-written."

I asked the Colonel's permission to put another question or two.

"When I saw you just after the explosion," I said to Staff, "you were wearing a gun. You haven't got it now."

"Well, yes," he said, and was smiling sheepishly and hunting for words. "I wondered if you'd noticed it, sir."

"Well, go on," I said. "Tell the Colonel and me all about it. Why were you wearing the gun?"

He gave a long-winded but feasible explanation. He was fed up, he said, by all that blether about Mortar being the only fighting soldier, and he had suspicions the note was part of the rag. What he meant by that was that he might get laughed at if he didn't stand his ground. So he made up his mind to sit tight in his room and await the coming of Mortar. If he came, and he tried any monkey business, then Staff was going to poke that gun in his belly and march him outside. There would be no doubt then on whose side the laugh would be.

I had to smile, though I hope I didn't show it. The idea of Mortar being intimidated by a gun held by Staff was really too comic.

"And why did you happen to be outside your room when the explosion actually occurred?" I said.

That, it appeared, was just one of those lucky things that happen. Staff had got fed up with waiting, so he determined to reconnoitre the enemy's position. So he opened his door a little, and then he heard muffled voices outside Mortar's door. I nodded, for the voices were mine and Ferris's.

Then he shut the door again and waited, and when after a few minutes he looked out once more, he saw and heard nothing, so out he stepped to reconnoitre. Nothing was to be seen, so he decided to look round at the back.

Just as he was turning the corner the explosion occurred and he was blown clean off his feet. It was a few moments before he recovered, and then he saw someone—who turned out to be me—coming towards him in the dark.

That was his story, and he stuck to it. Also he swore he had seen or heard nothing suspicious except what he had already reported.

"You didn't see Mr. Flick?" I asked.

"No, sir," he said, and then with surprise: "I thought he was at the lecture-room all the evening."

He and Harness went out, and the Colonel was at once clicking his tongue exasperatedly.

"Damn' young idiot," He did some more tongue clicking. "Seems to me, Travers, all sorts of things have been going on behind our backs. Most unsatisfactory. Most unsatisfactory."

"You can't treat men like boys, sir," I said. "In any case, now poor Mortar is gone things ought to be on a different footing."

I was hoping he'd argue the point, since the getting rid of Mortar had been, by his own admission, the one snag to the smooth running of things, but then there was yet another tap at the door and this time it was Collect who came in.

"I've got Feeder outside, sir, if you'd like to speak to him."

"Bring him in," the Colonel said belligerently.

"He doesn't know what's happened, sir," Collect warned him. "Also he's been drinking."

The Colonel nodded meaningly and waved a hand. In came Feeder, blinking a bit at the sudden light. When he caught sight of me he gave a cheerful grin of acknowledgment, and for the life of me I couldn't help a faint smile in return. For Feeder was looking very much the happy warrior. His battered face was rosily flushed, and his eyes were sparkling. That bit of a binge had certainly toned him up, and he was less likely than ever to be abashed by circumstances.

"Where've you been?"

Feeder's eyebrows raised at the Colonel's curt demand, then he gave a shake of the head and another cheerful grin.

"Just down town, sir, having a bit of a do."

"Stand to attention!" Collect reminded him sharply.

The look he received was not so cheerful. Feeder let his hands appear by the seams of his trousers, but there was no other smartening up.

"You know the regulations," the Colonel said. "Why did you break them?"

"Well, it was like this, sir," began Feeder, in the usual style and words of the Army defaulter. What he said was virtually what Ferris had told me, though he had sense enough not to mention Ferris's name. He admitted, with every bit as much cheerfulness, that he had broken camp regulations, but added with a confidence that I personally found most engaging, that he regarded himself as a kind of civilian, and therefore outside the rules.

"Well, you'll soon be a civilian again—a real civilian," the Colonel told him, and with wholly unnecessary cruelty, irritating though Feeder must have been. "I've got some news for you. Bad news. Captain Mortar's been killed."

Feeder had straightened up at the words *news*, then he had leaned forward, and when the last word had been said, he was staring at the Colonel like a man hypnotised. A moment or two and he was shifting the same intent gaze on me.

"It's true, Feeder," I said. "There was an accident and Captain Mortar is dead."

The intent look went and he was standing there with a kind of stupid lolling.

"Say something, man!" the Colonel snapped at him. "You're not too drunk to understand what you've been told?"

"I'm not drunk, sir," Feeder told him quietly. "I've been drunk but three times in my life, sir, and the last was at Rabat, and that was seven years ago."

He turned to me with a queer, natural dignity. "So the Captain is dead, sir."

I nodded.

"How did it happen, sir? Would you mind telling me that?"

I glanced at the Colonel before replying. "We don't know. We think he had some explosives in his room and was experimenting with them and they went off. There was a tremendous explosion at about nine o'clock."

"Explosives, sir, in his room?" He sounded so incredulous that I asked him why.

"There's not a thing in that room that I don't know of," he told me. "There was nothing in the room at twelve o'clock to-day, sir, and that I'll swear by all that's holy."

"You never knew him to have any explosives in the room?"

"Never, sir. Not even a Mills." He paused to give another incredulous shake of the head. "And why should he blow himself up with explosives, sir? He knew more about them things than any man living. Him and me's handled explosives all our lives, and never an accident to either one of us."

"Well, there we are," I said. "It's one of those things that happen."

"And where is he now, sir? Can I see him?"

"I'm afraid not," I said. "To tell the truth, Feeder, and you're man enough to hear it, there isn't anything of him to see."

I had caught the Colonel's eye again, and he motioned me to the far end of the room where we had a whispered talk. Feeder was to consider himself under open arrest and was to stay in his quarters till further notice.

When we came back to our chairs, Feeder was wiping his eyes on the sleeve of his greatcoat.

"Get along now," the Colonel told him, and with far more humanity than I expected.

"Just one little thing," I added. "Did he have any relatives, Feeder."

"Never a one, sir," he told me. "That was why he didn't mind where he went and what he did. That's what he told me once, sir."

Collect went off with him, and the Colonel was heaving a sigh as soon as the door closed on them. I waited for him to speak, and it was a goodish time before he did so.

"What now, do you think, Travers? Ought we to ring the War Office?"

"I think we ought, sir," I said. "And I think it ought to be done as quickly as possible. And from Harness's office, because what will have to be said is highly confidential."

"Right," he said, and was getting to his feet.

"One minute, sir. Don't you think we ought to be sure in our minds what precisely we're going to report?"

He gave that curious, wary look of his. "Just how do you mean?"

"Well, sir, in my considered judgment we're not going to report an accident."

"What do you mean?" he said, and stared again. "It's the accident we're going to report, isn't it?"

"No, sir," I said quietly. "We may have to report something that was meant to look like an accident."

"Meant? What do you mean by meant?"

"What I say, sir. Something that was meant to look like an accident, but wasn't. To be perfectly frank, sir, we may have to suggest that Captain Mortar was murdered."

## Chapter VII

THE COLONEL'S LOOK was one of horror, and I never saw a man so taken aback in my life, though surely everything we had heard was merely a leading up to a climax he should have recognized for himself.

"You mad, Travers?"

"Look here, sir," I said. "You and I have got to do some plain speaking, and I'd prefer it to be as man to man. You're the Commandant and you're entitled to ask my views and put me down to give evidence at a Court of Inquiry, but you can't force me to do anything else."

No wonder he was startled at that attitude of mine. I had blurted out the beginnings of what I thought, for the simple reason that I could see myself on the very edge of the devil of a hole. At the Greyhound I had been given information in confidence, and the Colonel might rightly say that if I had passed that information on to him, then Mortar might be still alive. What I somehow had to do was to still keep that information back both from the Colonel and from the Court of Inquiry. If I couldn't do the latter, then I had to play for time.

The Colonel had been frowning, and rubbing his chin. "Well—er—yes," he said, "All the same, I don't see what you're getting at."

"Then it's this, sir," I said. "All I might do now is ask if you want me any more, and then say good night, It's no business of mine to report to the War Office, unless you expressly order me to do so."

"But you agreed to help?" he said, and no wonder he was looking bewildered. I had never shown any bellicose tendencies, and he must have felt like someone suddenly savaged by his pet rabbit.

"Exactly," I said. "But if I help it must be in my own way. You'll pardon me if I recall that I've had experience of happenings along the same lines as this one. If you gave me a free hand, I think I could promise that all this business would be cleared up without any fuss or scandal."

"Why should there be fuss?" he asked, very much on his dignity.

"You're the answer to that," I might have told him. What I did say was that there wouldn't be any. "You and I have the same interests at heart," I said. "We want the school to function normally next week, and we'd hate like hell to have it get a bad name for accidents. Once rumours start, they run like wildfire."

"Yes," he said, and was nodding heavily. And then we were disturbed once more; this time by Compress.

"I don't think I can do any more to-night, sir."

"Any definite results?" the Colonel asked him.

"Plenty, sir," Compress said. "We can definitely identify him. But what I wanted to ask, sir, was about procedure from now on."

The Colonel glanced at me. I had been in that same predicament about procedure myself, and luckily I knew all the answers.

"The War Office will be giving instructions later," I said. "As soon as they come through, the Colonel will let you know."

Out went Compress and we got on with our little chat.

"As I was saying, sir, I think I know a way to get this bad business settled domestically, so to speak. I even think we can avoid a pukka Court of Inquiry."

"No-o-o!" said the Colonel incredulously.

I convinced him, at least sufficiently to let me make the attempt, which was enough for the moment. Had I known even a part of what was going to happen, I should not have been so cocksure.

It was not too far off midnight when we got a reply from the War House, and it was another half-hour before we were through to the Colonel Henrison with whom I had had dealings before. I had to do the talking, and I did as much repetition as possible so as to keep Topman in touch with what was being said at the other end.

Colonel Henrison remembered me well enough, for before taking up an appointment at the outbreak of war he had been an official at the Yard. What was finally settled was this. By hook or crook he'd get George Wharton sent down, and the inquiry would thereupon become a confidential one. If we were at the end of the line at nine hours in the morning, he would give further news. He agreed on the spot, however, that we should proceed with the rebuilding of the demolished rooms.

The Colonel was delighted, as he had reason to be. Then the last elements of uneasiness asserted themselves. "This Superintendent Wharton; what's he like?"

I knew what answer he hoped for, and I gave it.

"He's a mightily important man," I said, "and more than competent. What's more, he's tact itself, and he's the sort to go down well with the Home Guard."

"Good, good," he said. "But how are we going to explain him away?"

I suddenly smiled. Somehow I always smile when I think of George. "Let him give a special lecture on Security," I said. "He was an Intelligence officer in the last war, and I think he'd do it."

"You mean, make it appear that he's one of the staff?"

"Exactly," I said. "Even if his lecture's never delivered, it'll be a first-rate camouflage. He can be called a civilian expert."

Well, that was all settled. A successor to Mortar would be arriving on Monday at the latest, and the Colonel and I were to meet after breakfast to make any rearrangements of syllabus. Harness was to go to Peakridge and make with a building firm there a case of priority for the rebuilding of the shattered rooms, and as the work was chiefly timbering, it might be rushed through in two or three days. In his address to the new Course, after dinner on the following night, the Colonel was to make a subtle allusion to the danger of tampering with electric lights or explosives, and he would pronounce a brief oration over poor Mortar. The Colonel and I were to compose the actual wording at that after-breakfast conference.

"Come and have a drink, Travers," the Colonel told me both genially and with concern. "I feel as if I could do with one."

"Thank you very much, sir," I said, "but I don't think I will. I'm devilish tired and I think I'll get straight into bed."

"Perhaps you're right," he said. "A long day ahead of us to-morrow."

So we parted at Harness's office. The Colonel had one or two matters he wanted to discuss with his Adjutant, and I made my way to my room. A window or two had been broken by the blast from the explosion, and as I stood for a moment looking at them I fairly gave a leap, for a hand touched my shoulders.

"Could you spare a minute or two, sir?"

It was Ferris.

My batman had rigged me up a bedside light, so I turned it on and kept the stronger light off in case a gleam of any sort should be seen from the outside. I also cautioned Ferris to speak quietly. There was a double partition between the rooms and it was difficult to overhear, but I was taking no chances, especially with Collect.

I might have been doing him an injustice, but I thought him capable of flattening his ear against the partition.

"Any more news?" Ferris wanted to know.

I told him there was nothing important, and then he said he had seen Feeder.

"I thought he was confined to his hut," I said.

Ferris's lip drooped. I hated his doing that, for it changed his face into something malevolent and even cunning. It was curious how there should be three sides to Ferris, and that only one should strike me as the real man. There was the scholarly, good-looking Ferris, quiet in manner and dry in humour, and he, I somehow felt, was not the real man. There was the Ferris of the guerrilla lectures, with burning eyes, tense voice, and clenched, smiting fists. That was the real Ferris—the Ferrova who had commanded a Brigade in Spain and made his name a terror to Franco's men. It was also a Ferris for whom I had a tremendous, if sneaking, admiration. Then there was this other Ferris, with a sneer that almost bared his lower teeth. He was the night prowler, and something more savage even than the man of the twisted knife.

"Feeder wouldn't give a damn for an order like that," he said, "He's got ways and means the same as I have. He thinks the same as me. Mortar was wiped out, and we're going to get the one who did it."

"Look here, young fellow," I told him sternly. "I'm not going to listen to talk like that. This isn't Spain, and I'm the second-in-command of this school. From now on I warn you that I'm reporting every word you say."

His eyes were fixed so burningly on mine that somehow I was forced to turn mine away.

"Be sensible," I told him. "Don't you think I'm as eager as you are—and Feeder—to see this business through? I liked Mortar, and if I can do anything to help hang the one who killed him, by God I'll do it! If he *was* killed, that is."

He gave that same sneering smile again. Suddenly I remembered where I had seen that smile before, and what made it so distasteful to me when I saw it on the face of Ferris. It was in 1930, when I was having a holiday in Donegal and got friendly with a guest at the same hotel. I thought him a good fellow, generous, genial, and a good friend to myself and to Englishmen generally. Then most indiscreetly I happened to speak disparagingly of the Irishman's love of trouble, and in a flash I was horrified and frightened by the expression of his face. The landlord told me later that he had been in the thick of the Rebellion and that no man was a more fanatical hater of everything English.

The look went from Ferris's face and all at once he was what I might call his first self.

"I see that, sir. And I think you're quite right. Are you going to let out about the Northover that nearly got him and the Mills that nearly got me?"

"I don't know," I said. "But I will tell you this, and in the strictest confidence. You'll know why I'm telling you as soon as you hear the name. A special investigator is coming down, and nobody's to know who he is. Wharton—Superintendent Wharton of New Scotland Yard."

He stared, then gave a lame sort of smile. "Good heavens, sir, how did you—"

He was speaking far too loudly and I held up a warning hand. Then I explained, and I pledged him to absolute secrecy.

"So you see," I said. "I can tell him in confidence what I as good as swore I wouldn't tell anyone else—what you and Mortar told me in the Greyhound."

"Good," he said, and nodded. "You tell him everything, sir. But speaking of stamps, there's one thing I'd like you to do for me. I believe the Colonel thinks I was trying to get into that burning room of Mortar's in order to try and get Mortar out. I don't want him to think I was a ruddy hero. I wasn't doing anything of the sort, sir. I knew there couldn't be much of Mortar to get out. What I was after was rescuing my stamps, and I believe I might have done it if it hadn't been for that interfering fool, Brende."

"Good Lord!" I said. "Those stamps of yours. Pretty tough luck, that."

"Several hundred pounds," he said, but far more philosophically than I should have spoken. "Luckily I've a few duplicates but—well, there we are. They've gone and that's that."

He was getting to his feet and I rose too. My hand went to his shoulder. "Take my advice," I said. "Leave everything to Wharton. If you have to think, keep your thoughts to yourself."

He nodded. Then his eyes narrowed. "I'll tell you this, sir, and you can do what you like about it. If you see me pally with Store, don't be surprised."

"Store?" I said, and stared. "What on earth could he have to do with it!"

"He's pally with Brende," he told me almost offhandedly. "That Mills that nearly got me came out of the magazine, and so did whatever killed Mortar. Store may have faked the books. One other tip, sir. Don't forget Flick. He should have been running films off to-night, and he wasn't."

A whispered good night, and he was letting himself out. As I closed the door and went over to my bed, I was trying to make sense of what he had just told me. I never had liked the look of Store, who struck me as one of the shifty kind, and as for Flick, I knew already that he had not been running off films all the evening. But when it came to good hard thinking, my brain refused to act, and I knew that the only thing for me was sleep.

Inside five minutes I was snuggling down in my camp bed, and then was asleep before I knew it. Yet I had one of the worst nights in my life, and it is essential that I should tell you why.

I hate to read about other people's dreams, but my particular nightmare was something different.

Did I tell you that when the fougasse was let off during rehearsal week, I was the one who did it? Well, I was, or I should have been. There was the box with electric contact ready to be made by the simple depression of the plunger. Perhaps I was wool-gathering, or maybe I hadn't listened sufficiently closely to the instructions, but when Mortar who was standing by my side, called. "Now!" I merely fumbled round. As my hand fell on the top of the plunger, his hand closed on it to help me. He saw my hesitation, in other words, and as the explosion was timed to a second, he was covering up my hesitation by depressing the plunger himself, and unknown to the others, whose eyes naturally were on the bank from which the blazing barrel would emerge.

At any rate his hand closed over mine, and never had I felt anything so icily cold. My own was warm, for it had been in the pocket of my British warm. And that was what I was to dream about all that Saturday night, or so it seemed. There was I, getting into hopeless muddles over that fougasse—muddles that varied chaotically from dream to dream—and always Mortar's ice-cold hand would settle over mine, and then I would wake with the perspiration literally streaming down my face. Only towards morning did I know what it was that caused those dreams. My bed was an old iron type, and in my restless sleep my hand would keep going beyond the bed clothes and coming to rest on the cold iron framework of the bed! The hotter I was, the colder the iron seemed.

In the morning I was up early, and I flattered myself I was easily the first in to breakfast. Then the orderly told me that Harness had breakfasted more than an hour before, and when I came out to the parade ground I saw him coming back to his office. It appeared he had already put in half a day's work, and that after being up most of the night, and there he was fresh apparently as a daisy.

Everything was going well. A Sapper officer and a sergeant were due at any minute to make the official search of the debris in order to determine the nature of the explosive. The building contractor at Peakridge would have men on the job of rebuilding that very afternoon, and his lorries would be delivering material within an hour. Harness had also seen the undertaker at Peakridge, who would get a full-sized coffin ready at once, and Harness told me that after I left the previous night, the Colonel and he had decided that unless anything unforeseen happened, the funeral would be at Peakridge on the Monday afternoon. The Course would be in the lecture-room, unaware that a funeral was taking place.

I had overtaken Harness short of his office, and I saw the sentries doing their patrols round the shattered building, for I had been too busy with my thoughts to notice anything when I left my room to go to breakfast. In Harness's office we had a good look at all correspondence concerning Mortar and could get no information about next-of-kin. Every officer, however, is required to fill in for the War Office a comprehensive account of himself and his previous service on a special long form, but Harness had not yet had time to get the forms filled in by officers at the school. A new hand, that is; an officer who had served before in this war, would have made one out at his previous place of appointment, and the War Office would have a copy. Harness said he would get the number of Mortar's previous School of Instruction and they could refer to the form, if they still had it.

Nine o'clock was zero hour for that call from the War House, and well before the time the Colonel and I were at the telephone. The call came through promptly enough, and what Colonel Henrison had to tell us was, as far as I was concerned, simply splendid. Wharton would be leaving London that morning by train, and he would arrive with the full authority of the War Office behind him. Every facility should be given him for inquiry, and within the bounds of his own discretion there was apparently nothing he was not empowered to do.

"One thing I want to put up to you," Henrison said. "Would it be a help if he came in uniform? For camouflage, I mean? He held a captain's rank in the last war, and, personally, I think it would be a help."

I was absolutely flabbergasted. Somehow I didn't dare trust myself to think of George in uniform, but Topman had never seen George and his moustache and his private paraphernalia, and he jumped at the suggestion. Wharton would be one of the staff, and the new Course would be completely in ignorance of what he really was.

Henrison said he'd fix things at once. He also gave permission, subject to Wharton's approval, for the funeral to take place on the Monday afternoon.

"A real good job done, Travers," Topman said when we had at last hung up. "I think we might as well keep the staff in ignorance, too, about who this man—this Captain Wharton really is."

I said it was an excellent suggestion, though I was already sweating as to whether Ferris's discretion could be relied on. Then I put it to the Colonel that as the train from the junction would be crowded with the new Course of students, it might be as well if I met Wharton at the junction by car. That would also allow me to give him some ideas before his arrival. The Colonel thought that was an excellent suggestion, too.

Then we adjourned to the Colonel's room for the conference, which was over in no time. We amended the syllabus, even if we had to throw more work on Ferris, and towards the end of the Course we fitted in a lecture on Security by Wharton. Then we decided on the wording of the allusions the Colonel would make after dinner that night to both the accident and Mortar himself. I left the Colonel committing the speech to memory'.

Next I had a look round and decided to take a brisk walk in the direction of the town. Then Harness collared me to introduce the Sapper major and the highly efficient-looking sergeant, who were just beginning their search of the ruins, helped by a couple of our men. Then, when I got going again, I ran into that cinema operator assistant of Flick's.

Before I tell you what we talked about, I might as well make something perfectly plain. When I was first associated with George Wharton, I took my stand on the question of lying. In my callow way I thought we should play cricket, and all that. To tell deliberate lies and create false situations in order to entrap even a criminal seemed to me to be hardly playing the game. George, who regarded me with the contempt I deserved, said he'd stop lying, as I called it, if the criminals began first.

It took me a goodish time to come round to his way of thinking; indeed I still wince inwardly a bit when I perpetrate some terrific untruth in the cause of justice. But on the whole I have become a fairly fluent liar when a situation seems to me to demand it, even if I can't quite separate such private and necessary duplicity from personal morals. Mind you, George still has me stone cold in the Ananias line. At times he will even lie on my behalf, and I find that he has committed me to the most outrageous statements.

"Well, how'd the films go?" I said to this operator of Flick's.

"Pretty well, sir," he said.

"I just peeped in," I said, "but Mr. Flick wasn't there. Or perhaps I didn't see him."

"Oh, no, he wasn't there," he said. "He had to go away, and we carried on."

"You gave him a report afterwards?" I suggested.

He showed a momentary surprise and then said that I was right. Mr. Flick had asked for a detailed report on each film—a kind of synopsis, in fact.

The artistry of lying—according to Wharton—is never to overdo it, so I nodded cheerfully and moved off towards the town. On the way I passed a big lorry loaded with timber, and on my way back a second one overtook me. What I thought about on that hour's walk is—like what the soldier said—not relevant evidence. Then when I did get back I went across to the ruins where the Sappers were still at work.

"Any luck?" I asked.

"Oh, yes," the major said quietly. "We know what caused the explosion." His voice lowered. "This is not official, of course, and even you had better keep it under your hat. It was that Blacker bomb."

Then he was giving me a queer look as I stood there blinking away and polishing my glasses.

"Don't tell me you'd guessed?"

As a matter of fact I had had from the first ideas at the far back of my mind, though I had never let them get farther than that. For one thing the shattering roar of the explosion was more than could have been made by a whole box of Mills bombs.

"I knew it was possible," I told him. "After all, your chaps were never able to find that bomb for us."

He nodded and frowned. "That chap Mortar must have been a first-class lunatic to've gone tampering with a thing like that."

I shook my head and said nothing, then we stood for a minute or two watching the progress of the tail-end of the search. All the floor-boards of the three huts had long since been ripped away, or at least the charred ends that showed where the boards had been, and most of the ashes had been sifted. Small sacks, properly labelled, stood ready to be taken away for analysis and further research. Suddenly the Sapper sergeant was straightening his body and having a good look at something. He wiped it carefully with his handkerchief, then held it to the light again, and was shaking his head and frowning.

"What's that you've got?" the major called.

The sergeant came over to us, and he spoke very quietly. What he handed over was something I could recognise—the cartridge used to propel a Blacker bomb from the bombard.

"Damn queer?" the major said, and then to me: "That bomb you lost was actually fired?"

"Of course it was," I said. "It struck low and ricochetted off, which was why it didn't happen to go off."

"I know," he said, patient with my stupidity. "But if the bomb was discharged from the bombard, then the cartridge was exploded. Then what's an unexploded cartridge doing here?"

I could only gape a bit foolishly.

"Lord knows," I said lamely, and then in the same moment I knew where the sergeant had found it. The search of what had been Mortar's room was over, and so was the search of Ferris's. That unused cartridge had been found, therefore, under what had been the floor of Staff's room. What it had been doing there was a question for Staff to answer—and to George Wharton.

# Chapter VIII

IF I HADN'T BEEN right on top of George when he got out of his compartment, I should never have spotted him, so smart was his appearance. I don't know why, but I had anticipated him in battle-dress, but there he was in a well-cut uniform and wearing a Sam Browne as dark and polished as a general's. As I came smilingly up, I was still puzzled by some other difference in him, and then I saw that he had probably spent his hours in the train on curling back his walrus and making it into something of an old-time Guardee. But a bulge in the breast pocket showed that he was still carrying the antiquated spectacles.

"Hal-*lo*! George," I said. "What's all this? Kidding yourself you're a soldier?"

He grunted. "I was soldiering, young fellow, when you were in your cradle."

"Then it must have been in the Boer War," I said, and relieved him of one of his two handbags. Instead of a British warm he was carrying a fine serviceable waterproof, and his back had miraculously straightened.

When we were in the rear of the comfortable saloon, and I had told the driver to take it easy on the way home, I had to swivel round for another good look at him.

"Well, I must say you're looking smart," I told him.

George actually smirked. "We old war-horses can prick our ears up," he told me, and gave a sideways nod of approbation.

He was wearing the three British war medals and a French one. I was so pleased at the general sight of him that I could only express it by trying to pull his leg.

"What did they give you that Croix de Guerre for?"

"Saving the wine ration," he said, and chuckled.

"Well, it'll give you a point of approach to Feeder," I told him. "Who's Feeder?"

"I'll tell you," I said, "and I'll start at the beginning."

It had taken us three-quarters of an hour of fastish driving to reach the junction and I thought now that I should have an hour in which to give George a full story. I had also drawn the plan of the camp you will have found earlier in the book.

"First of all," I said, "I'd better tell you that no one in the camp except the Colonel and I and Ferris—you remember telling me about Ferris?—knows who you really are. You'll be accepted as a War Office expert who's inquiring into the explosion, and you'll be also put down for the students' benefit as a member of the staff. You'll be put down, in fact, for at least one lecture."

He shot a look at me from under his shaggy eyebrows. "A lecture on Security," I said. "Don't tell me you've got the wind up?"

"Wind up!" He snorted. "I can do that standing on my head."

"Then you'll be highly popular," I told him. "Still you needn't go into training. Your effort's down for very near the end of the Course—a kind of threat over the students' heads—so you probably won't have to strain your blood-pressure system after all."

Well, I went over each member of the staff, trying to impress each one on his mind so that at the general introduction he'd have each one firmly fixed. Naturally, I included Feeder. Then I gave my personal opinion of each as formed in the three weeks' acquaintanceship. When he had thoroughly digested all that, I went through the first week's rehearsal, and the gradual forming of two hostile camps within the staff.

"You and I talked about that when we were having lunch that Friday," I reminded him. "You remember—the day you proclaimed to the room that you were a democrat. But I wouldn't like to say that the division in the school was of Regular and Not-so-Regular. That was behind it, perhaps, but there were other things that caused the split. The principal one was Mortar himself. If one man loudly proclaims to all and sundry—and with a damn-your-eyes attitude—that he belongs to one class, then you can expect the other class to take counter measures, even if those measures are passive."

"You're a bit beyond me there," George said. "You get on with what actually happened and I'll do my own theorising."

So I came to the two so-called accidents and my meeting with Mortar and Ferris in the Greyhound. George knew a Mills bomb as well as most, but I had to explain the Northover in de-tail. Brende, I said, would show him the actual works, and would arrange for him to let off a round or two if he so wished. George was already wishing; I could almost hear the old war-horse pawing the ground.

Then I came to the events of the Saturday—Mortar's birthday. There was much frowning, and pursing of lips from George, and he made me go over everything twice, following various movements on the plan. Next he wanted details of the bombard, but again I preferred to say that Brende would show him more in five minutes than I could tell in thirty.

"Brende won't let you fire that weapon, though," I had to add. "It's a terrifically powerful thing. A twenty-pound bomb and nine pounds and more of high-explosive inside it. What you'll have to do is wait till it's fired at a demonstration."

He saw that all right and switched back to a quick memory test on what I'd already told him, and by that time we were about fifteen minutes from the camp.

"Now we'll get down to brass tacks," he said, and held his pencil poised. "Have you got any ideas? Real ideas, mind you, not any goddam theorising."

I've told you about that perennial point of difference between us, and how George expects me to produce every time something that hits the nail clean on the head. If I do happen to get a clean hit, then he classes it under ideas. If I miss, then it's a theory.

"I've told you why I think Mortar was murdered," I said. "You haven't said if you agree or not."

"You don't think I'm as big a fool as that?" he said, and leered roguishly. "I've got to justify being down here, haven't I? And I mustn't let you down? Very well, then. Let's take it for granted he was murdered. What I'm asking you is, if you have any ideas about who did it."

"I know who didn't do it," I said. "It's a very short list—myself and Ferris. I don't like to add Feeder, because you never know. He may have had some private quarrel with Mortar which I never got to hear of, and we haven't yet heard what sort of an alibi he's got."

"It was only Feeder's evidence that proved there weren't any explosives in the room, wasn't it? If Feeder was lying, then the whole thing takes on a different complexion."

"That's a good point, George," I admitted. "Break down Feeder's evidence, and you may arrive at death through negligence instead of murder."

"I know all about that," he said. "And who else couldn't have done it?"

"No one," I told him. "Even the Colonel might have done it, if you want my answer to include the fantastic. But I don't see why Compress should have done it, or Nurse Wilton."

George grunted prodigiously, made a note or two in his book, and then was at me again.

"And who's your favourite for the job?"

"I haven't any," I said. "What's more, I'm not going to have any. I've given you the facts and it's up to you to do the theorising—and the suspect-eliminating. What'd the taxpayers buy you that beautiful uniform for?"

"You always will have your little joke," he told me cajolingly. "Don't tell me you haven't a favourite for the job."

"What I will tell you, George," I said, "is this. I'm too old a pet nowadays to be led round on a string. All I'll repeat is that I saw Collect looking where that bomb was supposed to be, and after that the bomb couldn't be found. I'll repeat that I didn't like Staff's manner when I ran across him at the end of the hut there, and I thought it damnably queer that he didn't put that anonymous note in his pocket. And it was queerer still that he should be out of real harm's way when the bomb happened to go off. I'll also repeat that Flick wasn't where he should have been that night, and that Brende more than once gave Mortar a look as if it'd be a pleasure to blow him sky-high. And when that accident occurred with the Northover, it was Brende who got his fists on it and said he'd take it away—remove the evidence, if you like—and have a real good look."

"Now that's the very kind of thing I wanted," George said unctuously. "And this is Peakridge, is it?"

He replaced his spectacles in their antiquated case and ran his eye over the little town as we went through it. The driver quickened pace and we overtook a couple of vehicles bringing students from the station.

"A couple of minutes and we'll be at the camp," I said. "You'll just have time to tell me if you've any ideas yourself. Not that I expect you to have any already."

That brought him out, as I'd hoped it would do. "And why shouldn't I have ideas? What've you been talking away for the last hour for if it wasn't to give me ideas?"

"Splendid," I said. "And what ideas have you got?"

He hesitated for a moment, and I knew why. George likes climaxes. I told you he was a showman. Not a buffoon, mind you, for no man can so maintain the dignity of the Law when he is so minded. But he has a weakness for tricks. He likes the glare of the lights, the flourish of the hand, and the "Hey presto!" before he produces his rabbits from the hat. But now we were in sight of the camp and he had no time to work up to a climax.

"Well, here's something you've missed," he told me grudgingly, and as if it were my fault that the car was slowing down. "Brende stopped Ferris from going into that burning room, didn't he?"

I nodded, wondering what was coming.

"To stop him getting burnt to death?"

"Obviously," I said.

"Are you sure?" he said, as the car came to a halt. Then his voice lowered. "Why shouldn't it have been the other way round? *Why shouldn't there have been something in that hut Brende didn't want Ferris to see?*"

The Colonel was waiting at his usual spot. George gave the walrus a final curl, and then the salute he gave the Colonel was as smart as a man could ever wish to see. The Colonel was undoubtedly impressed at once, and favourably. He was smiling quite genially as his hand went out.

"How are you, Captain Wharton? Damn those fellows there! They make so much noise you can't hear yourself speak."

He was referring to the contractor's men, who seemed to be swarming like ants about the burnt-out centre of the staff quarters. George's eyes were that way, too. Then Harness came up, and George seemed to recognise in him a kindred spirit, for he gave a grasp of the hand that made Harness wince.

"We're having tea in the Mess to-night," the Colonel bellowed, and off we moved. There was a special batman, by the way, for George, who was being accommodated in a spare room in the hospital.

Shorty was on duty and produced tea as soon as we entered. Collect, Staff, Flick, and Compress were already there, and I did the formal introductions. Neither George nor Ferris gave a flicker of recognition, but I doubt if he got far in his deductions, for George was already at the top of his form. He had a part to play and he was playing it for all he was worth; quietly, deferentially, urbanely. Flick I was watching with interest, and as something of a stranger, for it was two whole days since I had seen him other than at meals.

We all sat chatting over our meal, with George playing the hardest part of all—that of listener. Collect must have seen something congenial in him, for he brought up a chair alongside George's, and I could just hear them talking about experiences in the last war. Then, when the meal was over, George and I adjourned to the Colonel's room, and George's manner underwent a subtle change after he'd presented his credentials, so to speak. He considered, and rightly, that he'd given an exhibition of perfect discretion, and indeed of discipline. Now, in the Colonel's private quarters, he was the representative of what he was accustomed to call the Big Bugs, or the Powers that Be. It was the Colonel's turn to be deferential.

"Would it be too much to ask, Superintendent—"

Wharton held up a warning hand at once.

"Never that word, sir. When I play a part I like to *be* the part. Captain Wharton, sir, to you, and everybody, and wherever we happen to be. A slip of the tongue has ruined many a good investigation. And now, sir, what was it you wanted to know?"

"Well—er—just an idea of your plan of campaign, so to speak," the Colonel said.

Wharton bowed graciously. "And a very proper question, too. What I propose to do, sir, for at least a couple of days, is to go everywhere and say little. I hope to pop in at lectures and see the demonstrations, and even mix discreetly with the Home Guard. In other words, sir, I want to get this school into my skin. By that time the ideas ought to come of themselves, as they say. If not, then my name's Robinson."

He had glanced at me when he talked about getting to be a part of the school itself, and I knew he was recalling an investigation at a camp of my own. But when we got outside and I was accompanying him to his room to see he had all he wanted, I had to do a little leg-pulling.

"You're putting up a great show, George," I told him, and then while he was still purring: "And still clinging to the Maigret business?"

Maigret was the only detective of fiction about whose quiet exploits George had frankly confessed he liked to read. And no wonder. Physically the two seemed the spit of each other, and each was a product of the same hard school and imbued with what I might call the depths of domesticity.

"Maigret, my foot!" George snorted. "I was working that line and wearing out my flat feet long before Maigret was thought of. Maigret be damned!"

"Right-ho, George," I said. "We'll consider him damned."

Then he was giving a grunt as the batman showed us into the room, and I believe it was a grunt of disappointment at finding nothing for complaint. It was certainly an airy, comfortable room, and far more like home than my own. He had even been provided with a portable typewriter, a lockable desk, and special lighting, and there was a hospital bathroom across the corridor outside the door.

When we had both cleaned up we took a stroll round the camp, and there was plenty for George to see, what with the place swarming with the students of the new Course, and George's various identifications of buildings he had seen only on my map. Then the salutes of the students got rather a nuisance and we sheered off in the direction of the ranges. There was a kind of natural entrance, where the crescent of the hills narrowed, and once inside there and round the corner, George got on top of a handy mound and had a good look about him.

"The red flags still there, then?" was his first comment.

"Yes," I said. "The bomb was never officially found."

He nodded, then was giving a twisted grin which was meant to register a cynical distrust of other people's infallibility.

"I suppose you haven't wondered just where we'd be if that original bomb should ever happen to be found?"

"Thanks for the *we*, George," I said. "But to tell the truth I hadn't thought of any such thing. Losing twenty-pound bombs isn't like losing collar studs."

"Maybe," he said. "All the same, you'd look a pretty fool if it turned out that Mortar was killed by a different bomb altogether."

"Good," I said. "So you're up to your old tricks already. When it's a question of someone being a fool, it's *me*. When there's a job of work to be done, then it's *we*. But get this into your head from the word go. My job here is as laid down by the War House. Anything I can do to help in my spare time—well, here I am, even if it's to be something for you to sharpen your wits on. That's all I promise."

"Never knew such a chap as you are to take offence," he was grumbling at once. Then he glared. "What're we hanging about here for? Where was it you saw that chap Collect when you thought he was looking for the bomb?"

We set off that way, George grumbling at the going. Then I halted.

"You can't have it both ways, George. If that bomb's still somewhere here, then we oughtn't to go any farther."

"What's the idea? Wind up?"

"No," I said airily. "Merely a respect for regulations."

But he didn't go on by himself. All he said was—and in his best placatory manner—that there was no point in a couple of amateurs going over what the professionals had searched. So we turned towards the centre and I showed him the actual firing-points, and the scene of the queer affair of the Northover, and the very crater that had been made by the Mills that might have got Ferris. By then the first dusk was already in the sky, and when we were back at George's room, it was time to smarten ourselves up for the first real event of a new course-dinner in the dining-hut. When I picked George up to take him there, I saw he had been doing some heavy and efficient work on his moustache again. What had been a walrus was now a first-class buffalo.

"All set?" I said.

He gave a last complacent smirk in the mirror, and was so annoyingly pleased with himself that I had to try to knock him off his perch.

"Just one thing I ought to mention," I said. "I may be your stooge in the business of investigations, but outside all that, don't forget our relationships. You're trying to be a soldier and I'm trying to help you."

He gaped a bit. "For instance," I said. "I'm your superior officer. Don't forget in public to call me a —"

George glared, then called me something very different.

Collect had done some more rearranging of places at the high table, and George was placed between Collect and Flick. I could see he was enjoying that first public appearance, and though I had lost much of the thrill of the real opening of a new Course, I could still find a warmth of pleasure at the sight of the crowded room. The Home Guard seemed much like the last lot: just as fit and keen, just as busy already at talking shop, and just as silent when the full plates were in front of them.

The loyal toast was drunk at last and then the Colonel rose to make his usual opening speech. He was a man of little imagination but retentive memory, and his second effort was—but for circumstantial alterations—word for word like the first. There were the same gestures, the same inflexions of the voice, and it was fascinating to guess when he was going to smile, when to sink to an impressive inaudibility, and when to look round at the staff for some wholly unnecessary confirmation. The little speech we had decided on that morning had also been committed to memory.

It was a masterpiece of evasion. The students were told that at the school they would be taught the correct and safe handling of explosives, and that it was a matter of life and death neither to omit nor to exceed instructions. Carelessness was the enemy, and one little moment of forgetfulness might mean the death not only of a fool but of the innocent and trustworthy. If an officer of the staff, after years of immunity in the handling of the most deadly explosives, had had to pay the greatest price of all for an aberration—perhaps—

And there the Colonel broke artistically off. There was no need to labour the point, he said. He was sure that no man there had the wind up. Simple precautions were one thing, and nervousness another. But one thing remained to do. Captain Mortar, whose loss the school mourned, needed perhaps no tributes paid to his memory, but the last Course, who had worked under him, would always remember him as a magnificent instructor, and the staff were mourning the loss of a colleague. Captain Mortar always spoke of himself as a fighting soldier. That was a true summary of a varied and honourable career, and no man could wish for a finer epitaph.

So much for that. There was an unrehearsed silence of a few seconds and then came the rest of the speech. Then the Colonel rose and, with the staff at his heels, passed out through the lines of standing students. I had somehow got well to the rear, and as I stepped out to the darkness of the parade ground, a hand touched my arm, and Ferris was drawing me aside.

"Did you ever hear such damned hypocrisy?" he said.

That knocked me a bit off my perch. "You mustn't let yourself be jaundiced," I told him. "Certain things have had to be said in the interests of the school, and it's bad discipline for you to question them. What you've got to do, at least openly, is to let the dead bury the dead. You come along to the Mess and have a drink with everybody. The way you're behaving is the surest way to call attention to yourself."

He didn't say anything, but he turned my way.

"How's Feeder?" I asked him, as we quickened our pace in the cold.

"About the same," he said. "He was asking me when the funeral was going to be and if he might go to it."

"I expect it could be arranged," I said, and then suddenly had an idea that made me stop in my tracks.

"By the way," I said, "why shouldn't I try to take on Feeder as my private batman? That would keep his mind off brooding while he has to stay here. And he'd be nice and handy if a certain gentleman wanted information."

"I think he ought to like that," he said. "He always had a soft spot for you, sir."

"Then you see him and play on it," I told him. "But don't let him know I'm using him for ulterior motives. As soon as the hut is ready for occupation again I'll mention the matter to the Colonel. That strikes me as a favourable time. And, by the way, how are you getting on in the writing-room with Staff?"

He gave a little grunt and I could imagine the sneer. "Oh, we say good night and good morning."

I grunted too. "You open out a bit," I said, and rather testily, "and don't wear your grievances on your sleeve. A very few hours and you'll be confidentially questioned. That'll be the time to get things off your chest."

He did seem a little more friendly and even cheerful in the Mess that night, where, thanks perhaps to the presence of Wharton, there was quite a lot of business at the bar. I had never found the bar so animated a spot, and I was feeling quite cheerful myself when I turned in. It was fine to think that Feeder might be my batman in a day or two, and, frankly, not because of one of the reasons I had given Ferris. That reason had in fact been given in order to cover up a streak of sentimentality in my make-up, even if it was true that Feeder, as my batman, would always be on tap for questioning. But I liked Feeder, in spite of his unprepossessing appearance and various aberrations. He was the antithesis of red tape and convention and, like his late master, he was a fighting soldier.

# Chapter IX

I FORGOT TO TELL YOU that the Colonel had agreed to a readjustment of duties in order that I might have more time with Wharton, if he needed me. Collect was being called in to do a job of work at last, thank heaven, and he and the Colonel would undertake most of the supervisory duties.

I was up at an hour which I considered very early indeed, but when I went to Wharton's room he was not only up and dressed but doing a job of work, if you can give that description to the careful examination of what looked like a very high-class camera.

"What's it for, George?" I asked quite unnecessarily. "Taking a few pictures," he told me, equally unnecessarily. "I knew I'd have to be my own photographer and finger-print man, so I borrowed it and brought it along."

"Going to use it this morning?"

"Straightaway," he said. "The doctor'll be here in a couple of shakes, or he should be."

Then he did some explaining that fairly made my flesh creep. While I have grown somewhat accustomed to the grisly sights of violent and disintegrating deaths, I knew I could not bring myself to be present at what George and the doctor were about to do. But I had to admit that George was putting to the test a brilliant idea, and one that would never have occurred to myself. The Maigret business of absorbing atmosphere and then trusting to ideas to come was all very well, but George was only too aware that certain essentials came first.

When Compress came in I heard all about it.

"Sorry to get you out of bed at this unearthly hour," Wharton began, "but there's something that has to be done before this afternoon's funeral. I want to photograph and I want you to label every portion of the body you've recovered—that lies under the sheet, in fact."

Compress had looked a bit surprised. I was also gathering that Wharton must have already dropped him a hint as to who he actually was.

"Well, it's rather a mixed lot," Compress said. "He caught the full blast of the explosion and most of him practically disintegrated. I can't put it more clearly than that."

"Well, a word in your ear," Wharton said, wagging a paternal finger and with a fine pretence of humour. "This business is highly confidential. I know what you're going to say—that it's your creed to keep confidences, but it's my official duty to warn you. Now I can be frank with you about what we're going to do."

As soon as he said that I knew only too well that frankness would consist in revealing the obvious and keeping the rest well up his sleeve.

"Here's where we start," Wharton told him, and laid the camera down. "According to what's left of the body we might determine the exact position of Captain Mortar in relation to the explosive at the very moment of death. Suppose, for instance, he'd been found with his head blown off. That might have proved—*might*, mind you—that he was crimping a fuse into a detonator with his teeth instead of using nippers. If the legs were gone and the trunk left, then he probably kicked against something on the ground. But you say the torso's gone."

"A few bits and pieces left," said Compress casually. "Extremities of limbs and so on."

"Well, the expert to whom these photographs and things are going has had tougher jobs than the one we're giving him," Wharton said. "But here's something that mayn't have occurred to you."

He tore a page from his notebook and drew a couple of diagrams.

"This first one is a hand and part of a forearm found after the explosion, and we assume the arm was in a normal position at the owner's side when the bomb went off.

"Now then. The blast of an explosion is upwards and outwards, provided there's anything to check the downward blast, and in this case there must have been the floor. Very well then. This first drawing severed the arm in such a way that the owner must have been facing the explosive point. In this other diagram, it's just as plain that he must have had his back to the

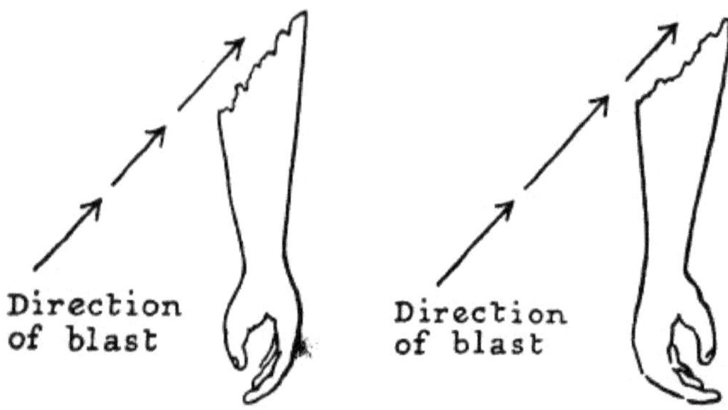


explosive point. Is that perfectly clear? It is? Then we'll get on a bit.

"You say the torso doesn't exist. That proves conclusively that he was slap up against it when it went off. You might even assume the middle of his body was in actual contact. Very well then. Our photographs should show whether he was facing the explosive or had his back against it; isn't that so?"

"It looks so to me," I said. "If Compress has enough fragments and you can take clear enough photographs, you ought to find out a whole lot about that explosion."

To my surprise Compress had a kind of objection to make. "But how could he have had his back to the explosive?" He saw George's lifted eyebrows, and hedged a bit. "I mean, I was given to understand that he was doing something with explosives. You can't have your back turned and be doing something at the same time."

"You be patient with an old gentleman," Wharton told him. "Explosives can go off by delayed action. Most bombs go off with a fuse. Mortar might have inadvertently set off the action that started the fuse burning, and then have turned his back to do something else. Still," and he waved an airy hand, "that's neither here nor there. If you're ready I think we might make a start. The light looks like being good and after breakfast we can go right ahead."

"You won't want me," I said hopefully, but already I was talking to George's back, for he had grabbed the camera and was off. I sidled out, then moved at a more stately pace back to my room, and hoped for the breakfast bugle.

After breakfast I kept out of George's way. When the parade had moved off to the lecture-room I watched the progress of the rebuilding of the centre of the hut, and I was not surprised when the foreman told me that the job would be entirely finished that evening. Then I thought I would take a walk which would lead me by the magazine, and present an opportunity of seeing Store. So far I had never seen him at really close quarters, for his work was largely connected with and taking place in the magazine, from which he issued material either live or dead for use at lectures, demonstrations, and actual firing. He also was responsible for the keeping of the highly important records of issues and expenditures.

The door of the magazine was open and I made no bones about walking in. Store was there, and he was trying to be humorous and official at the same time as he waved me back to the door.

"Sorry, sir, but I daren't let you in here." As I backed out again, he explained. "I have to search everyone who comes in here, sir, to see if they've any matches or stuff like that on them."

"I'm sorry," I said. "The last thing I want to do is to break regulations."

I don't think I described Store to you, though I did say that he was a Second-class Warrant Officer, and addressed therefore not as Mr. Store—as one said "Mr. Brende"—but as Quartermaster-Sergeant. But you can picture him in a second; a shortish, powerful-looking man with ramrod back, a minute Chaplin or Adolf moustache, and a sallow complexion. Perhaps that moustache prejudiced me against him, for I hate all topiary work in moustaches, and above all the movie-star streak. But I also didn't like the look of Store in other ways. I didn't like his mouth, and his eyes struck me as shifty. I didn't care too much for his manner either, which was far too hearty and decidedly cocksure.

"Now then, sir," he said. "What can I do for you?"

"I don't know that you can do anything, as you put it," I said somewhat frigidly. "As second-in-command of the school I felt it my duty to see at least something of the magazine and the armoury."

"Come on then, sir," he said. "No matches or inflammable matter on you?"

There was nothing but a petrol lighter, which I left outside. Store led the way in, and I saw at once that it was no place for a man who might suffer from nerves. If nine pounds of high-explosive had blown Mortar to smithereens, then if the collection at which I was looking happened to go off, there wouldn't be enough of me to scrape up. Mills were there in hundreds, all beautifully oiled, and there was a row of murderous-looking Blackers, as well as cases of Stickies and the big Anti-tank that looks like a full-sized thermos. There were plenty more that I didn't recognise.

"What happens when you lose anything?" I asked.

"We can't lose anything, sir. The system's too good. Everything that leaves here, no matter if it's a dummy, has to be signed for. Whatever's unexpended comes back and I sign for it. The difference has to tally with the written certificate of the officer who expended the difference."

"Well, there's the first loophole," I said, maliciously delighted to have the chance. "When you get down to brass tacks, your real safeguard is the integrity of the officer who expends the explosives."

"How's that, sir?"

"Heavens, man, think!" I told him impatiently. "An officer might think he'd like a Sticky for himself, to experiment with. Right. All he's got to do is certify that he's exploded the ten with which you issued him, whereas he'd have exploded only nine."

"There're other safeguards," he said. "Always at least two officers there, sir."

"And each keeps a record and counts the bombs as they go off?"

"They're supposed to, sir."

"I see. So we arrive at a possibility of collusion. Let's suppose something that's utterly fantastic; something that didn't happen because everybody's confident of the integrity of the two officers concerned. Let's suppose that two officers put their heads together—Captain Mortar and Mr. Ferris, for example—because they think they can improve a bomb. It'd be child's play, wouldn't it, for them to retain an unexploded bomb?"

"Well, if you put it like that, sir, I suppose it would. Only you can't make regulations for things like that."

"Agreed," I said. "Yet one curious thing does remain. Captain Mortar blew himself up, shall we say, with some very powerful explosive. Where'd he get it from?"

Store smiled confidently. The question had evidently been discussed and he had an answer ready, and one naturally that would redound in some measure to his own credit.

"Probably brought it with him, sir, from that other school he was at. They aren't so particular there, so they tell me, as we are here."

"Well, that's excellent hearing," I said. "What are those little chaps up there?"

"Bakelites," he told me.

I said I ought to have recognised them, but my bat eyes were always playing tricks on me. Would he mind letting me have a look at one at close quarters?

He fetched a very short ladder and brought me one from the shelf. When he had replaced it I said it was getting late and I'd have to be going. I thanked him for showing me round and I congratulated him on the scrupulous cleanliness of everything.

At the door I turned. "Strictly in confidence, I think I'd better return you these."

With something of horror he watched me lug the two Millses from the pocket of my British warm, and he took them as if they were a couple of snakes.

"Gawd, sir, where'd you get these from?"

"Just put them in my pocket while you were getting me the Bakelite," I said.

An extraordinary' expression flashed across his face. It wasn't suppressed anger, or surprise, and it wasn't sheepishness at having been caught out, even if trickily. It was more like suspicion, and as if he were wondering just how much I knew.

"I suppose I could have slipped a Blacker under my arm," I said.

"Not a heavy thing like that, you wouldn't," he told me, and was shaking his head. "But that wasn't a fair test, sir, if you don't mind me saying so. I wouldn't think of watching an officer like you."

I smiled consolingly and apologetically. "Of course it wasn't a fair test. Forget all about it, except that when anybody comes in here in future, imagine he's as big a rogue as I am."

He had quite recovered his aplomb by the time we were outside. He even showed me of his own accord the subsidiary magazine which lay some hundred yards farther north, and housed the inflammable stuff like the S.I.P. bottles. There were scores of yards of all sorts of fuses, and electrical apparatus used for remote detonation, and when I finally left him I felt I had had a very interesting hour.

I dropped in at the Mess where Shorty made me some mid-morning coffee, and it was well after eleven hours when I went in search of George again. He had finished his job with Compress and was now in the room that had been Mortar's. Feeder was there, and the camp Quarter-master, arranging a new issue of furniture precisely like the old. Feeder was assuring Wharton that the room was exactly as it had been on the Saturday morning, except for private baggage. Wharton went to the trouble of having two bags of his own brought in to represent those destroyed.

While he was waiting for them to come he explained that the photograph of the room would supplement the photographs of the body, and that Compress had already marked on a ground-plan of the room the spots, as nearly as he could remember, where each portion of the body had been found. The fire had been the really disastrous concealer of evidence.

If I go into that a little more fully, it is because you may not know even the general action of explosives. When a high-explosive goes off, there is an instantaneous production of an incredible amount of gas, and the efforts of that gas to accommodate itself in space, by expanding, may be taken as a simple explanation of what we call blast. Now the expanding gases naturally take the line of least resistance. If the explosion occurred, for instance, on the floor, then the floor-boards would offer some resistance, and more blast would occur upwards than downwards. But there would still be a considerable blast effect downwards, for the quantity of explosive was considerable, and the floor-boards flimsy by comparison with, say, a steel sheet. If there had been no fire, then, one could have seen the hole in the floor and known *precisely* where the explosion occurred. If it had taken place on a shelf by the partition or outside walls, there would have been similar evidence left. But the fire had burnt practically every bit of timbering, and all evidence had gone. What the Sappers had discovered beneath the ashes was a small depression that might have been a crater, and it was situated near the middle of the partition wall that separated Ferris's room from the one where we stood. As Mortar's bed had stood by that wall, Wharton and I were inclined to agree with the Sappers that the depression was not a crater but a natural hole under the floor-boards, which the original builders had not thought it necessary to level.

As for the evidence that might have been given by the furniture of the room, all the wood had gone up in flames and the metal was a twisted mass. One thing only seemed a lucky find. Of Mortar's two bags or trunks, one had gone almost entirely and only fragments of it had been found. The other had been blown through the partition into Staff's room, where it had been found beneath the general debris, though badly shattered and very much burnt. Wharton's opinion therefore was that when the bomb had gone off it had been in the first bag, and it had been standing, according to Feeder, at the foot of the bed and near the chest of drawers.

Feeder was dismissed before Wharton took his photographs of the reconstructed room. A motor dispatch rider was waiting to take the whole series to the Yard, and as George was busy with that and other things, I didn't see him again by himself till after lunch, when we strolled back towards the Colonel's room. Then I told him about the trick I'd played on Store. He wasn't nearly so enthusiastic as I'd hoped.

"I get all your points," he said, "but I rather wish you hadn't done it. A plausible chap like that oughtn't to be put on his guard."

"Dammit all, George," I said. "According to that line of argument there'd never be any inquiries."

"Didn't you say Ferris was tackling him?"

"I did," I said, surprised enough. "But he's doing it entirely on his own. Why should he pass anything on to you? Or have you co-opted Ferris as a member of the investigation committee?"

He shot me a look. "Not yet," he said. "But don't you see? You've been seeing Store and with a very plausible excuse, and you think he was suspicious. In fact, he's rumbled you. Probably he'll rumble Ferris, too. What chance shall I have if I ever have to tackle him?" We waited for the Colonel and went into his room for a brief conference. I got permission to employ Feeder, and Wharton saw to it that the regular Sappers were asked to make another immediate and concentrated search for the possibly unexploded bomb. The Colonel didn't see the point. Surely it was beyond doubt that Mortar had found that bomb and removed it to his room.

"Let alone the fact that Feeder swears it never was in the room," Wharton said, "the fact remains that in this kind of job, sir, you've got to be dead sure. A man's neck may depend on it."

"Then you actually think it murder?" the Colonel asked, and the final word came out with an effort.

"I'm not prepared at the moment to tell you anything, sir," Wharton said. "The less we all know, the better. For instance, we three are the only ones in the camp who know that Mortar *was* killed by a Blacker bomb. Even Harness doesn't know. Very well then. Suppose some officer on the staff mentions to one of us that it was bad luck, say, that Mortar should get killed by a Blacker bomb. I've never mentioned the fact; you haven't and Major Travers hasn't. Very well then, sir. There's the man we want to interview. How'd *he* get to know it?"

"Inspector Hornleigh investigates," I nearly said, but the Colonel was obviously pleased. When Wharton told him about the morning's gruesome work, he was tremendously impressed.

"So long as we keep the old fellow amused, that's all we need," George told me later. "I'd say he's a chatty old bird, and what he doesn't tell somebody or other in confidence is what he doesn't know. And that's going to be the devil of a lot."

I didn't see him again till after the funeral. I had to attend it as representing the Colonel. Ferris couldn't possibly be spared, but Feeder was allowed to go. There were also a couple of buglers to sound the Last Post over the grave, and a detachment of our men to make a decent military show. In the town I collected the wreaths that had been ordered: one to which all the staff had subscribed, one from the general staff, and one from Ferris.

On the whole it was what modern jargon calls a good show, though I found it melancholy enough, especially when the bugles sounded on the sharp autumnal air. Feeder was very distressed. As we dispersed prior to the return, I could hear him telling all and sundry what a great character Mortar had been, and I thought it might be just as well if I brought him back in my car, however unorthodox the act might appear.

"You realise you'll have to stay in the camp for a few days?" I said to him. "When the inquiry's over, then you'll be at liberty to go."

He understood that, he said, and was giving a dour shake of the head. I guessed he was thinking that those arrangements suited only too well the playing of his hand. The last thing he wanted was to be sent away from the school. Then I asked him if Mr. Ferris had mentioned a certain proposition to him—that, in fact, he should act as my batman during the rest of his stay.

"I'll be real pleased to do that, sir," he said. "All the hanging about nearly drives you off your chump. I'm a good batman, sir. The Captain would have told you that."

"I'm sure he would," I told him, and then nothing was said till we were almost in sight of the camp again.

"You won't mind if I ask you something, sir." He didn't wait for my reply but went right on. "You wouldn't mind if I attended to some little things I want to do. I shan't neglect you, sir, only I mayn't be always on hand just when you think I ought to be there."

"In your spare time you do as you like," I said, and he assured me that was all he wanted to know.

But when we got out of the car I motioned him aside. "You can keep a still tongue in your head?" I began.

"No man better, sir, though I say it myself."

"Then keep a still tongue about what I'm saying to you now, which is this. Drop that damn-silly idea of yours about squaring any accounts for Captain Mortar. Higher authorities have got that little job in hand and they'll do it far better than you."

He merely nodded and said nothing. I said no more either, for I had sense enough to know that the advice had fallen on remarkably deaf ears.


Wharton spent at least some of his afternoon listening to one of Ferris's lectures, and he was tremendously enthusiastic.

"Whoever would have thought it!" he said. "That chap's a fighter, if ever there was one, and he knows his stuff."

"Naturally he does," I said. "He had all that experience in Spain, and he did two or three Courses, including one at least at a Weapons' School, before he came here."

"Weapon Schools!" he said, and snorted contemptuously. "Take that young fellow Staff. That's your schools. Smart young officer, I grant you, and knows his stuff, but no real guts."

"So you heard Staff too, did you?" I said. "The fact of the matter is this, George. You and I are attracted by men like Ferris and Mortar because they make us think we're younger than we are. When they talk, we're daredevils again. No carpet slippers for us on cold dark nights. We want to be out mopping-up tanks, and sticking knives into Huns."

"Isn't that the line of talk you want for the Home Guard?" he asked indignantly.

"It is," I said. "And the fact that Ferris made you chuck out your chest and straighten your back just shows what a spell-binder he is. Anything else have you seen or heard, by the way?"

He said he had seen Brende, who had gone over both the Blacker and the Northover with him. He had also been introduced to Mortar's successor, who had arrived while I was at the funeral. He described him as colourless, and as he does not concern this story, that one-word description will serve.

When I slipped into the Mess before dinner, Ferris was there. He asked me to have a drink with him, and I had it. Then he told me something that really pleased me.

"I think I've changed my mind, sir, about something we talked about," he said, and just a bit shamefacedly. "I think I'll try and mix in a bit more."

"Good man," I said. "Have another drink."

He said he wouldn't, and in the same breath was doggedly insisting that he'd always have tried to be a good mixer if it hadn't been for others. I said I knew that. And would he join Wharton and me at the cinema after dinner. Flick was showing some brand-new films, and both Wharton and I were in need of a little relaxation. He said he'd be delighted.

The three of us sat by ourselves well at the back of the huge room and we did no talking, for the films were as good as promised. It was after twenty-two hours when we came out to the parade ground, snapping our eyes a bit after the strain, and glad to breathe the clear air after the smoke and fog of the room.

As we drew near our quarters I asked Ferris if he were pleased to get back to his old room again.

"I suppose I am," he said. "I hope it won't be ghost-ridden, that's all."

"I'm a pretty good ghost layer," Wharton said. "Which reminds me. Tomorrow you'll be on the carpet officially. Instead of spending your night looking out for ghosts, you'd better get all the answers ready."

"Don't let him scare you," I told Ferris. "He's the gentlest Inquisitor who ever twisted a rack."

We said good night to George and then went back to our rooms. As Ferris dropped me at mine, he said a curious thing. "A very enjoyable show to-night, sir."

"It was," I said. "And most instructive."

"Flick's a good hand at his job," he said. "I wonder if Wharton knows, by the way, that he's a stamp collector?"

# Chapter X

I WANT TO CONDENSE those interviews of Wharton's with the staff, and give nothing but the relevant facts that emerged. They took place in his room at the hospital on the Tuesday morning, when, by a slight adjustment of times, every person concerned was available. I was present throughout, as a kind of liaison officer.

When Wharton put it to the Colonel that his evidence was merely being taken *pour encourager les autres*, so to speak, he was only too ready to give in. As a matter of fact he and Collect said precisely the same thing. Each, as I knew, had been up to the eyes in the work which the end of a Course involved; each had been in his own room from after dinner onwards, and each recalled the explosion by the fact that the lights had gone out at the same time. Compress made a statement much to the same effect, except that he had been in his room writing a letter to his fiancée. All three had at once rushed out into the open and had met where I first saw them.

Wharton's handling of those three witnesses had been as matter of fact as their evidence, but when Ferris came in everything was very different. The atmosphere was chatty and informal, perhaps because he knew he was dealing with a decidedly touchy specimen. There was a bit of general gossip to begin with, then Wharton was asking how Ferris liked life at Peakridge. He made a wry face.

"Well, to get down to business," Wharton said. "No need to tell you that everything said here is as secret as the grave. And I needn't ask you what your movements were on the Saturday night, because Major Travers knows all about them. By the way, you and he had a narrow squeak? If you'd stayed gossiping by the door you'd have both been in Kingdom Come."

"To be perfectly frank," Ferris said, "I go hot and cold all over when I think of something else. Suppose there'd have been a booby-trap connected with the electric light!"

"Good God, yes!" Wharton said, eyes bulging. "I remember you talking all about booby-traps in that lecture of yours, and remarkably interesting it was. What you mean is, a booby-trap connected with the switch. Meant for Mortar, of course, only it so happened that one of you turned the light on."

"That's right," Ferris said. He was about to say something else, then he hesitated and looked at me. "Do you mind if I get a whole lot of things off my chest? There mayn't be any truth in them. They're just what I think myself."

"This is Liberty Hall," said Wharton largely. "Say what you like without fear or favour."

"Well, my idea is this," Ferris said, "and it's been worrying me nearly to death. I think I was responsible for killing Mortar." He smiled at our startled look. "What I mean is this. Everybody on the staff attended that particular lecture where I went into the making and use of booby-traps. What I did was to show someone how to kill Mortar."

Wharton was looking remarkably serious. "Would it have been as easy as all that? No special knowledge required?"

"The whole thing's child's play," Ferris said. "That's why I said I went hot and cold all over when I thought of Major Travers and me inside Mortar's room. At any second either of us might have touched or kicked against the very thing that set the trap off."

"Yes," said Wharton slowly, and pursed his lips. "It's a damned unpleasant thought. But suppose Mortar was killed by a booby-trap. Who knew his room was empty that night and that he was working with you?"

Ferris shrugged his shoulders. "His door was open. I know that because we found the key inside. All anybody had to do was to look in and see he wasn't there."

"You're making me go hot and cold too," I said. "But, repeating Wharton's reminder about secrecy from the other angle, I think I ought to tell you something highly confidential. It was a Blacker bomb that killed Mortar."

His mouth gaped, and then he was licking his lips. "My God, you don't say so! What a bloody fool I was." He was shaking his head. "I ought to have known it from the noise it made. But wait a minute. Was it that bomb that didn't go off that day? The one that wasn't found?"

"Possibly," I said. "It still remains to be proved."

He was shaking his head again. "How the devil could anybody hide a thing like that? Twenty pounds weight to hide and then to carry it to the room."

"Would the booby-trap be easy?" Wharton asked. "That part'd be easy enough," Ferris told him. "Merely the arranging of some kind of electrical contact with a detonator. You kick against a trip-wire or pick up some object or other, the contact is made and up she goes. It might easily have been done through the electric fire and the power switch."

"Then thank heaven we didn't turn it on," I said whole-heartedly.

"Well, I may have to have a long talk with you later about rigging up traps of that kind," Wharton said; "but all I want at the moment is your assurance that it wasn't beyond the power or intelligence of any member of the staff."

"If anyone couldn't do that sort of thing, especially on top of my lecture on the subject, then he was an absolute fool in electrical matters," Ferris said.

Wharton nodded. I cut in. "I hope I'm not abusing any confidence, but there was a somewhat cryptic remark you made to me last night—about Flick being a stamp collector, like yourself Still in the strictest confidence, has that any bearing on the subject of this morning's investigations?"

His eyes narrowed and he looked away for a moment or two before he spoke. "I don't know. I hardly like to tell you because it shows I have a very unpleasant mind."

"So have we all—at times," said Wharton helpfully.

"Well, here goes then," Ferris said. "I don't know if either of you collects anything, but if you do, you know that the last person to trust is a fellow collector. They're the biggest thieves in the world. No matter how moral they are in everything else, they'll slip something into their pockets and not turn a hair. I showed Flick my stamps because he said he was a collector."

He paused again. "I hardly know how to go on. It'll all sound so damn-silly."

"Let's hear it, silly or not," Wharton said.

"Well, after the explosion that night I grubbed about with a torch in the dark and I couldn't find a trace of either of my albums. They were in a drawer right up against the partition wall of Mortar's room, but I hoped something might have escaped. Then I asked the doctor if he'd seen anything, and that Sapper officer. None of them had seen even a bit of the cover of an album."

"In other words," said Wharton, leaning forward eagerly, "you think it wasn't impossible that Flick lifted those stamp albums before the explosion?"

"And that it was he who arranged the explosion—not thinking it'd kill Mortar—to cover up the theft?" was my addition.

Ferris again shrugged his shoulders. "I'll leave it to you, gentlemen. I will say this. When Major Travers and I were helping poor old Mortar across to his room we saw Flick go past the end of the hut. Did you notice anything else, Major?"

"I can't say I did," I told him. "My eyes are pretty bad in the dark."

"Mine are pretty good," he said. "What I saw was that Flick was carrying something under his arm. I won't pretend I know what it was because I didn't know then and I don't now. All I've done since is put two and two together."

Staff was the next one in, and he repeated the story he'd told on the Saturday night, adding that he remembered now that he put the anonymous note on the top of his chest of drawers with a tobacco tin on top.

"Who did you think wrote the note?" Wharton asked.

"I thought it was Flick perhaps, or Ferris." He smiled apologetically at me. "Ferris wasn't a bad sort when he was out of Mortar's company. I don't mean he wasn't decent then, because he was. I mean he never egged Mortar on, or was offensive."

"Have you spoken to either of them about the note?"

"Oh, yes," he said. "And to Brende, and Compress. Nobody knows a thing about it. My idea is that Mortar wrote it himself as part of the rag, so that he could say he'd scared me into staying in my room."

"You say you questioned Flick about the note," I said. "Was it the same night?"

"No, it wasn't," he said. "I wanted to question him, but I knew he was busy at the cinema."

"You didn't think of looking in his room in case he might be there?"

He smiled. "He wasn't there, sir. I mean, you can hear old Flick barging round like an elephant. I always know when he's in his room."

"And what about Captain Mortar's room that night?" Wharton said. "Did you hear anybody in there?"

"Nothing at all, sir. I did think I heard somebody once, so I put my ear to the partition and listened. Not snooping, sir, but because I wanted to know what he might be up to. When I listened I couldn't hear a thing."

"Well, you certainly had a lucky escape yourself," Wharton said. "That explosion might have made a nasty mess of you." Then he was peering over his spectacle tops. "You're a bit of an expert on explosives, I take it?"

"I, sir?" He smiled. "I don't know a thing—except what one picks up in the ordinary way. They didn't do that sort of stuff at Sandhurst in my time."

Out went Staff, and it was Wharton's turn to do some head-shaking. "That young feller gets my goat," he said, and almost despondently. "Talks like one of those B.B.C. tenors. And takes himself a damn-sight too seriously."

"One very interesting fact is beginning to emerge, George," I said. "It's a problem that may have to be decided and very soon. Was that note a fake? I mean, did it exist only in Staff's prepared story? If it didn't, then why was Staff kept in his room that night?"

"Do you think I haven't thought of all that?" he growled at me. "The idea was to kill two birds with one stone. But for the grace of God—and assuming all the time that the note wasn't a fake, of course—Staff should have been blown up too."

"And Ferris, if it comes to that. A regular holocaust, George."

"Why not?" he said pugnaciously.

"Well, for this reason, for one thing. It makes things too easy. All we'd have to find would be someone who hated all three sufficiently to try to murder them. But that doesn't make sense. I told you that this place was divided into two camps—the Regular and Not-so-Regular, or the Mortarites and anti-Mortarites. Very well then. While I can imagine someone trying to wipe out the whole of the Mortarites—Mortar and Ferris—at one swoop, why include an anti-Mortarite like Staff?"

"We're not here to theorise," George told me impatiently. "We want to get this preliminary investigation over. Take a look out and see if Flick's handy."

Flick was handy. In fact he was talking earnestly to Staff at the south end of the hut. I called to him and when he came in he apologised for being late.

"That's all right," Wharton said. "Sit down there and make yourself at home. Smoke if you want to."

The usual assurance about secrecy, a few deft blandishments about the cinema, and he was putting his first question.

"You were at the cinema all Saturday night, I believe?" The reply came pat. "As a matter of fact I wasn't. I didn't feel any too good, so I left a man of mine to carry on." He smiled at Wharton's look. "I know I look as if I never had an illness in my life, but honestly I do get some queer spells. Sort of singing in the ears and giddiness."

Wharton nodded sympathetically, and then inquired about the cure.

"The only thing to do is to get out in the fresh air," Flick said. "That's what I actually did. I just took a quiet stroll along the Peakridge road. When I got back, I had a wee crack with a feller I met and then I was just in time to hear the explosion. As a matter of fact it was myself who warned the fire squad."

"Good work," said Wharton, and then was pursing his lips. "Still, we'd rather hoped that you'd been in your room some part of the night, then you might have heard or seen something. You might have seen Captain Mortar, for instance, or someone going into his room."

"Sorry I can't help you there," he said, and that was virtually all.

When he'd gone I told George there was a suggestion I'd like to make, even at the risk of being ticked off. It was this. If Flick had really stolen those stamps, then he'd have sent them away at once, as far too dangerous stuff to keep in his own room. In that case the camp post office might be induced to disclose the fact that Flick had sent away a parcel on the Monday or even the Sunday morning.

"I was thinking that myself," George said. "It's a ticklish business but I'll try it."

Brende was next on the list, but when I looked outside there was no sign of him. Wharton fumed a bit, then impatiently had a look for himself. I heard voices as he came back, and whom should he be bringing in but Nurse Wilton.

It was George's boast that women were his most successful witnesses. I don't know if he had that inscrutable quality known as IT, or its even later variety known, I believe, as OOMPH, but he certainly had something to justify the claim. I have tackled women witnesses, using every art of deference, courtesy, and even flattery, and have got nowhere. George has taken over and, with what I regard as wheedlings, displays of forlornness and longings to be mothered, has had the same witnesses eating out of his hand.

He was beaming as he came in. "Do you know we'd absolutely forgotten you?" he was saying to Nurse and looking accusingly at me. "Mind you, I did say to Major Travers that you might give us some help, but he rather pooh-poohed the idea."

She had given me a charming smile when she came in, and now she seemed rather amused. She had a round face with the most delightful dimples, by the way, and her smile had always struck me as roguish and provocative.

"I think Major Travers is a woman-hater," she said.

"Merely uxorious," I said as I made a cushion for her chair out of one of George's blankets. "Will you have a cigarette?"

"Will I not?" she said, and when it was alight, settled her elbows comfortably on the table. "Now, what do you want me to tell you?"

Wharton grimaced, then scratched his head. "To tell the truth, I don't know."

"Don't tell me you inveigled me in here under false pretences?"

Wharton chuckled, then was peering at me over his spectacle tops.

"What was it we wanted to ask Nurse Wilton?"

"Only if she saw Captain Mortar on the Saturday night," I said. "Or perhaps if she saw anybody go into his room."

She was shaking her head at once. All days were alike to her, just as they were alike to the Course. She had had dinner in her room, then dressed the hand of a man who'd cut himself opening a tin. Then she had read a book for a bit, after which she had taken a very short walk along the Peakridge road. As she was entering the camp again she was overtaken by Flick, and she had hardly got back to her room when the explosion occurred.

"Flick saw you as far as here, didn't he?" I said. "I only mention the fact because I saw him going back to the lecture-room at about that time."

I think I have indicated that she had all the aplomb in the world, but that apparently innocent remark of mine made quite a different look flash across her face. My own idea was that she wanted to deny the fact, and then was suddenly seeing no harm in admitting it.

"Oh, yes," she said. "I didn't want him to come, but he insisted on seeing me to the door."

I tried to look roguish too. "What was it he was carrying when I saw him? It wasn't a baby was it?"

A slight flush ran across her face; there was not a shadow of doubt about that. It couldn't have been outraged modesty at the mention of babies, and she was flicking off her cigarette-ash to gain time.

"I don't remember him carrying anything," she said. "Why did you ask?"

"For no reason at all," I said, "except that I'm a grossly curious person."

There was a tap at the door and Brende peeped in. Nurse Wilton rose at once and said she would really have to be going. Wharton ushered her out and was saying he was intending to see more of her. I could hear him telling her he was a lonely old fogey, and then the voices died away. I asked Brende if he'd be so good as to wait just a minute, and I heard Wharton saying the same thing as he came back.

"What'd you think of her?" he fired at me as soon as he got in.

"I told you about her and Flick," I said. "I think Flick took her for a walk that night. That Peakridge road yarn was all bunkum."

He nodded in agreement. "Why was she all hot and bothered when you mentioned Flick carrying something?"

"You spotted that, did you?" I asked.

He snorted. "What d'you think I'm here for? And let me tell you something else. When Flick went out of here he went straight to her room. He sheered off when he saw me and that's why I got her to come here. When I went back just now he was still hanging around. I'll lay a fiver they're comparing notes."

"Well, they may be trying to conceal the Saturday night walk," I said, "and if so they're taking it mighty seriously. What I'd like to know is, what Flick was actually carrying when he left her. It couldn't have been the two albums of stamps. She wouldn't have been hot and bothered about them because she wouldn't have known what they were, even if he'd been fool enough to let her see them."

Wharton said there was no use in theorising and we'd better see Brende. His manner with him was purely business-like. What did he think the explosion was when he heard it.

Brende said he was absolutely flabbergasted. If the sound had come from the opposite direction he would have thought the magazine had gone up.

Brende said he and Store had spent the evening in the sergeants' mess, listening to the Saturday night music-hall show, but at the actual moment of the explosion he was outside, having gone to the lavatories. When he'd recovered from his first bewilderment he had run towards the hut, then had seen the flames and had run back to warn the fire picket. Mr. Flick was already doing it.

"Where did he come from?" I asked, as if I hadn't known.

"I saw him run out of the lecture-room, sir," Brende said.

That was all the information we got from him. Wharton thanked him profusely and said he would probably have another private lesson on explosives at some convenient time, and then out he went.

"His evidence was straightforward enough," Wharton said. "He didn't look the least bit uncomfortable to me. That bit about Flick darting out of the cinema fits in. He'd have gone to the cinema to see how things had been getting on while he was away."

"And to ask if anybody had been making inquiries, so that he could have an excuse ready to explain his absence," I said.

Wharton glanced at his watch and said we'd just have time to see Feeder. I went out to find him, but he was not in my room. Another batman told me he'd seen him leave the room an hour or so previously, and he hadn't seen him since. Wharton was very annoyed.

"It's no use getting annoyed with me, George," I said. "Feeder made a start with me only this morning, so perhaps he hasn't got used to my ways. But I distinctly impressed on him that he was to be handy at midday."

"Well, we'll give him a minute or two," he said, "and then if he doesn't turn up I'll see him to-night."

I remembered then what Feeder had told me the previous afternoon on the way back from the funeral, that he might have various private affairs of his own.

"Should he be taken seriously?" I asked. "And Ferris too for that matter. Is it only hot air, that threat about taking the law into their own hands?"

"There'll be none of that while I'm on the spot," Wharton said grimly. "The first crack out of Feeder and I'll pop him in clink, if there's a clink here. Have another look outside, will you?"

I had a look and Feeder wasn't there. George gathered up his notes and said he'd spend the next half-hour collating them. I ventured on one suggestion, and it was hardly that.

"What strikes me about all this business, George, is the dirty, underhand nature of everything. No real killing, like stabbing or shooting, but dirty little tricks. The Northover affair and the Mills bomb, for instance, and the way Mortar was got rid of."

"Well, and what's the inference?" he rapped at me. "Let me enlarge on it a bit first," I said. "It's all been cowardly and sneaking. Something has been done in each of the three cases, and all the one who did it had to do was to lay the trap and then keep out of the way. It's as if he didn't have the guts to witness the actual killing. It's like a poison case where the poisoner plants his stuff, and after that what happens seems something wholly impersonal."

"Well?" he said impatiently.

"Well, this then," I told him. "Anybody, particularly a woman, can be immediately a suspect in a poisoning case. These three events have been of the same cowardly type as a poison murder. What I claim is that anybody might have been responsible therefore, even people who give the impression of being remote from murder types or likely to have a murder mentality. Just a minute," I said, for he was about to burst in impatiently. "Let me instance Collect. Who in his senses would suspect him of murder? Yet I say he's capable of the kind of thing I've been mentioning, and I did see him looking for that Blacker bomb."

"Now you're getting somewhere," Wharton was gracious enough to say. "It's an idea and it's worth thinking about."

He was already settling down to that collating of his notes, so I left him. That afternoon he was spending at the ranges, where there was to be an exhibition of flame-throwers, fougasse, and mines, and I knew he was looking forward to it. But I had told him that the real treat was to come on the Friday, when there was to be an entirely new demonstration. It had been ready for incorporation in the syllabus, but up to now the Air Force had not been able to co-operate. On the Friday, however, two dive-bombers were coming. Their pilots would report on camouflage and concealment, for one thing, but the principal object of the demonstration was for the Home Guard to experience the thrill of being dive-bombed, if only with flour bags, and to practise the rapid sighting and firing of machine-guns and even the Northover in defence and attack.

I was to be busy myself that afternoon in a different way. I was due for a lecture when the Course returned from the ranges, and the trying thing about my lectures was that they had constantly to be brought up to date, which made a considerable amount of preliminary work. Once a week at least some new A.C.I. would reach me and throw a spanner into the old works, and there would be those specially infuriating ones that consisted wholly of corrections and deletions to those that had gone before. Still, one ought, I suppose, to cultivate an attitude of philosophical resignation. After all, if it weren't for corrections and deletions, quite a few decrepit old gentlemen at the War House would be out of a job.

I did have a scout round for Feeder after dinner, but none of the batmen said they had seen him. After my lecture, which ended at eighteen hours, I had a wash and clean up and then went round to general staff quarters, where a man said he had seen him go out a few minutes before, and wearing his greatcoat. Dusk was well in the sky by then so I didn't trouble to institute a search. What I did make up my mind to do was to have a heart to heart talk and a very definite understanding with Feeder in the morning.

I went to George's room to make a report, but he wasn't there. As I came by the south end of the hut I heard his voice inside the Colonel's room, and as I was entering my own room I saw him come out. There was no need to call him, for he had been coming in search of me in any case.

"Just been buttering the old boy up," he said, and gave a chuckle. "We're getting as snug as two bugs in a rug."

He gave a conspiratorial look round, then his voice lowered.

"I got an idea. I think I know how Mortar might have been blown up."

My fingers were already at my horn-rims, and if I had known I was going to spoil his show I'd never have spoken.

"You mean, by remote control?"

He glared, then looked infinitely hurt. Then he bucked up.

"Depends what you mean by remote control."

"Sorry, George," I said. "You tell me all about it."

"Well electrical contact," he said, in the off-hand manner of one who conceals the fact that he is only partly informed. "You operate one of those plunger things. Just press it down and the bomb goes off when the contact is made. You can be at any distance you like, provided you have a long enough wire or cable."

I nodded.

"You see the beauty of it?" he was going on. "The bomb is prepared and the wires are connected to the power-point of the electric fire. Of course it's a kind of booby-trap, really. Whoever's going to set it off has just to make certain that Mortar's in his room, then down goes the plunger and up goes Mortar."

Then he was heaving a sigh. "The trouble is, it doesn't make things easier for us. It's no use trying to make sure where everybody actually was that night, and eliminating those that weren't alone at the time. There's more to it than that. A man might have been sitting in his own room and have pressed down the plunger from there. The wires would be blown sky-high and there wouldn't be a trace. If there was any slack wire left he could pull it in."

"In other words, Staff might have done it."

"Anybody might," he said. "Brende, for instance, when he was supposed to be relieving nature. Or even your pal Collect."

"Yes," I said, "or even Flick. What he was carrying mightn't have been a couple of stamp albums but the preparations, so to speak, for the crime."

# Chapter XI

I woke at my usual hour of seven the following morning, verified the fact from my watch, and wondered why Feeder was not bringing tea, for outside I had heard the steps and voices of batmen. Ten minutes passed and then I decided to investigate, so I put on a dressing-gown and looked out of the door Staff's batman told me he hadn't seen Feeder at all that morning, and another batman who came up confirmed that Feeder had not been near the cookhouse. But he said he'd try to find him, so I fetched my own hot water and got on with my shaving.

Another ten minutes and the helpful batman was coming in with a cup of tea, and obviously bursting with news.

"I got this made fresh for you, sir,"—and in the same breath— "they say Feeder was out of camp all night."

I didn't say anything except to thank him for the tea, but I was furious with Feeder, to whom I'd tried to be friendly and decent. Like master, like man, I thought, and always making enemies and trouble. Confined to camp for breaking regulations, and now breaking the same regulation again, and in the most flagrant form. When he did turn up I made up my mind that I'd tell him that as far as I was concerned he could henceforth go to the devil and at his own pace.

Just as I had finished dressing there was a tap at the door and Ferris came in. He also was all excitement. "Have you heard about Feeder, sir? Brende's just told me."

"I've heard," I said. "What's happened to him, do you think?"

"Happened?"

It was my turn to stare. "Well, where is he? I thought you were telling me he'd been out of camp all night."

"I didn't know that," he said, and scowled. "My God, he's a dirty double-crosser!"

"What *is* this?" I said. "Why's he a double-crosser?"

"That's what I came to tell you," he said. "Last night he asked to speak to Brende, so Brende says, and he told him he'd been lying about Mortar not having ex-plosives. He said Mortar had that Blacker bomb in his room and he told lies about it because he didn't want Mortar to be badly thought of."

"Oh, my hat!" I said, fingers already at my horn-rims. "That's thrown a spanner into the works. It definitely makes the whole thing out to be an accident."

"He's a liar and a double-crosser," Ferris told me vehement-ly. "He's either been got at or he's spinning that yarn to save his own skin in some way. I ask you, sir; why should Mortar have had that bomb in his room? And if he had, was he the sort to blow himself up?"

"He was pretty tight," I said. "And you'll remember he did say he had something to do before he went to bed."

"I know what he meant," Ferris said, with something like contempt. "He meant—well, after all he'd been drinking, he must have wanted to get rid of some of it."

"But you'd locked the room up," I said. "How could he have got out to the lavatory?"

"I didn't think of that till later on," he said. "While we were walking across to the Mess I remembered it, and that's one rea-son why I said I'd go back and see if he'd turned his light off."

"Excuse me," I said, "but there's Brende going by now."

Brende was making for the Adjutant's office, to make a re-port on Feeder. I told him to stand fast till I'd fetched Wharton. George was absolutely flabbergasted by the news, and no won-der, for every theory was knocked cockeyed.

"Tell me just what happened," he said to Brende.

"Well, sir, I was just coming across the parade ground, not too far from the Home Guard N.A.A.F.I., when Feeder comes up and asks if he can have a word with me—"

"What time was it exactly?"

"Exactly?" He frowned. "About eighteen hours fifteen, I should say, sir. I know it was getting a bit darkish. Then he said he had to own up he'd given wrong evidence to the Colonel and Major Travers, sir, and how Captain Mortar did have some explosives in his room that night. He even said it was that Blacker bomb that we couldn't find."

Wharton grunted. "And what did you say?"

"I told him he'd better make an official report, and if he didn't, then I would. I ought to have said, sir, that he spoke to me confidentially like. I also warned him that he'd be lucky if he wasn't for the high jump."

"Then no wonder he bolted," Wharton said, and gave another grunt or two. "Was he stone sober?"

"Absolutely, sir, and very respectful, so to speak."

"He certainly went off immediately afterwards," I said. "It couldn't have been more than a few minutes later when I was looking for him and was told he'd gone out of his hut with his greatcoat on."

Wharton said he would make the necessary report to Harness, and Brende needn't stay. Harness was furious with Feeder, and then was wondering if the Colonel could deal with him or if he should be handed over to the civil power.

"Oh, no," Wharton said. "We don't want any outside meddling. I'll see that he makes a statement on oath, and then the sooner we get rid of him the better. Mind if I use your telephone? What time was there a train for town last night?"

Harness, who knew the local service by heart, said there was one at twenty hours. It was a slow to the junction and there made a connection which brought one into London in the very early morning hours. Wharton rang Peakridge Station and asked if a man of Feeder's unmistakable description had boarded the train. Peakridge said the men who might know were now off duty, but they'd send a reply at the earliest moment.

"He might have jumped a lorry," Harness said. "There's no end of traffic through Peakridge at night." Wharton said he'd be getting along to breakfast, and might the report be brought as soon as it came.

I was going too, when Harness stopped me. "I've managed to get all the forms for officers who've returned them before. I wondered if you'd like to have a look at them, sir."

"After breakfast, I think. If you don't make a move you'll be getting none yourself."

He posted a telephone orderly with instructions and then we strolled across to the dining-hut together.

"What was Captain Mortar's record?" I asked him. "As long as your arm," he said. "Wherever there was a scrap anywhere, that fellow seems to have gone. No doubt about it, sir, he wasn't far out when he said he was a fighter. Why, he was wounded at least four or five times. Those Mexicans thought a lot of him. They gave him three or four decorations. Of course he couldn't wear them—not over here."

"I expect a good few Mexicans wouldn't have minded giving him some decorations of another kind," I said, thinking of that pitch-dark night when he'd blown up that house on the canal, and sent it and a good few rebels soaring sky-high.

After breakfast I hurried to overtake Wharton.

"Looks as if I'll have to alter my time-table this morning," he said. "Would you mind seeing if there's anything through from Peakridge yet?"

I said I'd see to it. I added, only too obviously, that Feeder's confession had altered the whole complexion of the case.

"Don't I know it?" he told me, not as disgruntled as he might have been.

"There is an alternative," I told him consolingly. "Brende may be telling lies for his own reasons."

Wharton halted in his tracks. "Yes," he said slowly. "I hadn't thought of that. You see what it implies?"

"Only that Brende possibly got Feeder to go away because he had some evidence, not yet disclosed, which Brende didn't want disclosed."

"There's more in it than that," he said, and was scowling away as we moved on again. "Brende must have known that a man as conspicuous as Feeder couldn't get clear away. Wherever Feeder is, we'll have our hands on him within forty-eight hours, or my name's Robinson. No," he went on, with a shake of the head, "there's something I don't like the look of in the least. If you ask me, there's more unlikely things than that we'll never clap eyes on Feeder again."

He waved his hand impatiently and I duly sheered off to Harness's office, and I was thinking that what George had said was contradictory. Then I saw what he meant. If Brende was lying, then Feeder was dead. We might clap eyes on Feeder again but he'd be no good as a witness, and it was a thought that made me go hot and cold all over. Somehow I wished I'd never suggested that alternative to Wharton.

"Nothing through from Peakridge yet," Harness told me. He was getting into his Sam Browne prior to the inspection of markers before the eight-hours thirty parade. "If you like to wait, sir, you can be having a look at those officers' records."

There was no mistaking the pale blue forms on his table, so I began to run an eye over them as soon as he'd gone. Staff's happened to be on top. That was of no particular interest to me, and I was just about to place it at the bottom of the pile when something caught my eye. Colonel Staff—our Staff's father—was described as a director of Staff and Blackett, quarry owners, of Fenderby, Yorkshire. Staff's private address was Fenderby, Yorkshire.

Now I happened to have heard of Staff and Blackett before, and in connection with a sister of mine who had been making extensive alterations to her garden before the war, and needed a very large quantity of crazy paving and other stone work. She had been recommended to try that firm as being one of the largest in the country. And why, you may ask, did the name interest me? Well, because blasting would always be going on at the quarries, and quarries, mark you, near Staff's home. And yet he had assured Wharton that he knew nothing whatever about explosives except what he'd picked up at the week's rehearsals at the school!

I passed on to the next form, which was Flick's. His father was dead, but his mother, I was interested to note, lived at a place called Rathgore, which is in Wicklow, which is Eire, and Flick had been born there. I also noted that Flick was a Territorial officer who had joined up just before the outbreak of war. His civil life job was described as being a film company executive, which seemed to me to cover a rather large tract of ground.

Then the telephone bell went and the orderly-room sergeant was handing me the receiver. Peakridge was reporting that no man of Feeder's description had taken the train from Peakridge. According to them there wasn't a shadow of doubt about it. I asked if the station was well blacked-out, and when they said indignantly that it was, asked why Feeder couldn't have jumped the train unnoticed. They said he'd have been spotted on the train, where his ticket would have been examined. I let it go at that, but thought, as I later told Wharton, that there were seats to hide under and lavatories in which to conceal oneself.

What I did then was to ask the sergeant to get R.T.O. at the London terminus, to find out if Feeder had reached town, for however well he might have dodged the authorities on the journey, he'd have had his work more than cut out to get clear of the train and station under the eyes of red caps and other emissaries of the R.T.O. Then I thought I'd better report to Wharton.

Wharton was good enough to say I'd done the right thing. Then he was looking highly gratified at what I told him about Staff.

"Everything hasn't altered as much as you'd think," he said "Even if Feeder did tell us lies, and Mortar had that bomb in his room, there'd still be the possibility that somebody else set it off."

He pursed his lips in thought and then announced that he'd go to the Colonel's room and use the 'phone from there. He'd get in touch with the police at Fenderby and have inquiries made to find out just how much Staff knew about explosives and letting off charges by remote control.

While he was gone I sat in his chair, stoked my pipe, and tried to do some thinking for myself. Somehow my thoughts never got far away from the events of the evening when Mortar was killed. Something suddenly occurred to me, so I went to Harness's office again. He was back from parade and soon found me the reports on the last Course which had been rendered by the various lecturers and instructors. What I wanted were those returned by Ferris and Mortar, and as soon as I saw them, I knew my suspicions confirmed. Mortar's work at which he had ostensibly been too busy to attend dinner, had all been done by Ferris, though Mortar had appended a rather shaky signature.

That gave me a bird's-eye view of that Saturday after-noon. Mortar had been as good as tight when he got back from Peakridge. Ferris had shrewdly made him come to his—Ferris's—room, and to work like everybody else at those reports. But he had been useless and Ferris had made him get on the bed and sleep, and had then worked like a nigger at both sets of reports. His hurried writing on his own reports showed that. Then when Mortar had ultimately woke up he had still not been in good enough shape to be seen at dinner. The scrawled signature proved that clearly enough. Finally, Ferris, hoping some good from the hair of the dog that had bitten him, let him go to the Mess, from which my help had been needed to dislodge him.

Wharton had made his telephone call one of urgent priority, and was back in his room sooner than I had expected. Then it appeared that his thoughts must have been running in much the same direction as my own, for he had sent for Ferris, who happened to be free. When Ferris came it was to corroborate everything, and to add something mightily important.

Mortar had slept on Ferris's bed till about eighteen hours. Then he had insisted on having a drink. Ferris refused. Then Mortar said his bladder was bursting and he was going outside.

"I told him to get to hell outside then," Ferris said. "I was fed up with him, and that's the truth. I got on with my job, and then I thought he was the devil of a time, so I went to explore. I found him in the Mess—with Flick."

I raised my eyebrows. "I thought they weren't on speaking terms?"

Ferris shrugged his shoulders. "I gathered there'd been some sort of reconciliation, but I was damn' fed up and I got him away. I was furious with Flick, too, though I didn't say anything. You see, they were drinking Guinness."

"Good Lord!" I said. "And he'd originally got tight on whisky?"

"That's it," Ferris said. "The worst thing he could drink was Guinness after whisky. It's as bad as giving a man knockout drops."

"Did it knock him out?" Wharton asked.

"Not as luck would have it," Ferris said. "I arrived just in time. Mortar was as sick as a cat in my room. I made him lie down again, and he did. Then I thought I'd let him have just one nightcap, and that was when I couldn't get him out of the bar again and came in to get you to help me, Major."

I clicked my tongue. "You certainly had a hell of a day. But who told you I was in the writing-room? Shorty?"

"That's right, sir. He gave me the tip when Mortar was trying to make him have a drink."

That was virtually all that Ferris had to tell us, and when he'd gone, I was asked to get hold of Shorty. I found him cleaning up the Mess, and when we got to Wharton's room the orderly-room sergeant was there. He had brought a message from the R.T.O. at terminus that nobody of Feeder's description had got off the train from Derby.

"I don't like the look of things a bit," Wharton told me, while Shorty waited outside. "You'd have thought that if Feeder went anywhere, it'd have been to London. Mind you, he may have had relations elsewhere. He may have taken a different train from the junction, if he ever got as far."

He frowned in thought for a bit, then said he'd get a description issued throughout the country. Within a few hours every cop in England would be on the look-out for him. Then he was asking me, or rather directing me, to bring in Shorty.

Shorty was a little, snub-nosed, good-humoured fellow, by name, Tom Smith, and he was a first-class witness. You could tell that by the cheerful way he listened to Wharton's admonitions on secrecy, and the veiled threats.

Yes, he said, Captain Mortar had come hurriedly into the Mess and had asked for a double whisky. Just then Mr. Flick came in, but at the sight of Mortar had turned back. Mortar hailed him affectionately, so we gathered. He even got Flick by the arm and literally dragged him to the bar.

"What was Captain Mortar's condition like?" Wharton asked.

Shorty said he was all right. He'd obviously had a few, but he was all right. "He said to Mr. Flick, sir, that he liked him and he liked all the Irish."

"Just a minute," Wharton interposed again. "Can you remember the exact words that were used."

"I'm not getting nobody into trouble, am I, sir?"

"Of course you're not," Wharton snapped at him.

Shorty grinned, then licked his lips and thought back. A moment or two and he said that what Captain Mortar had said was that he'd killed the Irish and fought alongside the Irish, and they were all good chaps. "Good chaps, them was the exact words he used, sir," he concluded.

"And then?" Wharton asked.

"Mr. Flick said he *would* have a drink, sir, and said his was a Guinness, and Captain Mortar said to make it two Guinnesses. Then Mr. Flick said, would Captain Mortar have another, and they had two more. Then Mr. Ferris came in, sir, and he looked at me as if he'd like to slosh me one, sir, and that's all there was to it." He gave me a look and then added: "Except later on when you came in, sir."

"What were he and Ferris drinking, then?" Wharton asked me.

"Now I come to think of it, I believe it was Guinness," I said.

"It *was* Guinness, sir," Shorty said. "Captain Mortar wanted a double whisky, but Mr. Ferris says to him, 'No, you don't. You had Guinness last,' he says, 'and you stick to it!'"

"That was wise," Wharton said, and then with a peer at Shorty over his spectacle tops. "Didn't you think so?"

"Me, sir?" Shorty said, and then grinned. "I reckon it was, sir. He didn't want to go mixing up his drinks again."

"He had the one Guinness and then he didn't want to go. Wasn't that it?"

"That's right, sir," Shorty said. "Mr. Ferris could do anything with him usually, if you know what I mean, sir. Just quiet-like, you know, sir."

"Used to talk to him like a father."

"That's it, sir."

"Anything else did he and Mr. Flick talk about earlier in the evening before Mr. Ferris got there?" Shorty licked his lips in thought, made as if to speak, then shook his head.

"Come on," said Wharton jocularly. "Everything's in confidence here. What else were they talking about besides the Irish?"

"Honestly, sir, I don't know," Shorty said. "You see it wasn't my place to stay at the bar if I wasn't actually serving a drink. If I did hear anything, sir, I wasn't supposed to take notice, if you know what I mean."

"Yes, but what did you hear?"

"Not nothing, sir, not really proper. It was something to do with a lady, and that's all I know, sir. Soon as they began talking I went round behind."

Wharton nodded. "I know. Into that cubby-hole of yours. And you didn't hear anything else?"

"No, sir. Mr. Ferris come in almost at once."

"Well, you've been a good witness," Wharton said, and glanced at me for confirmation. Then his eyes narrowed and the gratified smile left Shorty's face. "One single word from you about what's been talked about in this room, and God help you. You get that?"

"Yes, sir."

"Right. You can go."

Then at the door he was halted. "A chap with your responsibilities ought to be a lance-corporal at least."

"Yes, sir," said Shorty promptly.

"You've got sense, too," Wharton added. "For instance, if any officers of the staff happen to be talking at the bar about any-thing—well, interesting; anything to do with what we've been talking about this morning, you'd keep it in your mind and let me know?"

"Yes, sir," said Shorty, again promptly, but with wariness in his eyes.

"I knew it," Wharton said, and nodded again for him to go.

"That was flagrant blackmail," I told George. "You've no power to get him a stripe."

"Haven't I?" he told me belligerently. "If I thought it necessary I'd have made him up to full sergeant, and before this day's out."

"Very good, sir," I said. "But if you're chucking out promotions why shouldn't I come in? I could do with colonel's pay and allowances."

"You always would have your little joke," he told me, and was replacing his notebook as he got to his feet. "Looks as if I'll be tied down to the telephone for an hour or two."

"The police at Penderby are handling the staff inquiry?" I asked.

"Oh, yes," he said. "Later on I'm going to see your pal Store and find out if he's shy of a cordite cartridge for a Blacker bomb."

I had forgotten about that cartridge that had been found among the debris beneath Staff's floor, but I did suddenly think of something else.

"Suppose Feeder's retractation was genuine, George. Who else but Ferris and Feeder knew that Mortar had the bomb in his room?"

"Why should Ferris know?"

"I told you he was friendly with Feeder."

"That proves nothing," he said. "There must have been plenty of things these three didn't have in common." He paused in the act of replacing his spectacles in their battered case. "And now let me put something up to you. You didn't see why somebody should try to wipe out both Mortar and Staff, for one was a Mortarite, as you call them, and the other an anti-Mortarite. Isn't that so?"

"I did put up that argument," I admitted.

"Well, let me put something up to you. In my humble way," he added, and I knew I was in for something unexpected. "Is it unreasonable to suppose that that bomb went off right against the partition wall?"

"It isn't," I said. "For one thing we know—unless Flick stole them—that Ferris's stamp albums were blown to smithereens."

"Very well then," he said, replacing his glasses with an air of finality. "The intention was to kill both Ferris and Mortar. Ferris's bed was alongside Mortar's in the next room."

I was polishing my glasses and Wharton was regarding me quizzically as I thought that out.

"It's good logic," I said at last. "But why was Staff kept in his room all night by that note?"

"Maybe the note was a fake after all," he said. "It existed only in Staff's imagination. Everything's much clearer if we assume that Staff set off the bomb."

"Yes, but just one minute," I said. "Neither Ferris nor Mortar would be expected to be in their beds at so ungodly an hour as nine o'clock. They were both night birds. The Mess has to be closed at twenty-two thirty, but they were usually in there till then. Then why set off the bomb to kill one, when it was intended to kill two?"

"Simple," he said. "Whoever had that bomb ready to set off saw what he thought was Mortar and Ferris entering Mortar's room soon after nine o'clock. He daren't show himself for a good look, and that's why he didn't see you. By the time he'd got ready to do the job, Ferris had gone, and as he was naturally keeping himself concealed, he didn't see him—and you—go."

Before I had time to ask for further enlightenment, or show a few of the holes with which that theory was riddled like a colander, he was on the move. Feeder's description had to be circulated, for one thing, and there were the Big Bugs to ring up.

"Just when I wanted a few minutes to get a few ideas together, too," he said rather plaintively. "This time next week I'm supposed to be giving a lecture and I haven't got a word down on paper."

"Anyone so fertile in ideas as you, George, oughtn't to need any paper," I told him. "And why worry about fiddling while Rome's burning?"

I heard his chuckle, but once more I was talking to his back. What I really knew was that the talk about that Security lecture was some sort of red herring. George had got an idea, and if so, he was already engaged in heavy camouflage work. When I next heard about it, it would be when the idea was solid fact. Even that careful selection of Staff as the principal suspect might be all eye-wash too, and indeed it probably was. Why, for instance, should the hidden watcher have mistaken three people for two? Both Ferris and I were assisting Mortar to his room, and I am a taller, and presumably more conspicuous sight than Ferris.

Then I suddenly thought of something. Perhaps Wharton had been mercifully sparing me when he made the suggestion. Perhaps the watcher had seen three people. Among the three were Ferris and Mortar—the two he wanted. I might be there, but I didn't count. But for having left the room with Ferris, I might have been added to the holocaust too!

In other words, the problem now was to find a murderer who was little inclined to hold his hand for my sake. Someone who had little use for me, in fact, and there I could begin with Collect. But I didn't go any further. To be frank, it was rather devastating to the self-esteem of one who had regarded himself as a reasonably good mixer, to have to work out a list of possibles who had found him so much a bore as to be worth no consideration in the matter of a Blacker bomb.

# Chapter XII

AT FOURTEEN HOURS that afternoon I was due for my second lecture, and as one of the abominated kind of A.C.I.s had come in, with no end of deletions and amendments, I was not at all sorry to leave Wharton to his own devices, crafty and otherwise. I also wrote a couple of letters in the writing-room of the Mess, and then, with half an hour to go before lunch, thought I would rest my brain by switching to the *Times* crossword.

So I drew up a comfortable chair to the electric fire, got out my special pencil with the pessimist's rubber at one end, and reached for the paper. Then I saw that Staff, as sometimes happened, had been before me and had filled in half a dozen clues. That rather put me off my stroke, for I am selfish enough to like a virgin page. In a minute or two I was laying the paper aside and my thoughts were back on the case.

I am not going to give you a long, logical disquisition. For one thing I found myself unable to use much logic at all. All, indeed, that I could arrive at was a series of questions, and here they are as I finished writing them in my private notebook just as the lunch bugle went.

1. Where is Feeder?
2. Did he bolt out of fear of punishment for giving false evidence, or was he the killer?
3. Did Brende make up the Feeder story?
4. Where did the Mills come from that nearly got Ferris?
5. If from Store's magazine, has Store managed to replace it?
6. Is he also short of a cordite cartridge?
7. Since the cordite cartridge found beneath Staff's floor was a live one, and therefore unconnected with the setting off of the Blacker bomb, what was its significance?
8. Why was Collect looking for that bomb?
9. What was Flick carrying that night?
10. Why was Nurse Wilton hot and bothered?
11. Did Brende keep Ferris from the burning room for fear Ferris should see something? And if so, what?

I might have found a few more questions to add, but those are enough to be going on with, and I was cocksure enough to tell myself that their answers would be more than enough to clear up the case. I didn't think about them after lunch because I had to have another quick look through my amended lecture. Then as I made my way to the lecture-room just ahead of the parade, Harness hailed me. All he wanted to know was, if I intended opening a private account in Peakridge as some of the other officers were doing.

Out of that a sudden idea came to me, but I had to approach him warily.

"Well, it'll be good to see one's name on a Pay List again," I said. "Only a day or two now."

"I hope they'll be prompt," he said. "They sometimes aren't in a new camp."

"It's costing the very devil of a lot to run this show, you know," I said. "Even the officers' pay and allowances must come to a tidy penny every month. And most of us married too. But wait a minute, though. Staff isn't married, or Ferris, or Flick— or Compress."

"Hold hard, sir," he said. "Mr. Flick's married. I ought to know. I sent his details to Pay Office."

"Foolish of me," I said. "Somehow I got the idea he wasn't the married kind."

He laughed. "He isn't so old as you and me. He doesn't show it yet."

"There's plenty of time," I said, and then remarked that if it weren't October I should have said we were in for snow. Then we went our respective ways, and I had to forget all about Flick, for when men are as keen as our Home Guard men, it is hard enough to give a lecture at any time, let alone be ready with answers to the questions that follow. But that afternoon lecture was my worst, for a hungry morning made men eat everything in sight, and my experience of the first Course had warned me that they might be somewhat somnolent unless my lecture was sufficiently enlivening to keep them awake. The hard seats wouldn't be enough to do that, for if you have imagined them as hard, then you've wasted your sympathy. Each, in fact, was provided with an additional seat of very thick Sorbo rubber, which made them even more conducive to sleep.

However, we got through it, and then as I at last emerged from the lecture-room I saw George coming across the parade ground, and headed him off.

"Everything been going all right?" I asked him.

"Can't grumble," he told me, "The Sapper's report's come in, by the way. No doubt about it being a Blacker bomb."

"And where're you bound for now?"

The post office, he said, to try to check up on registered letters. I remembered that my two letters were in my tunic pocket, so there was an excuse to accompany him. As a matter of fact everything turned out too easy. In the camp post office they kept a record of registered letters and parcels, so there was nothing to do but look through the list. The system was that all such registered mails were sent in a special bag to Peakridge, who did the official stamping and then returned the receipt to the camp, where it was later handed to the sender. In any case the camp list did not include the name of a single officer of the staff.

"That's that," I said to George when we came out.

He halted a moment, looked up at the sky, then gave a preliminary grunt.

"Feel like a bit of fresh air? I thought I might as well run down to Peakridge."

"A walk might do us both good," I said.

"Walk, my foot!" he said, or words to that effect, and went off to order the car.

It was a bitter cold day with a gusty wind from the north-east, and I remember that when we passed a haystack on the right of the road, the wind was playing Old Harry with the thatch. As we drew into the town—I was driving, by the way—I saw what looked like a drill hall, and on it some notices relating to the local Home Guard. I drew the car up at the side of the road. George was asking what the idea was.

Just as I finished telling him, I had a bit of luck, for behind that drill hall I caught sight of a man digging the garden. Something in his face seemed familiar, and men with short clipped beards are getting none too common. Out of the car I got, George at my heels, and through the gate and along the grass path. The man straightened his back from the digging, had a look at me and then smiled.

"Hallo, sir. Having a holiday?"

"I thought I recognised you," I said. "You're the platoon sergeant who attended our first course from Peakridge, aren't you?"

I remembered him because he had buttonholed me with a question that had taken some answering. At once he began scraping the soil off his boots.

"Like to see our drill hall, sir?"

I said we would, and introduced Wharton. When we had seen what there was to see and learned something of the local training, Ponter—that was his name—asked if anything had ever been discovered about that Mills that had almost scuppered Mr. Ferris. I said the culprit had never owned up.

"It's a funny thing, you know, sir," he said, "but when we had a check up of our Millses the other day we found we were one short. I wangled it on the books, but it's lucky the Company Commander didn't know." Then he explained why. "Everyone here got to know about that affair at the school and as I was the one to go to it from here, they might have thought I was the one who'd been up to monkey tricks."

"I can assure you that none of us ever thought such a thing," I said. "Where is your magazine, by the way?"

"It's only just been laid down that we've got to have a special magazine," he said. "Till they build it, we're making do with the old one. On top of the garage there."

It was always kept locked, he said, and being slap up against his house, was little likely to be burgled. I didn't say so, but I thought his missus must sleep uneasily at night if enemy planes were over. What I did say was that Store would give him a few tips on the running of magazines.

"He came along one evening and helped us no end," he said.

"When was that?"

"When I was on the Course," he said. "He and I walked down one evening. He showed our chaps how to keep the Millses oiled and made us keep the Molotoffs up the garden." He smiled. "Gave us a rare nice talk, he did."

We pottered round for a few minutes longer, then said good-bye. When we were in the car again I couldn't help feeling gratified.

"There was a stroke of luck, George. The first thing we've really been sure of in this inquiry. Now we know where that Mills came from that was meant to get Ferris."

"I wouldn't be so sure," George said. "All we know is that Store lost one from the magazine and took steps to replace it. Who took it from Store? Tell me that."

"Maybe it wasn't taken," I said. "Maybe Store obliged a pal—Brende, for instance."

"Much more likely that Store had it taken when his back was turned. Didn't you prove it could be done?"

"Sorry, George," I said ironically. "I was only doing my best. All the same I hardly think that would explain the startled look Store gave me when I produced those two bombs from my pockets."

"Of course it would," he said. "He wondered if you'd rumbled him, didn't he? Thought you might have got wind about his coming along here and lifting one of Ponter's bombs to make good the deficiency. You'd better hurry up, by the way. I might have to be a long while in that post office."

We were to be much longer than he thought. The post-master was fetched and Wharton presented his credentials and asked to be shown a record of all registered packages and letters. The postmaster seemed a bit reluctant, but at last produced it. We had a good look through, but found nothing of any use. Wharton tried another tack. Flick was most carefully described, and the date of dispatch was limited to the Saturday of the explosion, and the following Monday.

The assistant who had been on duty on the Saturday was now off duty. Later she might have to be fetched, Wharton said, but in the meanwhile he would like to interrogate the one who had been on duty on the Monday. She seemed a bright sort of person, but could only shake her head at Wharton's description of Flick.

"You see, we have such a lot of troops about here," she said, and looked at the postmaster for confirmation. "There's the Brigade just outside the town and men always on leave. You see so many it's hard to remember any particular one."

"Were you on duty on the Monday at about half-past two?" I asked, for I had suddenly remembered something. When I had the car drawn up at the florist's where I was collecting the wreaths, Feeder had got out of the lorry too. When I was coming out of the florist's I had seen him coming out of the post office, which was only two doors away. Her face lighted up when I described Feeder. Not only was he the kind of person one would never be likely to forget but it also appeared he was a garrulous soul and he had told her he was going to his Captain's funeral. He was still giving her an account of Mortar's life and adventures when his parcel was stamped and she had had to get rid of him tactfully because of a waiting customer.

My eyes bulged at that. I had mentioned Feeder only to find out what sort of a hand she might really be at remembering people.

"There was someone from the school then who sent off a registered package," I said, and looked triumphantly at George.

"You look it up in the book, Miss," Wharton said.

"All I want is the address where that parcel went to. By the way, what sort of a parcel was it?"

She couldn't remember that, she said, and was frowning away. She rather thought it was a flat packet, but she had recognised Feeder as the very chatty sort, and as a customer was on his heels, she had been trying all the time to expedite matters and get rid of him.

"Well, have a good look and try to refresh your memory," Wharton said. "A smart young lady like you ought to be able to put two and two together."

She simpered a bit and began looking through the book. Wharton explained to the postmaster in confidence that that particular man happened to be a deserter and he was anxious to lay his hands on him. The address to which the package was sent might be the one where the deserter was now hiding.

A quarter of an hour later the assistant had given it up. There were no fewer than twenty-seven registrations recorded, and for the life of her she couldn't find a thing to make her recall which of them had been Feeder's.

"Rather a lot of registrations?" Wharton said.

"Oh, no," the postmaster told him. "It was market day for one thing and we always get a lot of extra business then. Also people go in for registration much more these days. Posts are a bit irregular, and then there were the blitzes. What they think is that things will be quicker and safer if registered."

There was nothing for it but to take a complete list of addresses to which letters and packages had been sent, and copying them down took a goodish time. Wharton was in far too bad a humour when we came out. It was only with difficulty that I could induce him to have tea. I was dying for a cup.

"You ought to be bursting with excitement, George," I said. "Two strokes of luck in one afternoon."

"Luck, my foot!" he said, and brandished the list under my nose, to the vast astonishment of the waitress. "Addresses from John o' Groat's to Land's End. Best part of a week before I can get them all inquired into." Then he found another grievance.

"And it'll take me most of to-night to do the telephoning."

"It'll be worth it if we get our hands on Feeder," I said. "And there may be more to it than that, George. Feeder's package may have been Ferris's stamps. I told you Ferris made a kind of pet of him and I'll bet he showed him the stamps. A keen collector would be anxious to show anybody his stamps. And you know what scroungers and thieves old soldiers are. When Feeder knew those stamps were worth hundreds, he simply waited for a chance to lift them. And he posted them here instead of at the camp."

"You and your theories," he said. "Far more likely he'd scrounged something else out of the Quartermaster's stores and was sending it off to a pal."

Inside me I was sufficiently gratified to let George enjoy his pessimisms, even if he was failing to enjoy his tea. When the plate of toast had gone he was ignoring the cakes and wiping his moustache with the usual voluminous sweeps of his handkerchief as he got to his feet. I paid the bill and followed him down to the car, and then I was beginning to wonder. In a minute or two I thought I knew. George was far too irritable for that irritation to be genuine. George had discovered something then, and the irritation was a mask to conceal some intense gratification.

However, I didn't give the knowledge away, even when he tried some of the old camouflage on the way back. "All that telephoning," he said, "and just when I wanted an hour or so to myself to-night."

"Something special on?" I ventured.

"I've got to have a little leisure sometime, haven't I?"

"Of course," I said, and with what I hoped was suavity. "The Maigret business and all that."

He shot a look at me. "What about that lecture of mine? I don't want to get on that platform looking like a fool, do I?"

"Not if it can be avoided," I said. "But if you like I'll lend you a hand with your lecture."

"You!" he said. "A lot you know about Security. You can't even drive this damn' car. Nearly had us in the ditch then."

"That's because I can't help listening to your cheerful prattle, George," I said, and after that he was stonily silent till we were home.

"Oh, yes," I thought to myself. "George is certainly on good terms with himself. He's got hold of something, and it's something big."

But for the life of me, even after I'd racked my brains in the Mess, with and without some moist assistance, I couldn't be sure quite just what it was. Still, I ought to tell you that I had inklings.

In spite of all that telephoning George found time that night to attend the cinema. I didn't get a chance to collar him, for he disappeared before the end of the show, but I couldn't help wondering if he had been doing the Maigret business with Flick.

In the morning I woke up all excitement, for it was the day when there was to be that aerial co-operation for the first time, and it looked like being an uncommonly exciting demonstration. I called on George before breakfast and found him much his usual self, though a shade too genial for that early hour. He wanted to know, for instance, if I'd slept well, and he admitted he was intending to take a look at the dive-bombing.

After breakfast there was a call from the Yard. The preliminary investigation of Mortar's remains had been completed, and there was no doubt that the line of the explosion had been against his back. I won't go into all the gruesome details, but analysis of fibres and so on showed that the bomb had gone off very close to his bowels, and the explosive was that used in the Blacker bomb.

"That rather kyboshes things, doesn't it?" I said to George when we'd got back to his room. "It looks to me as if he had that bomb on the floor and was lying on his side examining it. He'd have been too tottery standing on his feet."

I had to lie down and show him just what I meant. George shook his head, though not at disapproval of my efforts. "That doesn't alter the fact that the bomb might have been wired for detonation by electrical contact. It might have happened to go off just when he lugged it out."

"But he must have seen the wiring," I said.

"Maybe he hadn't time. He got on his side to lug it out from where he'd hidden it and just at that moment someone pressed down the plunger and up it went."

"Then you accept Feeder's evidence that Mortar did have the bomb concealed in his room?"

He was far too dexterous to admit that. "What's the use of theorising?" he told me. "I don't accept anything, but I've got to look at everything, haven't I? What time does this bombing begin?"

I said it was at ten-thirty hours, and didn't add that he might have seen for himself the notices on all the boards. Then he said he had a job or two to do but if I'd call round at ten hours twenty or so, he'd be ready.

Long before that we heard the two big bombers doing their preliminary zooming in the sky. I and George got on a knoll near the ranges, and I had my field-glasses.

"What are those fellows doing?" he asked.

He was referring to a line of men moving slowly along the scrub in the distance, and I remembered that the Sappers had come that morning to make a final search for the missing Blacker bomb. Then we turned our eyes the other way, for the dive-bombing was beginning. All over the camp and the ranges men were in prepared positions. Some would be putting to the test the lessons on anti-aircraft attacks with machine and sub-machine guns, and practising rapid and accurate sighting. Some of the posts and pits were for aerial testing of camouflage, and I did my best to wish that Collect's hectic labours would not be reported on too badly by the close scrutiny from the air to which they would be subjected.

I said *close* scrutiny, and I meant it, for those planes zoomed down with a really terrifying noise and nearness that made one instinctively duck. One second there would be the roar and then up they would zoom and be out of range and almost earshot. Then they would circle low a mile or so back and down they would roar again from some new and unexpected angle, and more than once it seemed as if a wing must catch the top of a hut.

"A great show this," I hollered to George through the din. "And all free and gratis."

It certainly was a marvellous display of aerobatics, and there was more in it than that, especially when a bag of flour fell plump near one of the pits as an indication that its occupants had been well and truly bombed. There were shrieks of mirth as the umpires ordered the dead out of the pits, and the Home Guard were certainly enjoying their morning. So was George, and he even said he was sorry when it was all over. I was sorry, too, even if the bugle had long since gone for lunch.

Collect was a bit fidgety during the meal, and no wonder, with the report on his camouflaging still to come in. Then towards the end of the meal an orderly came in and whispered to Harness, who at once left the room. In five minutes Harness was back and making signs to Wharton. The meal had just concluded, so I shamelessly followed George out.

"Something in your line, I think, sir," Harness was telling Wharton. "It's the local police and the Air Station. I can't quite make out what they're getting at."

Wharton bustled across to Harness's office, I at his heels. An orderly handed him the receiver. It was evidently the police who were now on the line, for Wharton was giving his credentials. Then came various Ah's and Yes's and Very Good's, and at the end the assurance that he'd be there inside five minutes.

"It *is* something for me," he told Harness, and out we two went. "Get a car, and double quick," he was then snapping at me.

I collared the Colonel's car and just had time to get a cap and my British warm. Wharton was already waiting when I took my seat at the wheel.

"About a mile down the road, at that haystack," he said.

I shot the car off and was wanting to know just what was in the wind.

"It was one of those aeroplanes," he said. "When the pilot came down to ground-level he saw something lying on the ground on the far side of the road. Next time he came round he went right over to investigate. One of his crew said it was a man lying there, and in khaki, and as he hadn't moved when he came round the next time, he thought he'd better report the matter at the Air Station. They got in touch with the local police."

I had been hurtling the car on and we were practically there. Another car with a constable at its side was there too, and he opened the field gate for us. Round the corner of the stack were two men in plain clothes, one of whom was the local detective-inspector. On the ground at their feet a man was sprawled, a revolver by his outstretched right hand. Even at a distance of yards I could see that the man was Feeder.

# Chapter XIII

"You're Superintendent Wharton, sir?" the plain-clothes Inspector asked.

"That's me," Wharton said. He whipped out his credentials, flourished them and whipped them back again. "Anyone touched the gun?"

"It's just as we found it, sir."

Wharton circled round and had a look at the body. The shot had been fired apparently with direct contact of the muzzle and the right temple. Only a tiny trickle of blood had congealed along the jaw.

"How long do you make him dead, sir?"

"A couple of days at the least," Wharton said, not looking up, for he was gently raising the head and looking at the ground beneath. Feeder had certainly chosen a soft bed, for the winds of the last few days had whirled loose hay that had settled like a carpet when night dews had damped it and held it down.

"No signs of footprints?" Wharton asked, as he got to his feet.

"We looked as we came in," the Inspector said. "Too much hay about and the ground's too hard, sir."

Wharton took a series of photographs, then had the position of the body marked by pegs cut from some old thatching stakes. Then he made some measurements, and was asking us to lend a hand to move the body just round the stack corner out of the wind.

"Looks like plain suicide, sir," the Inspector ventured, as we laid the body down.

"Yes," Wharton said. "Everything looks fair and square to me. I knew him at the school. Got himself into a bit of trouble and took his own way out. That's what it looks like to me. Name of Feeder, by the way. Let's have a look at his pockets. Got any gloves?"

The Inspector—luckily for him, I couldn't help thinking—had his gloves, and in less than a minute Feeder's pockets had been emptied. Four pounds three shillings, a stout pocket-knife, two keys, a very dirty khaki pocket-handkerchief, and ration book and identity card were all that were found on him.

"Christian name Albert," Wharton said, and grunted. "Ration book issued at Enfield."

He copied down the identity number, had another look at Feeder's body, then said he thought that would be about all.

"You get him along to your mortuary," he told the Inspector. "Have your doctor extract the bullet, and test the gun for prints. Must make sure they were his own. I'll be along in about an hour. And you'd better have a photographer standing by. And one last thing," he said, and tapped his skull. "Keep everything there. Not a word who this chap is or where he comes from. Spin any yarn you like so long as it's not the truth. Got that?"

The Inspector said he had, and no wonder, for Wharton was glaring at him from under his shaggy eyebrows.

"That's all right then," Wharton said, and relaxed. "Lucky for us that someone like you was here. In an hour's time, then, at the station."

"Back to camp?" I asked George, as we came through the field gate again.

"That's it," he said. "And don't move this hell-wagon quite so fast this time. Better draw in on the right when we get there. I want to take over his kit and stuff."

Ten minutes later we had all Feeder's belongings in Wharton's room and were going through them. The tin trunk—an old one he had probably taken over from Mortar—was principally filled with souvenirs of various campaigns, and they ranged from a perfectly lovely lace mantilla to Moroccan necklace rosaries of the usual thirty-three beads. Of what one might call personal papers there were none, though there were photographs of women and studies in the nude, and one or two neatly folded copies of Spanish newspapers. There was a very fine mouth-organ and a jews' harp, some articles of civilian clothing, and the whole was held down by a spare pair of battle-dress trousers and quite a lot of underclothes of the official issue type.

"Evidently travelled with all his belongings," George said. "Probably hasn't got any relations or he'd have given away that mantilla. More than the official issue of underclothes, aren't there?"

I said undoubtedly there were, and George said he'd probably scrounged them from the stores, and that was why the trunk had been locked and padlock attachment used as well.

"A chap with his nocturnal experience and so on could scrounge anything," he said. "But no spare ammunition. Where'd he scrounge that gun from that he did himself in with?"

"What was it?" I said. "I didn't see it any too clearly."

"An old-type Webley .450. 1916, in fact. Six in the breech and one fired. I've also got the gun number. What we'll do is get a question put at dinner to-night, if anyone's recently lost a Webley."

"Tell me honestly, George," I said. "Do you really think it was suicide?"

The answer was coming pat and then he changed his mind. "I'll put all my cards on the table," he said. "You believe in hunches, don't you?"

"I'd follow one every time," I told him.

"Well, all I've got against suicide is a hunch. I said as much to you days ago, didn't I? 'What I reckon is, we'll never clap eyes on Feeder again,' that's what I said, didn't I?"

"In substance," I said.

"There we are then. Something told me there was a hell of a lot of jiggery-pokery about Feeder's bolting out of the camp, and I think I can tell you why. I'm working here and it's all underground work. Nobody knows what's being done. I've never announced a thing publicly or let out a hint. I wanted this inquiry to get on somebody's nerves—the somebody who was responsible for me coming down here. Now do you see it? If anybody was likely to know all about Mortar, and likely to give me a tip, it was Feeder. What I must have been telling myself was that someone had the wind up about Feeder. Someone really thought that Feeder might have put us on the right track, and so Feeder had to be removed. That's one side of the question. That's why I'd hate to think it was suicide."

"And the other side is that everything points to suicide."

"That's it," he said. "He was fretting about Mortar and, according to Brende, he'd told us lies. Then Brende, like an officious fool, told him he'd be for the high jump. Every reason why Feeder should bolt, and at once, before Brende could take action. Also the bullet went to the right spot and everything looked perfectly natural."

"Feeder didn't act as if he were contemplating suicide when I saw him last," I said. "He seemed quite delighted to be doing a job of work as my batman. He was as cheerful as I'd ever seen him."

"I don't know that we ought to let that influence us," he said. "You know what brain-storms are."

Then he said he'd go through those belongings of Feeder when he had more time. What he had to do at once was to call off the search for Feeder, and report to the Colonel. Would I draft the question about the Webley for Harness to put after dinner, and tell Harness in strict confidence what had happened. If Harness had further particulars about Feeder I might as well collect them, and then if there was time I might do the same confidentially with Ferris, who must have known as much about the dead man as anybody except possibly Mortar.

Harness tried to look grieved at the news and with no great success. He had no information not already in our possession, except the address and telephone number of the school at which Feeder and Mortar had been before posting to Peakridge, so when we'd drafted the after-dinner question, I went to the lecture-room where Ferris was working. According to the time-table he ought to be finishing in a few minutes, which would allow me to be back to get Wharton on time at the police station.

The lights were on and I took an unobtrusive seat at the back, and on a form, trestle, folding flat—the official designation—which had no detachable Sorbo seat. Just when I was beginning to wriggle uncomfortably, the lecture came to an end, and five minutes later we were walking across the parade ground.

"What were you doing, Major?" he said. "Having a busman's holiday?"

"I really came to tell you that Feeder is found," I said.

"Is he, be jabers!" he said, and stared at me. "Can I have a few words with him? In front of you, of course?"

"I don't know that you can," I said. "As a matter of fact, he's dead."

He stopped in his tracks. I couldn't see the expression on his face, for it was almost dark, with heavy clouds that looked like rain.

"How do you mean, dead?" he asked me quietly. Too quietly, in fact.

"Now don't go getting ideas into your head," I told him, and took his arm and moved on. "When we get to your room I'll tell you all about it."

I did tell him. Outwardly he seemed quite convinced, but I knew him too well to take that at its face value. There was a set of his jaw that I didn't like, and an occasional sneer.

"And that's that," I concluded. "And now here's where you can help. Had he any relations?"

"I'm pretty sure he hadn't," he said. "He once told me that he and Mortar was two perishin' Babes in the Wood—which were his own words."

"Well, that appears to settle that," I said. "And now, can you tell me anything about his career that might help?"

He could tell me nothing but what I already knew, and he seemed surprised that Feeder had not told me his family history and all about himself. I reminded him that Feeder had been my batman—in my company—for about ten minutes. Then he told me that he had seen Feeder with Mortar in Spain, but naturally had had no contact with him. Feeder had acted as Mortar's servant and as soldier at the same time, and when he and Feeder had yarned together the last few weeks, all the talks had been of engagements and experiences in the Spanish War.

"When's he being buried?" was one of the last two questions he asked, and I had to say I didn't know.

"How was he off for money?"

I told him, and he said he thought he ought to have had more. Mortar had always treated him generously. Then he asked if he might contribute anonymously to the funeral expenses. I said that was good of him and I'd let him know. Then I had to hurry off to Wharton's room.

* * * * *

The late moon was not yet in the sky so I drove very slowly towards Peakridge, and gave George all my news. He said the Colonel had shown no signs of hysterics at the latest tragedy that had fallen on the camp, and that he had also offered to contribute towards funeral expenses. He also gave me the news that Penderby had reported that even on his last leave, which was at the end of September, Staff had been at the quarries and had personally assisted in some blasting.

"You're going to have Staff on the mat?" I asked.

"You bet," George said. "There may be nothing in it, but that young fellow's not going to tell me lies and think he's got away with it. If I don't do anything else I'll knock a little of his cocksureness out of him."

We didn't do much talking because I had to keep my eyes very much on the road. At the police station Wharton went bustling in, with apologies for being late. Everything was set, the Inspector said, and exhibited the prints on the butt of the gun.

Wharton adjusted his spectacles and had a good look. It was far too long a look, I thought, and I was not at all surprised when he was asking the Inspector what he thought of them.

"I think they're a very clear set, sir."

"And natural?"

"Well, they looked so to me, sir."

Wharton pursed his lips, then asked me to have a look. I could see nothing unusual except that the print of the thumb was not so clear as the others. It was what I should describe as a dab.

"Ah!" said George exultantly. "That's just the point."

Then he was deciding to show no bias, for his voice was suddenly avuncular. "Let's try and work this out. Doesn't matter where the gun came from, whether it was his own or one he stole. The fact remains that he brought it with him to where we found him. Now then, Inspector, what do you gather from that?"

The Inspector moistened his lips, scowled, and then admitted that he hadn't quite got it. George was delighted to demonstrate that the Old Gent, as he would occasionally refer to himself, was far more spry than he looked.

"He brought the gun, didn't he? Then where are the prints when he handled it and loaded it? Even if he didn't load it himself he had to put it in his pocket and take it out again. The whole gun should have been smothered with prints."

The Inspector admitted ruefully that that should have been so.

"Well, that's the first fishy thing," Wharton said. "And now the prints that are here. The thumb's only a dab, as Major Travers says, whereas it ought to be as close a print as the fingers. Imagine yourself firing that heavy Webley with a loose thumb."

"You think the prints were superimposed after the shot?"

Wharton shrugged his shoulders.

"What I think isn't evidence. All these facts, and they are facts, are accumulations that make evidence. But we've a final test—the paraffin one. You've heard of it?"

"Yes, sir, but we've never had occasion to use it here."

Wharton picked up the paper with the dead man's prints and compared them with those on the gun. "They're his all right. Where's the doctor? Somewhere handy?"

The Inspector said he was extracting the bullet. He had been unable to get him till a few minutes before Wharton's arrival.

"Do you know the paraffin test?" Wharton asked me.

I said I'd heard of it too, but thought it had only been officially adopted as a test since the war. In any case I knew George would have been disappointed if he couldn't have given us a brief lecture.

"It's perfectly simple," he said. "When a revolver's fired, minute portions of the charge are driven back against the hand holding it. They're not visible to the naked eye, but they're always there, just under the skin. The way to prove it is by applying paraffin wax to the palm of the hand. The minute pieces of powder adhere to the wax and then the wax is chemically tested. If the reactions show the presence of a powder, then the hand fired the gun, and, of course, the reverse."

"The length of time after the shot doesn't make any difference?" I asked.

"I don't know the time-limit," he said. "What I do know is that the test wouldn't be affected by the short time our man was dead. The powder particles are actually forced beneath the skin. The dew wouldn't have washed them off, if that's what you mean."

It was not till an hour later that everything had been done. The local photographer had taken pictures of Feeder and of the gun and its prints. The paraffin, reinforced by a strip of linen bandage, had been applied to the right hand first, and then to the left, for Wharton was taking no chances. Both casts were carefully packed, together with the gun and the bullet, and a trusted man was taking them to town by the night train. The Yard had been notified and a man of theirs would be at the station.

We were going to be late for dinner, but George was on extraordinarily good terms with himself as we drove back to the camp.

"The Old Gent certainly scored one there," he told me. "And now what about my hunch?"

"Good work, George," I said. "Very good work, in fact. One question I'd like to ask, though. Do you think Feeder was killed where we actually saw him?"

"That's a question that can't be answered," he said. "But what do you think we were looking for footprints for? One little print might have told us if someone was carrying the body."

"A hefty someone," I said.

"Yes," he said. "I reckon Feeder weighed a good fourteen stone. But not so difficult if you go about it the right way. You ought to see London firemen doing one of their stunts."

"Then there's the question of transport," I said. "No man could carry that weight too far."

"I'm not worrying about transport," he said. "What I'm satisfied about is the wind. Blowing clean down this road from the camp the last few days, isn't that so? Therefore I say he wasn't shot in the camp itself or the sound must have been heard. I'd say he was lured in some way to come along this road and he was shot here because the wind carried the sound of the shot well away from the camp. Another thing. Wouldn't that stack make a good rendezvous?"

"It certainly would," I admitted. "But wait a minute, though. Who in the camp but Ferris was sufficiently acquainted with Feeder to make a rendezvous like that?"

"Now, now, now," he told me placatingly. "Suppose we do bring in Ferris. When I'm on a case I suspect every man Jack till I'm satisfied otherwise."

"And Ferris is still a suspect?" I asked witheringly.

"I wouldn't say that," he told me mildly. "But Ferris is the one who knows all the tricks and dodges of blowing people up. He got rid of Feeder that Saturday afternoon so that Mortar's room was safe. He more or less kept Mortar under his eye all the afternoon and evening till the bomb went off."

"Let me add a few," I said. "All that earlier stuff was nothing. The Northover affair was a natural happening and so was the Mills on the bombing ground. Ferris wasn't Mortar's pal. All that talk of his about getting the one who did Mortar in, was only damn-fine acting. Ferris was under my eye for the last ten minutes that mattered on that Saturday night, but that was nothing, of course. He set off the bomb by waving in the air, like those coves who produce music—I beg its pardon—on some of the less ghastly B.B.C. programmes."

"I didn't say I did suspect him," George said. "Not now, I mean. As a matter of fact you'd be surprised if I told you who my principal suspect was."

"Well, and who is he?"

"I said *if* I told you," he said, and chuckled.

We were getting near the camp so I had no time to think up a suitable retort to that. What I did ask was if he thought that paraffin test would prove that Feeder did not fire the Webley.

"Of course it will," he said, and then, like lightning. "Bet you a new hat?"

"No you don't, George," I said. "For all I know, the next case you're on may be something to do with the Navy and you'll be masquerading as a ruddy admiral. Those gold-braided hats cost a hell of a lot of money."

We apologised to the Colonel as we took our seats for dinner. The meal was well on its way, but by reducing the chewing to well below Gladstone's standard we made almost a dead heat of it with the others. After the loyal toast, Harness got on his pins.

"I expect you've seen the notices posted in the N.A.A.F.I. and elsewhere, asking if anybody's lost a Webley revolver. It's a Mark VI of 1916, and the number is 10735. If anyone has lost such a revolver, will he report the matter to me. I should also be glad to know if it was loaded at the time it was lost, and in how many of the six chambers. Thank you, gentlemen."

There was no sensation, even at the high table, and shortly afterwards we filed out. I was going to the cinema if George didn't want my services, for Flick had some new Russian films which he was running off. As I came out of my room where I had gone to collect a forgotten pipe, I saw two people ahead of me. Who should they be but George and Nurse Wilton.

"The crafty old rascal!" I said to myself, and had to smile. "No wonder he dodged me when we came out.

Nurse Wilton—her Christian name was Maisie, by the way— had the kind of laugh that is sometimes called infectious. It was certainly the kind of laugh that you'd expect from her, all gurgles and trills, and as shot through with IT as the front row of a modern chorus. George was chuckling away and having a great time generally, but my own face was suddenly straightened as I wondered something. Was Maisie Wilton George's chief suspect? Ridiculous, of course, for how could she have set off that bomb? True, she had been present at every demonstration, and what more easy than for one of her fascinating powers to cajole Store, say, into giving her a teeny-weeny bit of this and that on the pretence of wanting it for some electrical gadget?

Then I knew that my suspicions were more than ridiculous. What possible motive could she have for killing Mortar? No, what George was up to was ingratiation. Nurse Wilton was about to be made to prattle, and there was something that George hoped she would let fall. Then if she was only a minor objective, who was the main one? The answer could only be Flick.

The hall was dark and the two had disappeared somewhere inside by the time I made my way in, and as the last thing I wished to do was to spoil George's game, I edged along the side till I found an empty pew. I then reinforced my seat by brazenly taking the Sorbo seat from another chair and making a double pad for my stern, and then settled down to enjoy the show. When the lights went up from time to time, I remembered my old nannie's instructions on turning one's head. Doubtless George spotted me, but no gurgles or chuckles told me where he and his partner were actually seated.

It was not till close on twenty-two hours that the show ended. The time had come when one could stand up and look round without a display of bad manners. There were George and Nurse Wilton, making their way out, well in the van of the first departures, so I left them plenty of time to get clear. As I was making a slow way back to the Mess where there would be a small gathering, Harness overtook me.

"We've found the owner of the lost Webley, sir."

"Really?" I said. "Who is he?"

"Mr. Brende."

"Good Lord!" I said, fingers at my horn-rims.

"Stolen out of his billet, he reckons, sir. It was loaded in all chambers."

"What'd he keep it loaded for?"

"Well, he only had the six rounds, so he thought the best place to keep them was in the breech. He says his box wasn't locked, but he wasn't worrying about that. A man doesn't expect to have his kit stolen, sir."

"I know," I said. "But why'd he have the gun at all?"

"Well, it's really an issue for Warrant Officers in his class of job," Harness said, and I got the idea that he was covering up something. Maybe Brende had no right to the gun and had worn it in its holster on his belt and with the pouch to give the martial touch.

We went along to the Mess. The Colonel, Collect, and Staff were there and the Colonel insisted on standing us all a drink. Wharton came in just in time to be included. Staff ventured to suggest that there might be a whip round for Feeder's funeral expenses.

"Who told you he was dead?" Wharton demanded. Staff blushed up to the eyes and said he'd heard it. Gaining confidence he then said it was all over the camp. Flick arrived in time to hear what the topic of conversation was and said he'd heard it too. Then the Colonel said he would have to be getting along, and off he went with Collect at his heels. A minute or so afterwards Ferris came in, and we left him with Staff and Flick.

"That's Topman, the talkative old fool!" Wharton growled as we made our way to his room. "Wonder what else he's let out?"

I waited till we were under cover before telling him about the Webley.

"Brende, eh?" he said, and gave a grim sort of smile. "Stealing a gun from a Warrant Officer. That chap Feeder could have pinched his eyebrows."

"But surely it wasn't Feeder who pinched the gun?" I protested. "The one who shot him did that."

"Not necessarily," he told me. "If Feeder could be induced to meet somebody at a rendezvous, the same somebody might have told him to provide himself with a gun, and told him where to find one." Then he was waving all that impatiently aside. "The real point's this. Brende's let out as a suspect. If he'd done it he'd have brought back the gun, or left another in its place. Brende's the very one to know that any gun is traceable from its number."

"The gun was really a plant."

"That's about it," he said. "Whoever shot Feeder tried to incriminate Brende. He didn't think we'd issue a public notice about the gun but that we'd make private inquiries through the number and find out to whom the gun was originally issued. When we found out and asked Brende about his gun he couldn't have helped looking a bit startled." Then George was stifling a yawn. "Don't know about you, but I'm turning in. We've had a pretty heavy day."

I agreed and promptly said good night. As I came out into the night air again I remembered something, and deduced something. George had shoo'd me off because he didn't want to me ask what he'd picked up from the fair Maisie at the pictures.

# Chapter XIV

THE SATURDAY was to prove the vital day of the inquiry.

Up to then there had been a slow and cumulative amassing of information, and little more, though Wharton had certainly got the camp and his list of suspects well into his skin. One might say that what had happened was the assembling of stores, weapons, and ammunition for a big advance, but that advance could not be made for the simple reason that no main objective could be determined on. Information of various kinds had been brought in and various deductions made, but the enemy had yet to be accurately located.

The first thing in the morning brought us news of Feeder. The bullet that had killed him had come from the gun he was holding. As for the prints, they were his, as we knew, but the Yard expert considered it doubtful if his fingers had held the gun when it was fired. As for the paraffin test, that had given negative results for both hands. I had rather expected Wharton to be exultant, but he was not. Perhaps he was asking a question which I had already asked myself. We knew that Feeder had been murdered, but where did the knowledge get us? As the day wore on, sober reasoning made it plain that all we could find were yet more deductions, and deductions of that nebulous kind that makes you immediately aware that to follow them up and try to make them into fact would probably be a loss of valuable time.

Wharton actually gave me the news about Feeder when I met him on the parade ground after breakfast. He was on the way to the magazine, so I went with him. What he had in mind was an inquiry into the brass cartridge for the Blacker that had been found in the debris of Staff's floor.

Store was not at the magazine, but we found him in his quarters. He was full of an early morning heartiness for which neither of us was in the mood, and even more chatty than when I had seen him last.

"Funny about Brende's gun?" he said to Wharton.

"What's funny about it?" Wharton asked wryly.

Store waved a hand round the room he shared with Brende. "Well, it doesn't look any too good for me or the batman. I know he wouldn't suspect either of us, but there you are, sir."

"You never saw Feeder hanging about here?"

"Him!" Store said contemptuously. "You never knew where he was. Still, he'd have had a nerve to come in here and lift a gun out of Brende's box."

"The box was unlocked?"

Store said of course it was unlocked. The biggest crime in barracks is the stealing of a comrade's possessions, because barrack life means leaving things unlocked and trusting to roommates. Wharton told him with scarcely concealed impatience that he'd known that as long as Store himself, and the information that he wanted was at the magazine.

"What is it this time, sir?" Store asked, with a glance at me.

"Just a little check up," Wharton said, and that was the last he did say till we were inside the magazine.

"Cartridges, brass, cordite, Blacker bombs for the use of," said Store officially, running through the leaves of the ledger. "Here we are, sir. Bang up to date. Thirty-one, sir."

"And where are the thirty-one?" Wharton asked mildly.

"Here, sir, on this rack."

"Just count them," Wharton said.

Count them?' There was a slight lifting of eyebrows. "Certainly, sir."

A minute and he was frowning. A recount, and he had to admit that there were only thirty.

"When did you last count them?" Wharton asked.

There was a brief hesitation and then Store said he thought it was after the firing on the Wednesday. None had been issued since. Wharton gave him one of his Ancient Mariner looks.

"And what if I tell you that I know you were one short as long ago as last Saturday?"

Store blustered and said it was impossible. Wharton's stare persisted and he added that he had to leave certain things to his assistant, who probably had taken the balance for granted, seeing as how there were so few cartridges.

"And you made up the book on his word?"

"You have to sometimes, sir. You don't expect a sergeant to make mistakes, sir. Besides, I've only got one pair of hands."

Wharton nodded and left it at that. When he asked to be shown the magazine annexe, Store was so eager and officious that it was plain that he had had a nasty shaking.

"Plenty of flex and electrical stuff here," Wharton said as he cast an eye round. "Everything for detonations except actual explosives. No necessity to have such strict supervision as you have at the main magazine. No end of people come in?"

"Oh, but we do keep an eye on things," Store said. "I don't think anybody would have the chance of lifting much here."

Wharton touched what I call one of the plunger sets with his foot.

"That operates with its own batteries, doesn't it?"

"That's right, sir."

"Then if you had a power or light plug handy, you could dispense with the batteries?"

Store agreed. All that was needed was to set off the detonator by electrical current, and it didn't matter where the electricity came from. The boxes were handy when there was no grid or other electrical source into which to plug.

Being none too good at matters electrical I thought I'd use the opportunity to make my hazy knowledge far more secure.

"Suppose this bit of wood is a detonator," I said. "I fix the two wires in contact with it, and I attach them by means of a plug to a source of power. When I operate the light or heating switch, off goes the detonator, and not before."

"That's right, sir."

"But suppose I still prefer to use some sort of plunger?"

"That'd be all right, sir," Store said. "All it'd mean would be that the juice was on but the plunger action operated it instead of the switch."

"A perfectly simple thing to make, would it be?"

"Simple as ABC, sir." He picked up a smallish round tin and found a round piece of wood to fit it. "Let's imagine there's some metal on the base of this piece of wood, sir, and connected with the juice."

"By juice you mean electricity, of course?" Wharton said.

"That's right, sir. But the wires connected with the detonator are lying at the bottom of this tin and I fix the wooden plunger in so that it is still well clear of the wires. It happens to be a good tight fit, luckily. There you are then, sir. There's your home-made plunger set. The juice is on and all you have to do is press down the plunger. The metal at the bottom touches the wires, and off the detonator goes."

"Good," I said. "And I could buy any length of flex I wanted from any electrical shop. One of these days I'll try it."

"If you like, sir, I'll get this piece of wood and this tin fixed up for you."

I was going to say it wouldn't be necessary, but he was so eager to rehabilitate himself, as it were, that I said instead that I'd be most grateful, though I did add that there wasn't any hurry.

"I believe Mr. Staff's a bit of an expert on this kind of thing," Wharton cut in hopefully.

Store smiled condescendingly. "Oh, yes, sir. He's been in here once or twice, trying to tell me a thing or two. I believe his family are connected with explosives in some way or other. Now what did he tell me?"

Wharton didn't wait for Store to remember, but said we would have to be going. Then he put him on rather better terms with himself by adding that the visit had been unofficial. Then he added that it had also been highly confidential, and accompanied the statement by a look which removed the fleeting smile from the face of Store.

Before we could discuss in any way what we had learned, we caught sight of Harness coming from the Home Guard

N.A.A.F.I., and he waited for us. As we walked towards the office, Wharton told him in confidence the news about Feeder.

"My Gawd, sir, it fairly makes your flesh creep," Harness said. He had made as if to halt and his hand went out to Wharton's arm, but George was in the mood for haste.

"You mean, to think that a murderer's somewhere about the camp?" I said.

"That's it, sir. And who's he going to get next?"

Wharton was waving a hand by way of farewell, and sheering off towards the Mess. I didn't feel I ought to leave Harness so abruptly, so went on the few yards to the office.

"I'm real sorry about that Feeder," Harness told me with a shake of the head. "Take him all round, he wasn't all that bad. I think on the whole I'd rather have had him than his officer."

"Between ourselves," I said, "what was your main grouse against Mortar?"

He didn't need even a second thought. "He was a trouble maker. If I'd liked to make trouble myself, I could have had him before the Colonel."

"What for?"

"I'll tell you only *one* thing. When we were on parade one morning and I'd got the men moving right smart, Captain Mortar came across. He sort of rolled across, you know, sir, in that impertinent sort of way he had. 'Nice to see some real live soldiers again,' he says, and so that everyone could hear. Now was that discipline, sir? I ask you. I tell you it absolutely spoilt that parade and it made me so furious that if I'd had a gun I'd have shot him."

"Very annoying," I said consolingly. "I know he could be a very annoying person, and deliberately so. But he's gone now, Harness."

"Yes," he said, "and I've sometimes been tempted to say, 'Damn-good riddance!'"

I went to the Mess in search of George but he was not there, so I asked Shorty to make me a spot of coffee and went through to the writing-room. Thinking over what Harness had just told me, I had an idea. As I followed that idea up, it began to lead me into deeper and deeper morasses, and when I'd drunk my coffee I decided to put the whole thing up to George. As I came near the hospital, Staff was leaving it, and he was looking far from pleased with himself. George was in his room and making notes.

"Been twisting Staff's tail?" I said. George exploded.

"The damn' young whippersnapper. What d'you think he said? Said that he didn't consider the explosives work they did at the quarries came within the scope of my question. Within the scope, mind you. I gave him scope!"

"I bet you did," I said. "How d'you sum him up generally?"

His voice lowered and he was pursing his lips reflectively. "Don't know. My own private idea is that that cartridge that was found under his floor was another plant."

"Like the use of Brende's gun."

"That's it," he said. "Someone trying to throw suspicion first on one and then on the other. The trouble is that in each case we can't be sure. Staff may have had that cartridge there for some other reason and have forgotten all about it, and he must have had it well out of the way, or it'd have gone off when the room was burnt. We know he'd been in the magazine, and the same with Brende. His yarn about Feeder may have been a pack of lies from beginning to end."

"Well, I've had an idea, George," I said. "Perhaps it's one that has occurred to you long ago, but why shouldn't this case be looked at from a new angle—that of motive. Leave Feeder out of things for a bit and try to assess every possible motive that each possible person had for killing Mortar."

I rather fancied he was only too eager to clutch at any new ideas, for in less than no time he was writing down names. "Collect," he said. "You told me he was jealous of Mortar's popularity, and he'd never forgiven him for suppressing that Scoutcraft lecture. Is that all?"

I said it was, and he went on to Flick. There the only real point at issue between the two men had been Nurse Wilton, apparently. I added that Flick was something of a lick-spittle, and he had been very easily induced by the anti-Mortarites to transfer to their camp.

"But if we're to believe Shorty," Wharton said, "Mortar disclaimed all interest in the lady on the Saturday evening when he had those drinks with Flick. We simply must take that as true."

"Not only that," I said, "but would Flick, as a married man, take an affair with Maisie Wilton as more than philandering? His own affair, I mean. He daren't take it more seriously and risk the scandal and the effects on his military career. But leave all that out, George, can't you say about both Collect and Flick that neither had a strong enough motive to commit a murder?"

"Maybe," he said.

"Staff's a bit more promising. I've told you that Mortar badgered him till he was pretty desperate. But think of his career as a young regular soldier. I suppose you noticed his three pips, by the way? His promotion came through this morning."

George owned that he hadn't noticed the pips, but he did agree that even if Staff had the strongest motive so far, it wasn't a motive good enough. Then I told him what Harness had thought of Mortar, and that seemed no motive for murder. Lastly, there were Brende and Store. Brende had been discussed *ad nauseam* already. His motive seemed about as strong as Staff's, and had arisen from much the same causes, but if his gun had been planted, then he was let out altogether. As for Store, we knew no reason why he should have a murder motive at all.

George pushed the sheet of notes aside. "If this is your bright idea, I don't think much of it," he told me wryly. "It simply brings us up against the same dead end."

"I think it makes us see the whole case more clearly," I said. "You remember we talked over the nature of the Northover affair and the Mills, and then Mortar's death, and how all three had been underhand, sneaking sorts of affairs. A person could easily persuade himself in each of the three that they were no more than practical jokes, carried a bit too far. The bit too far wouldn't matter, because the perpetrator wouldn't be there to see the results. To see the blood and the torn limbs, for instance. But let's put all that on one side and go on to the murder of Feeder.

That comes into a different category. That's a cold-blooded, calculated killing. The murderer actually held the gun. He mayn't have seen the shattered skull, because it was a dark night, but *he* wasn't a practical joker. My point then is this. Have we to deal with a wholly different person from those on that list?"

"I get you," he said. "Was Feeder killed from a motive which we haven't even a suspicion of, and which had no connection with Mortar at all, and, as you say, by someone not on the general suspect list?"

Then he looked up at me with an expression of humorous resignation. "In other words, we may have to start all over again. Where? And how?"

I couldn't suggest a thing. He was shaking his head, and when he did say something else it was not what I was expecting.

"The funny thing is that I've got that on-the-edge feeling. There's just some little thing missing. You know, like when you've forgotten a name and it's on the tip of your tongue. At any minute I sort of know something's going to turn up. I felt it when we were with Store and I got it just now when you were talking. Then before I could pounce on it, it had gone."

He had some telephoning to do that morning so I didn't see him again till after lunch. He was then going down to Peakridge to arrange for Feeder's funeral on the Monday, and I should have gone to watch some firing at the ranges but for the fact that a fairly heavy rain was coming down. As I was not actually on duty I went to the Mess instead. Ferris and Flick were at the bar, and talking quite amicably.

Now you may have been thinking that I have made you plough through a lot of argument without bringing you anywhere. As devil's advocate I would retort that you, who heard Wharton and myself arguing about motives, were as wise as we. Not that I should expect you to arrive at the startling theory at which I arrived at the mere sight of Ferris.

"A new person and a new motive!" That's what flashed across my mind as I waved a hand in refusal of a drink and went through to the writing-room. Staff was there, and doing the *Times* crossword, but that didn't worry me in the least. I refused, and with not all the courtesy I should have shown, the paper that Staff offered me, and I drew up a chair on the other side of the fire and began to concentrate. I didn't have to think long.

A different sort of killer and a different sort of killing—well, Ferris was the answer. He was a killer all right, and whenever he thought the occasion warranted it. As for motive, it stood out like Beachy Head in the Channel. He had sworn to get Mortar's killer. Very well then. He had got Mortar's killer, *for Feeder was the one who had killed Mortar!*

Simple, wasn't it? And fairly watertight as a theory. Indeed, the more I examined it, the more I knew it was the correct answer to the whole business. All that remained to do was to find what motive Feeder had for killing Mortar. Incredible, you may say, that Feeder should have killed Mortar at all. What about his tears and genuine grief both in the Colonel's room and at the graveside? I can only say that such things prove nothing, and I speak from experience of murderers. Nothing is more explicable than a turgid and easily summoned emotion. A person who knows himself to be a murderer must have nerves at full strain, and emotion lies much nearer to the surface with him than it does with you and me.

I think I must have been shuffling uneasily on my seat for l looked round to see Staff's eyes fixed curiously on me. Then he went out and I heard Flick hail him from the bar before the door closed again. What to do about following up my theory was what was worrying me. I could hardly tackle Ferris direct, and yet what could Wharton and I do if we stuck to the recognised methods of inquiry? Ferris doubtless had some sort of alibi, and it was too much to expect that anyone might have seen him near the haystack that night, for since Peakridge was out of bounds and routine traffic had ceased, the road was always deserted by dusk.

But I sat on in my chair, worrying my wits and every now and then giving my glasses an unnecessary polish, and then when I was making up my mind to leave the whole matter to Wharton's judgment, the door opened and Ferris came in. In the brief glimpse I had of it I could see that the bar-room was empty.

"Hallo, sir," he said genially. "Taking things easy?"

"As a matter of fact I was just thinking of trying to find a job of work," I said, as he drew up his chair to the fire.

"No day for work," he said. "I pity those poor devils out there on the range."

"We'll all get our wet days now," I told him.

Nothing else was said for a few moments, and then he was asking when Feeder was going to be buried.

"On Monday," I said. "Were you thinking of sending a wreath?" I shot a look at him. His eyes had narrowed and his gaze was intent on the fire.

"No," he said slowly. "I don't think I'll be a hypocrite. I still think he was a liar and a double-crosser."

"Well, he's paid for it."

I shot another look at him, but his eyes were still intent on the fire. "Paid for it?" His lips curled. "He took the easiest way out."

"Are you sure?"

His eyes swivelled at last round to mine. "What do you mean?"

"This," I said, watching him like a hawk. "This is in more than strict confidence, by the way. I've no authority to let out official secrets but I'm going to do so—this once. Suppose Feeder didn't choose his own way out? Suppose he was murdered?"

"You're not serious?"

"Never more so," I said, and found it hard to keep my eyes on his, so concentrated and intent was their glare on mine.

"Any evidence?"

"I oughtn't to tell you this," I said, "but I will. It's beyond all doubt. The one who murdered him made several slips, and he didn't allow for modern police methods."

"I see," he said slowly, and his eyes were once more on the fire. "I suppose you haven't any idea who did it?"

"Wharton hasn't, if that's what you mean," I said, and then I added something else, and somehow I couldn't keep the words back. "That doesn't mean I haven't ideas myself."

I saw his body stiffen, and then his head slowly turned my way.

"Who was it—Brende?"

"No," I said. "I think it was you."

"I!" He stared blankly. "You're not serious?"

"I'm afraid I am."

I suddenly went to the door and looked inside the bar. I even had a look outside both windows before I sat down. When I looked at Ferris again he was shaking his head.

"That's a pretty foul thing to say."

"Maybe," I said curtly. "Feeder died a foul death." He turned on me, spreading his palms with a gesture that was curiously Continental. "But why should I kill him?"

"That remains to be proved—if you did kill him."

"Yes, but why this—this ridiculous charge against me?"

"It isn't a charge," I pointed out. "It's merely my own private suspicion. You told me, and you insisted that you were serious, that you'd get the one who did Mortar in. Can you blame me if I accept a statement that you're capable of murder? Moreover, I think your life in Spain has definitely made things like killing and murder of very little account."

"Just a minute," he broke in. "Is it fair to me to confuse my lectures, say, with my private life?"

"You're slurring the issue," I said. "It wasn't in a lecture that you said you'd get the one who got Mortar. You said it to me, and you meant it."

"I see," he said and let out a breath. "Then you think that Feeder got Mortar, and I found it out, and then I got Feeder."

"That's it," I said. "That's my private solution. I suppose it's no use asking you if it's a fact?"

He sneered. "What'd be the good? You wouldn't believe me, for one thing. And if I'd been such a fool as to have done it, I shouldn't be a bigger fool and own up."

"Did you do it?" I asked quietly.

His eyes were suddenly on mine again. "What would you do if I said yes?"

"Tell Wharton—later. Give you two or three hours start to get away. I'd owe you that much."

He smiled and shook his head. "You needn't worry, Major. I'm saying nothing and I'm not running away." Then he was getting to his feet and making his way towards the door. "I will say this, Major—that I'm grateful to you. And you've given me a really good idea."

The door closed. I sat on for a minute or two, and what I was wondering was why his voice had shaken as he made that final statement. Was it from anger, or had it been due to some private emotion aroused by that idea which he claimed I had put into his head? Then I began to wonder what possible idea I could have given him, and as I made my way back to my room I was wondering and worrying about something else—whether or not to mention my indiscretions to Wharton. Finally, I decided to say nothing, for the information that had arisen out of that unauthorised talk with Ferris had been purely negative.

But I did tell George of my latest theory, and it seemed to impress him. In fact, he admitted it was the most promising opening we had so far had. The problem was how to exploit the theory.

"Well, that's up to you," I said. "If you want me to do anything, just let me know. Now I'll leave you to do your telephoning."

He had plenty of other work to do too, he said, and he'd probably be in his room till dinner. Then, as I was going out, Harness came in to announce that owing to the rain and the need for men to change into dry clothes, the Advice Bureau would be closed for that evening. I promptly had a bath and a change myself, and then was at a loose end. It was still only five o'clock so I decided to go to the writing-room again and look through the weekly illustrateds. If I had not made that sudden resolution—and it needed a resolution to turn out in the pouring rain—I am confident to this day that we should never have known who killed Mortar and Feeder.

## Chapter XV

I THINK YOU HAVE gathered that Staff had put in a good session on the *Times* crossword that afternoon. He wasn't what I might call a crossword Mrs. Battle, with the root of the matter in him, but very much of a dilettante. For one thing he hadn't a pencil with a rubber at one end, and as he was also an optimist he would fill in clues without cross-checking. You can imagine, therefore, the condition in which he left an unfinished crossword, and the one that evening was a more horrible sight than most, and I made up my mind to give him a ticking off.

As I laid *The Times* aside again I remembered that there was quite a good one in the *Telegraph*, and pretty furious I was when I found that Staff had mutilated that too. But when I had a look at one of the illustrateds, there was what looked like quite a good crossword, and unfouled by Staff, so I sharpened my pencil and settled down to its solution.

You have probably long since gathered that my brain is of the crossword kind; that I know a very few things really well, for instance, and have a smattering of many more. Privately I have no respect for that kind of brain, though I would choose it every time for the fun it allows one to get out of life. As for the methods I employ in trying to solve a crossword, I expect they are the same as your own, which is to say that I read rapidly all the Acrosses and fill in any that are obviously correct, and then do the same with the Downs. After that, unless the puzzle is a snorter, its back is broken, and cross-checking does the rest.

After that first complete run through, here then is the puzzle as so far filled in. Ignore stray letters at the sides, because they represent the ends of clues already filled in and which do not matter. What you see is the bottom right-hand corner only, and I append all the necessary clues.

ACROSS

22 This poet has nothing in him.
28 No more than a second.

31 An Irish lake.

34 Fig out of sorts.

DOWN

20 Ordered appointments.

23 Nothing this and no prize.

24 Kosh dry, and get wheels.

26 The entrants have little laundry.

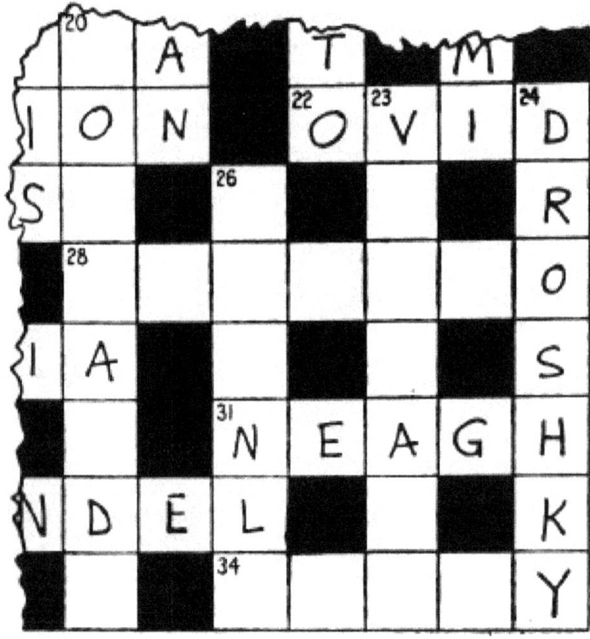

Now I ask you to follow my mental processes when I arrived at that bottom right-hand corner for the second look through.

"No more than a second. The O at the end is the no more. I've got it—MOMENTO."

In it went and I tried 34 Across.

"Fig out of sorts? Ends in Y. Fig? Of course, yes. SEEDY."

In it went, and then my eye caught something. If SEEDY were right, then 26 Down would have to end in NLS, and that seemed an impossible combination of 200 letters. Now the L was most certainly right, for it came from COROMANDEL (Coast) and the letters of that fitted everything else. The N was right, for I knew no Irish lake of five letters ending in H, except NEAGH.

"Leave it," I told myself, "and let's get on. 20 Down ought to be easy. Ordered appointments. Order . . . command. That's it—COMMANDS. Now 23 Down and what have I got? V—N—A—E. Nothing this and no prize. Nothing this. Nothing what? Simple VENTURE. Nothing venture nothing win."

Then I was saying, "Hallo, something wrong here. If the U's right, then the A's wrong. What about DROSHKY? Is that right? It must be. It's an anagram, and that slang word *kosh* gives it away. Then what about the last clue, 26 Down? The entrants have little laundry.—M—NLS. Must be SM, surely. I've got it. SMALLS. Little laundry, and Little-go entrance exam. Then 11 Across was wrong L—U—H. But how silly of me! Trying to be clever. No special lake but just the Irish name for lake."

Thereupon I filled in LOUGH, and the corner was complete. I smiled to myself at the mistake I had made, and on reflection decided it was a reasonably natural mistake. Now if the setter had said simply *Irish*, I might have put in LOUGH, but he said *an Irish*, which made me think of a special lake and a proper noun.

Then all at once I was lying back in my chair, and I was polishing my horn-rims. A curious idea had come to me, and on its heels another, and another. One more minute and I was hooking the glasses on again, and hoisting my long legs inwards. What had I better do? See Harness first and make sure, or see Wharton and both of us make sure? Another minute and I was making my way through the rain and the gathering dusk to Harness's office.

Five minutes later I walked, or rather bustled, unceremoniously into George's room. He was writing, and he peered inquiringly over the tops of his antiquated spectacles.

"I think I've got something, George," I said. "Don't look at me like that. I tell you I've really got something!"

"No reason why you shouldn't sit down, is there?"

"Well, no," I said, and took a seat. "But it's this way, George. Did I ever tell you about Mortar's original lecture and "

"You mean about blowing up a house by a canal and wiping out the whole collection, enemy, inmates, and all? The thing Staff poked his nose in about?"

"That's it," I said. "And here's where I went wrong later. Mortar said he'd change the episode to something else in Mexico. But he didn't say that at all—"

"Here, what *is* this?" George cut in. "You've got me tied in knots. Start at the beginning—if there is one."

"This is what happened," I said. "Mortar was in command of some irregulars who located an enemy headquarters. A night or so later on they came back with the explosives and blew up the house—a large private house, I'd imagine—to smithereens together with any civilians who happened to be in it. I thought it took place in Mexico, because when the Colonel asked Mortar to substitute something else for it in his lecture, what he said was: 'I'll put in something in Mexico.' I wasn't paying too much attention, but now I come to think back, what he said was: 'I'll put in something *else*, in Mexico.' You see the difference?"

Wharton nodded. "And where did the blowing up actually take place?"

"In Ireland," I said. "When he talked about a house by the lock, I thought it was l-o-c-k, because that was how he pronounced it. I imagined a canal lock therefore. What he should have done was to pronounce gutturally, then I should have known he was referring to a lough—l-o-u-g-h."

"I get you," he said. "And was he in Ireland?"

"Yes, with the Black and Tans. The job he'd have jumped at after the last war."

"Was Feeder with him?"

"There are no records," I said. "But he must have been with him. Mortar engaged Feeder immediately after the last war, and Feeder told me he was with him from then on. Feeder often used Irish turns of speech."

George shook his head at that. "Didn't you tell me there were a lot of Irishmen in that International Brigade in Spain? Besides, all these adventurers like Mortar and Feeder and Ferris add all sorts of words to their vocabularies. Long after the last war was over our men used to say *bon* and *napoo*, and so on. When we were fitting out Mortar's old room ready for the photographs, I heard Feeder addressing one of the Quartermaster's men as *amigo*?"

"We're getting wide of the argument," I said. "Waive all that and I'm still certain Feeder was in Ireland, and if so, there may be a motive for his killing Mortar. And something else I've discovered. I thought Flick was about thirty, but I've just found out he's turned thirty-six. He was born in Eire, and here's the address of his mother who's still living there. What I'm getting at is that Flick was old enough to have fought in the troubles."

Wharton grunted, but it was his best sort of grunt.

"And I'll put something else to you," I went on. "Mortar and Flick were friendly enough when we all got here first. Why shouldn't the cooling off—it came during the very first week here—have been due to Flick's putting two and two together about that lecture episode of Mortar's? Their quarrel needn't have been about Nurse Wilton at all."

"I'm beginning to get you," Wharton said.

"And to sum up, George, I'll say this. We agreed that Feeder's killing was something different. We're looking for a different kind of killer from the one who did Mortar in. We want a cold-blooded killer, and one with a cold-blooded killer's motive. We want him so badly that we can't afford to miss a chance."

"I might do worse," Wharton said, and frowned in thought.

"Worse than what?"

"Slip up to town and get an interview with the High Commissioner for Eire."

"It'd be worth trying," I said. "It might even be worth your while to slip across to Dublin, or question the neighbours at Mrs. Flick's home."

"Well, no time like the present," he said. "You arrange for the car to be outside the dining-room. We'll get our meal through early and then you can drive me to Peakridge to catch that eight o'clock. I'll do a bit of packing and see the Colonel.

At the door he gave me more instructions. "I shan't say where I'm going. All the Colonel will know is that I've been re-called to town for a few hours. I don't mind who knows that much. Perhaps it might make someone feel even more uneasy. And if I'm not back, you might take over the arrangements for Feeder's funeral."

Well, we got to Peakridge in time for the train. In fact we had to walk up and down the blacked-out station to keep our circulation going till the train drew in.

"I may have to arrange for any information about those registered packages to be sent here to you," Wharton told me. "I might be all over the place the next day or two. And there's something else you might do. It's unorthodox and I don't know if you'd care to take it on, but I think it might be a good idea to get this murderer as much on edge as we can. Have a little conference then, of everybody. Say I'm away following up a vital clue. If there's anything in this Ireland business, then the mur-derer will guess where I am. Watch faces and form your own judgment."

"How much can I let out?"

"Nothing," he said. "You pretend to be ignorant. I'm the one who has all the suspicions. We're dealing with a desperate man. I don't want anything to happen to you—just yet."

I had to chuckle at that. George said it was no laughing mat-ter, and added that if I cared to hint, very vaguely, of course, that someone might come forward with information and so avoid scandal, that might be all to the good too.

"You use your own judgment," he said as the train drew in. "I'll get in touch with you if I can, but I can't promise."

The whistle tooted and the train moved out.

"Good luck, George," I called.

The engine was puffing away and making the devil of a row, so that I couldn't hear what he was hollering back.

I gathered it was something about not letting the Colonel wash out that Security lecture.

*     *     *     *     *

That night I spent the last half-hour before bed in my room instead of in the Mess, and I was feeling a something I had felt only once in my life. When as a foot-slogger sergeant I did something in the last war, for which they gave me a D.C.M., I was no more conscious of fear at the time than if I'd been reading *La Vie* in a dug-out. Things moved too quickly for fear, but afterwards, when I came introspectively to recall the various happenings, I was cold with fright and horror, and for months afterwards I would wince if I even heard the name of the place.

Now I was cold with fear once more. George's anxiety about my safety was the thing that set me off, and yet somehow I was not being afraid for myself. Most of us have sufficient vanity to dissociate ourselves from the hostility of others, and what gave me that cold fear was the realisation, and once more after the event, that a killer was loose in the camp, and almost certainly among those with whom I sat each day at the high table. That killer was more than cold-blooded, for there had been something diabolically cunning about the ruthless blotting out of Feeder. Now that killer would know that Wharton was away, and following up a promising clue. Would Wharton's continued absence and silence fray the murderer's nerves to snapping-point? Would there be another murder, to cover up the killing of Feeder?

Laugh at me if you like, but that night I slept with my door locked, and I had my loaded automatic under my pillow. In the morning, when I had to rise to let my batman in, I felt no shame for either precaution, maybe because the rain was coming steadily down and it was a morning for depressions. At breakfast I regarded my fellows at the high table with a new interest, though with little profit, and every now and again I would be wondering where Wharton was at that precise moment.

After the meal the Colonel asked if I could spare him a few moments, and we went back to his room. I knew he was going to pick my brains about Wharton, and extract the whys, wheres, and wherefores, but I was wrong. What he did was to unlock his desk and take out a quarto envelope.

"Give me your opinion on that, Travers, will you?"

I polished my glasses and had a look at the two type-written quarto pages. They were the report on Collect's camouflage as seen from the air, and on the camouflage of the whole camp, for which it appeared he had been responsible.

In less than a minute I was raising my eyebrows. Then I kept my thoughts to myself till I had read through the whole thing.

"Well, what do you think of it?" the Colonel asked.

"I think it's the most damning thing of its kind I've ever read," I told him.

"Yes," he said, and sighed heavily as he locked it up again. "What's to be done about it? It ought to have gone to the War Office yesterday but I held it back for you to see."

I shook my head, and then mumbled something about it being too dangerous to suppress. The War Office would have to have it some time or other.

"That's just it," he said. "What'll be the outcome, I don't know. He's an excellent fellow in many ways, you know, Travers. I'm not saying so because my girl married his boy. Besides, we've got to be loyal to each other as far as we can."

Somehow I was getting the idea that he wouldn't after all be too grieved to see the back of Collect. I ventured to say that no man, even himself, if he'd pardon the liberty, was so valuable that he couldn't be replaced. Thereupon he sighed heavily once more, thanked me for my help and said that, however regretfully, there was nothing for him to do but to get the report off. Meanwhile would I keep everything to myself.

Since the iron seemed remarkably malleable, I mentioned that short conference Wharton had suggested, and said that as Sunday was a comparatively easy day, with no Advice Bureau, eighteen hours in that very room might be a convenient time and place. He looked extremely disconcerted when I only hinted at some of the things I should have to mention, and his eyes fairly popped at my request that both Brende and Store should be present. I think it was only because I said I was merely Wharton's mouthpiece that he gave way about that.

I went to see Harness about notifying everybody concerned, and just as I was leaving his office there was a telephone call for me. It was Wharton, ringing up from town.

"Don't tell me you're up already!" he began.

"Two hours and more," I said. But I knew the geniality concealed something, and asked what the good news was. His voice was lugubrious at once.

"There's one registered package that might be interesting but they're only just following it up." Without giving me a chance to get in a word, he switched the topic. "What I forgot to tell you is that if I want to communicate with you, I'll do so through Peakridge police. Everything all right your end?"

"Yes," I began, and then he cut in with the plea that he couldn't waste the taxpayers' money on a second three minutes, and off he rang.

I was much more cheerful as I came out to the parade ground again. The rain had actually ceased, and though it was bitter cold, a watery sun was trying to break through the clouds, and somehow it seemed a good omen. As I nodded to myself and moved on again, I suddenly heard a voice. Just disappearing round the end of the hospital were Flick and Maisie Wilton. She was in uniform and walking with head in air as if unaware of Flick's persistent presence. He seemed to be gesturing and trying to convince her of something, or explain something away, and then the two disappeared, and that was that.

While I waited for everybody to get comfortably settled, I ran a preliminary eye over the company assembled in the Colonel's room. Store looked most uncomfortable and out of place, Brende was stolid and evidently expecting a talk on routine work, Flick seemed a bit suspicious and darted more than one look at me, Staff was fidgeting with the ends of his moustache, and Ferris seemed just as cool and collected as ever, though he did try more than once to catch my eye.

"If you're ready, gentlemen," the Colonel said, "Major Travers has certain matters which he has to put up to us on behalf of Captain Wharton, who's been called away for a day or so."

He nodded to me and I got to my feet. I am not going to bore you with what I said, though I will give you the general trends. First of all, I made no mention whatever of the Northover and Mills affairs, but divulged generally the fact that Mortar had died as a result of the explosion of the Blacker bomb which had been fired by Brende and never recovered. The Sappers had reported a search of every inch of ground, and were confident that the bomb had been found by someone, and removed.

And so to the second bombshell. Captain Wharton was of the definite opinion, and for his undisclosed reasons, that Mortar had been deliberately killed by an explosion of that bomb as controlled by the killer. Everybody shuffled uneasily in his seat, and Ferris's eyes had that look of fierce intensity that one saw when he illustrated the use of the knife. Flick was looking surprised and no more. Store's face had reddened, Brende was looking at me intently, and Staff was nervously lighting a cigarette, though the Colonel had not given permission to smoke.

Still quoting Wharton, I said that Feeder had not committed suicide but had definitely been murdered. I didn't know, I added, but I had an idea that Wharton was away following up an important clue to do with that murder. For Brende's comfort I did disclose that though his gun had been found by Feeder's hand, Feeder himself had not fired it. Then I realised that the statement was no comfort to Brende after all, for it might have been a subtle hint that Brende had fired it himself. Brende himself seemed astonished, but no more.

"May I say something?" put in Collect in his slow, precise voice. "These are most terrible, horrible things we've been listening to. Surely Captain Wharton doesn't suggest that anybody in this room is responsible for them?"

"I'm not in Captain Wharton's confidence," I said unblushingly. "I acted with him last week merely because the Colonel thought that as I knew the camp and everybody I'd make a good liaison. What I will say is this. Everything that's said here is more than highly confidential—"

"I ought to have emphasised that," broke in the Colonel. "If a single word gets out, I shall take most drastic action. The one responsible, whoever he is, will be put under close arrest at once."

"Thank you, sir," I said. "And what I was going to say was that Captain Wharton may not have had any idea of associating anyone in this room with the things which have happened. Horrible things, as Major Collect has said. His idea may have been to request your co-operation. He knows, as we all do, that any further trouble here may mean the dispersal of the present staff and drastic changes. Some of those changes might have had a bad effect on some people's careers. I think that's why he requested me to ask any of you who had any information of any kind to come immediately forward. You can give that information in public or in confidence."

"If I knew anything I'd get on my legs and say it now," the Colonel announced belligerently. "If it were my own brother, I'd hand him over. It isn't ratting, gentlemen. It's a question of plain duty. We owe it to everybody—the Service, the school, to ourselves, and everything." Everyone looked round at everyone else. I polished my glasses and an uneasy silence settled on the room. Then at last someone spoke. It was Collect, voice dry and precise as if he were a schoolmaster addressing his form.

"I think I should say that I noticed one unusual happening myself. I mean, a happening that seemed unusual. Not at the time, but now."

"What was it?" the Colonel was firing.

"Well," said Collect, and stammered slightly. "I prefer at the moment not to say."

"You mean it concerns someone in this room?"

"Well, yes—in a way."

Flick's plump, clean-shaven face had gone a vivid scarlet. He caught my eye and was at once blowing his nose violently. The Colonel glowered at him.

"I mean, I'd rather give the person concerned a chance to make his own statement," Collect was going on. "That seems to me the honourable way." His eyes ranged the room. "I expect he knows what I mean and doubtless he'll think it wise to make a statement to Major Travers, or to Captain Wharton when he gets back."

The Colonel snorted. "He'd certainly better. It's his last chance. What Captain Wharton will do with him, I don't know." Then his eyes bulged as he swivelled his chair round on Collect. "You don't mean to suggest this man was the—was responsible for these murders?" Then he was glaring round the room. "Blunt words, gentlemen, but the time's come for plain speaking."

"Oh, no—not necessarily," Collect said. "Perhaps the person concerned could explain it. I don't know. I'm not suggesting for a moment he was a—er—murderer." That virtually concluded the meeting, for nobody else but the Colonel said a word. In any case it was time for dinner and when the Colonel gave the word go, everybody simply shot off.

At the meal everybody was remarkably subdued. I had a word with Flick as we came out, and gathered that the films that night would be well worth a visit, so I went back to my room to put on an extra pair of socks and a size larger shoes, for there was the very devil of a draught along the floor of the lecture hall at night. Something else delayed me for a minute or two and then I switched off the light and stepped out to the black of the parade ground. It was at that very moment that I heard the noise.

# Chapter XVI

AFTER THE LIGHT of my room the night was incredibly dark. What was happening I had no idea, but the sound was like that of a dog worrying something. Then there was all at once a kind of strangled shriek that made my blood curdle.

"What's going on? Who's there?"

I hollered and listened. There was that muffled shriek again and then a faint thud. I was trying to run towards the sound and then as I stumbled I listened again and there was no sound at all. Then it began again and near me, and as I moved forward cautiously again, there was a man.

He seemed to be bent double and was clutching at his throat and making queer gurgling noises. I had no torch but as I took him by the shoulders I knew who he was. "What's the matter, Collect? What's happened?"

It was a moment or two before he could get out anything at all.

"Someone attacked me." He gulped and tried to clear his throat again, and he was trembling as if from fever.

"Let's get along to your room," I said. "Let me lend you a hand. That's it. Take it easy."

My eyes were more accustomed to the dark and I could see the black bulk of the hut against the clouds. Inside his room I lowered him into a chair and asked if there was a handy drink. He pointed to the low cupboard, where I found a bottle of whisky. The two inches neat took a bit of swallowing, and now he had turned back the collar of his British warm, I could see the bruises on his throat and neck.

"Feel like telling me what happened?"

He was still shaking like a leaf; his face was pale and he looked ten years older. It must have taken him five minutes to tell me his story, for it hurt him to talk, and what he had to tell wasn't much. He had intended to go to the cinema, and all at once he was seized from behind. An arm was round his throat and he was as terror-struck as one is in a nightmare. Then by the grace of God he had remembered a ju-jitsu trick and had tried to hoist his attacker over his shoulder. What he had done was to loosen slightly the grip on his throat and had been able to get out that strangled shriek. When I hollered, the assailant had taken fright. Collect had been literally hurled away and he hadn't even heard the noise of the assailant's feet as he disappeared.

"Someone trying that trick of Mortar's on you," I said. "Lucky for you he didn't go right through with it."

It was curious how much more animated Collect became when he told me what redounded to his own credit. Like a flash he had known that someone was trying to kill him, and as Mortar had described, and that was why he had tried the ju-jitsu trick. All the same he admitted that if the thick collar of the British warm hadn't been turned up round his ears, he must have stood a poor chance.

"You've not the faintest idea who your assailant was?" He shook his head. He was a big man, he thought, and he didn't even know why he thought that. After all, he was shortish himself, and a man of his own height could have got him round the throat.

Then he said he'd have another drink, and he was firm enough now on his pins to get it for himself. I had a weakish one, and chiefly because I wanted to talk to him in confidence, and a drink always helps.

"One thing's certain," I said. "Someone tried to break your neck, and you know why. Because you'd announced you had information to give me or Wharton."

His eyes were so firmly fixed on his glass, and he was thinking so hard that I guessed his thoughts. I was wrong, at least partly, for what he said surprised me.

"The curious thing is that when I came to think it over afterwards, I thought it wasn't important at all. I wish I hadn't mentioned it."

"What was it?" I asked.

"No, really, Travers. It was nothing. I made a mistake."

I smiled. "All the more reason you should tell me what it was."

But he stood his ground, and I knew why. He was scared dead stiff. The suddenness of that attack in the dark had absolutely demoralised him, and his nerve had completely gone. In the morning, he said, he would apologise to everybody about making a mistake.

"Listen to me, Collect," I said. "Someone tried to kill you. Is that someone going to believe you? Won't he consider it a put-up job?" I shook my head. "You and I are going to the Colonel, and you're either going away for a day or so, or be under protection till Wharton gets back."

"No, no," he said quickly. "I won't have that. I won't have the Colonel told."

I let out a breath. "Very well then. Here's my ultimatum. If you don't tell me what you were referring to at this afternoon's talk, then I shall go to the Colonel."

He refused, so I got to my feet.

"Well, it was this," he said, and by the way he avoided my eyes I knew he was lying. "I thought I saw Ferris looking for the Blacker bomb."

"I see," I said. "And what was unusual about that? Wasn't he the kind of person who ought to look for it?"

You never saw anyone more grateful for such a suggestion.

"I know. That's why I realised afterwards that it was silly of me to have mentioned it."

I thought for a moment or two, then got to my feet again.

"Well, we'll keep it to ourselves. If you care to apologise in the morning, do so, but if I were you I'd slip a gun in my tunic pocket and keep it there. You've got a gun?"

He was only too eager to show me his automatic, and then I think he rather guessed what I was thinking about him, for he tried to be heroic and said he could look after himself.

"When you're in here alone, lock that door," I said. "Put that gun under your pillow to-night, and every night till Wharton comes back. How're you feeling now? Fairly all right?"

He said he was, though the hand that held the glass was still shaking. I said I'd get him a gargle for his throat, and he said it wasn't the throat exactly, but the larynx that seemed to be hurt. What he'd pretend was that he had a cold. In the morning it ought to be easier.

I left him like that, and I was feeling like a man who has been given three urgent jobs to do at once, and knows he's making a hopeless mix-up and muddle of each. But I did slip my own loaded gun into the pocket of my British warm. Whoever had been trying to kill Collect must have known my voice. It would follow therefore that if I had rescued Collect, then Collect must have told me all he knew. Therefore the assailant of Collect now had two objectives—Collect and myself.

I made a careful way to the cinema. One of Flick's men was operating, but a minute or two later I saw Flick near the projector. I had edged along the wall and taken a seat somewhere at the middle left-hand side, and as the picture was one I had seen before, my thoughts were switching back to what had just happened. I asked myself what it was that Collect was concealing. I could admit that there was reason for him to have the wind up, for the experience must have been a terrifying one, but that was no reason why he should have lied about the information in his possession, or have refused so adamantly to go with me to the Colonel.

Then suddenly I had an idea that made me fumble at my glasses. Was it all a fabrication on Collect's part? More than possible, I thought. He knew I was going to the picture, for he had heard me say so at dinner. Then he might have waited at a convenient distance till he saw me emerge from my room, after which there was only to make gurgling noises, fall on the ground, shriek, and, when I came nearer, try to get up and be clutching a supposedly injured throat, the redness and bruises on which had been made by himself. What about the trembling? Once more perhaps a case of turgid and easily summoned emotion. Collect's nerves were on edge and it was easy therefore to counterfeit shock. And, most peculiar of all, when I had driven him into a corner with my ultimatum about going to the Colonel, he had said his information was only about Ferris looking for the bomb. Since my first suspicions against him had been *his* looking for the bomb, didn't that show which way his thoughts were running?

So satisfied was I with that theory that I stopped worrying about Collect's safety. When Wharton came back I would report on what had supposedly happened, and George could take what action he liked. As I was thinking that, the film came to an end and up went the lights. I hooked my glasses on again and had a decorous look round, Flick was standing by the projector. Nurse Wilton was not in her usual seat. Staff and Mortar's successor were a row or two in front of me. Then as I looked round to the right, there was Ferris kneeing his way along my row. His shoes, I noticed, were perfectly clean.

"Hallo, Ferris," I said. "Enjoying the show?"

"The new stuff's just coming on," he said, and took the seat beside me. "Poor house to-night."

"That's because Peakridge is in bounds on a Sunday," I said, and then off went the lights again, and since the film—a Russian one—had a sound track, we didn't say a word till it was run off, by which time it was twenty-two hours and closing time. We waited till the exit rush was over. Ferris was bound for the Mess so we strolled across together.

"What'd you think of the Reverend's performance this afternoon?" he suddenly asked.

"Damned if I know," I said. "In any case Collect's confidences are for Wharton, not me."

"If you ask me," he said, "he's trying to grind some axe of his own. He's got his knife into somebody and he's out to make capital of something he's seen. He's a vindictive old devil."

"We're none of us perfect," I remarked sententiously. "But, confidentially, how's that idea of yours coming along? The one I was supposed to give you."

That irritating sneer crept into his tone.

"That's rather private, just at present. And what about your own theory? The one I was mixed up in."

"Very much private," I said. "Never have a theory, Ferris, unless you can side-step it. Theories, like many other things, should never be allowed to become obsessions."

"Meaning that I have obsessions?"

"Don't get touchy," I told him. "Have a drink instead." Flick was already at the bar and his shoes were reasonably clean. In the morning, I told myself, I would have a good look at that spot where the attack on Collect had supposedly taken place.

Collect was not at breakfast. There was nothing surprising about that, for breakfast was an irregular sort of meal, but I did have a lucky word with Compress as we came out.

"He's got rather a bad throat," he said, "and I'm keeping him in bed for a bit." He glanced round and his voice lowered. "I think he's been experimenting with the old-fashioned remedy of tying a stocking round it and he's rather overdone it."

I was gathering that Collect had found some method of hood-winking the doctor, but I made no comment, for I was too busy trying to locate the spot where the attack was supposed to have taken place. But the whole of that area, lying as it did in a direct line between living quarters and lecture- and dining-rooms, was a mass of footprints, and as I didn't want to be seen making a close examination, I did no more in the matter.

I was busy, too, that morning, for I had to run into Peakridge to make final arrangements about Feeder's funeral. Then I dropped in at the police station, and at a very lucky moment.

"We were just trying to get you at the camp," the station-sergeant told me. "This message just came in."

It was from the Yard, but it conveyed very little to me, except that Feeder's registered parcel had been traced and inquiries were proceeding. So off I went back to the camp again. The Colonel agreed that perhaps we ought to have buglers at the funeral, though he drew the line at a detachment, and I didn't tell him that I had made my own arrangements about wreaths. Then I went along for a look at Collect, but Nurse Wilton said he was asleep.

"I haven't seen much of you lately," I said, with an attempt at roguishness.

"Whose fault is that?" she asked me.

The question was accompanied by a look so provocative that I believe I blushed.

"I hope it's mine," I said gallantly. "All the same, I don't know what we're going to do about it."

"Your wife keeping well?"

I blushed again, I hardly know why. She gave me a smile and a nod and left me with that parting shot. A most attractive woman, I couldn't for the life of me help thinking. Then I was wondering just where she came into Wharton's scheme of things. And that reminded me of something else. I still had no idea who was Wharton's pet suspect.

Well, the afternoon was even more melancholy than Mortar's funeral had been, for a drizzling rain had come on. I had brought the buglers in the car, and when we got back to camp I found a message that Harness wanted me. He had a telephonic communication from Wharton, forwarded from Peakridge, and it was in telegraphic form.

*Hope return afternoon to-morrow Tuesday Stop Announce to-morrow have seen Emerald Stop Am not hopeful.*

*Democrat*

"Nothing serious I hope, sir?" Harness said with a look of concern. I stopped frowning. Thanks to Wharton's ironic pseudonym he had no idea that the message wasn't private.

"Oh, no," I said. "Just a little personal matter."

But it was not till some minutes later that I had Wharton's cryptogram unravelled, at least to some sort of satisfaction. In the morning, and presumably not before, I was to let out that he had been in Ireland. What was definitely disheartening was the hint that inquiries there had gone none too well. Or was it that they had gone very well indeed, and George was taking preliminary precautions, and for his own inscrutable reasons, to conceal both evidence and results?

November had come in almost imperceptibly and one realized with something of a shock how early the nights were now drawing in. The Colonel had mentioned that we ought to make some modification of the time-table, and having an hour to pass, I went to his room after tea. His batman told me he was with Collect, so I thought I'd kill two birds with the one stone.

Collect was sitting up in his camp bed with a dressing-gown round his shoulders, and he and the Colonel had been having tea in the room. From the quick look that Collect gave me I judged that he was apprehensive of my letting something slip about the attack, but I played my part in the best tradition. He said he was feeling much better. The soreness had gone from the throat and he was hoping to be out and about in the morning. He also asked about Wharton and when he was coming back. I divulged to him and the Colonel that the return would probably be at lunch-time the next day.

We had a little chat and then the Colonel got up to go.

"Poor Collect," he said, as we walked a few yards to his room. "I'm afraid we shall be losing him. I didn't have the heart to tell him just now, but he has to report to the War Office on Wednesday."

"As a result of the report?" I asked.

"I'm afraid so," the Colonel said. "Still, I'm hoping they'll find him something to do."

I was a bit restless and excited that night and found sleep hard to come by. As I lay waiting for it to come I was thinking of a good many things: how the school had changed in a brief week or two, with Mortar and Feeder gone, and Collect going. As soon as Wharton arrived I would tell him of the attack on Collect, and maybe I would not add my suspicions but leave George to suggest himself that the attack had been a fake. Then I thought to myself that George would probably come by the early train from town, so I would take the car to Peakridge and meet him, even if it meant being very late for lunch.

In the dead middle of night I suddenly woke, and it seemed that I had heard stealthy footsteps. At once the gun was out from under my pillow and my finger was on the switch of the bedside lamp. There was another faint sound from somewhere outside and I listened, breath held, and then after some minutes of silence I got quietly out of bed and listened with my ear to the side partitions. There was never a sound from either room. Then I made sure that my door was really locked and got back into bed. Perhaps the excitement of the day had tired me, for when I next woke it was to the sound of my batman knocking at the door.

I was not aware of it, but the final day had dawned. At breakfast, when all the staff except Collect happened to be present, I mentioned in the general hearing that Wharton was due back at lunch-time or thereabouts. Harness helped me by asking if he'd been in town all the time.

"As a matter of fact," I said rather loudly; "his wire to me was from Ireland of all places. What he's been doing there I don't know, but there we are."

That started the Colonel off on some fishing experiences in Donegal, so that even if I had wished I could not have looked round to see how Wharton's erratic peregrinations had affected the high table. After breakfast I was giving my final lecture of the Course, and I was glad of that to pass my time. Then I mooned about generally till the hour had come to meet Wharton.

They told me at Peakridge that the train was running late on account of fog, and I had to wait on that cold, draughty station for an hour. Then when the local train drew in, Wharton was not on it after all. In the empty dining-room at the camp a waiter told me he had arrived by car soon after I had left, so I made a hurried meal and went in search of him. His bag was back in his room, but no one seemed to know where he was at the moment. Then Maisie Wilton, who was just off to the ranges and whose eyes were better than mine, asked if that wasn't he standing at the entrance to the magazine, talking to Store.

I met George on his way back and he pretended to be uncommonly glad to see me. In fact he hailed me like a long-lost brother, and was all apologies for my wasted lunch-hour.

"You went to Eire?" I asked.

"Well, yes," he admitted. "I went by plane."

"Good," I said. "What did you find out?"

He frowned. "It's hard to say. You wouldn't believe me, perhaps, but in one way we aren't much farther forward."

"In what way?"

"Well, there's nothing definite. There's nothing solid on which to take action. What I'm going to do is to test things out this evening."

"You're tighter than a clam," I told him. "What're you going to test? Somebody or *something*?"

"Both," he said. "If it doesn't work, then I'll take action to-morrow, and risk it."

We were entering his room and who should be there but two men fitting a telephone extension. George fussed round them for a minute or two and then was handed the receiver to make a final test.

"Hallo? That you, Store?"

Apparently it was, and I was wondering what the devil he was doing with a private line to Store's office, and where Store himself came in. Before I could prise out more of the clam, George was questioning me, and as if he were anxious to try out his new toy.

"You got this afternoon's time-table on you?"

I said I knew it by heart and at once he was asking where Flick was.

"Off duty," I said.

"Ferris?"

"On the ranges." I held up a finger. "You can hear the plopping. He and the new man and Brende are all there. And Compress and Nurse Wilton."

"Brende there? Damnation!" He clicked his tongue. "Well, I shall have to get him later. Collect hasn't been well, they tell me."

Then at last I was able to get in a few words. He listened with an extraordinary intentness to my story of the attack, and to my surprise made no suggestion of its having been a fake.

"I knew I was taking a risk," he said, and then glared at me. "See what I was talking about when I warned you to keep your eyes open? I told you it wasn't a laughing matter."

"What's this telephone for?" I asked bluntly.

"So that no one can listen in," he told me impatiently.

There was a tap at the door and in came the camp Quartermaster, carrying a huge thin something covered with brown paper.

"There you are," said Wharton delightedly. "All ready to get it fixed?"

It turned out to be a sheet of stout tin, painted black, and I saw at once that it was intended to make a safer black-out than had been afforded by the dark curtain. The Quartermaster bored holes at each corner of the window and one in the centre of the mullion.

"I'll leave you the screws and the screw-driver, sir," he told Wharton, "and then you can fix it for yourself."

"What about the corner?"

That was in order too, he was told, and I could see that Wharton had been referring to a corner that had been cut away from the tin, leaving a little triangle. I imagined at the time that there was some obstacle in the corner of the window round which it was designed to fit, but I couldn't see any too well.

George hid the tin and the screws behind the cupboard. Then he was putting on his greatcoat.

"What's the time?"

"A quarter past four," I said.

"Well, I'm going to be busy," he said, "and I'm late now. You listen and mind you don't slip up. Got a gun?"

I nodded.

"Keep it in your pocket, and load it. If you move in the dark and anybody tries any monkey tricks, stop him dead. Have tea in the dining-room and then go to your own room and stay there. See the black-out's perfect if you want the lights on, but it'd be better to sit in the dark. Don't open the door to anybody. You got that? Not to anybody—except me. I'll tap out that Victory sign with my knuckles. When you let me in, see no light is on, and don't say a word."

"At what time will it be?"

"Perhaps not at all. Perhaps soon after dusk."

I did what George told me and soon after seventeen hours I was in my room with the door locked. For once in my life I found nothing ridiculous in a situation that had more than a melodramatic touch. George's injunctions had been too curt and his face too grim for me to doubt the seriousness of things. I took his advice and had no lights on, though I did switch on the electric fire when I had made sure the black-out was perfect, for the room was icily cold. I also took good care to make no noise.

As the dusk merged into dark the suspense was becoming intolerable. My heart began to beat at an alarming rate. Then my restlessness grew beyond control, and on a sudden impulse I switched off the fire and tiptoed to the door and opened it to the merest slit. Towards the hospital was nothing but blackness, and I was telling myself that George's tin contraption was highly effective. In the same moment I saw a flash of light away in the distance by his room, and I knew someone was moving about with a torch.

The light flickered and came my way. I closed the door, quietly locked it again, and listened with my ear to the panel. The steps neared, passed my door and went on, but all the sounds were so faint that I could not tell if they had stopped or had moved to beyond earshot. What I did know was that my heart was racing like a mad thing and that my forehead was wet.

A quarter of an hour went by and then, with a noise that seemed a thunderclap, there was a rat-tat-tat-tat on the door. In a flash I had it open and George was nipping inside. As he did so I noticed something in the distance—a pin-point of light.

"Something wrong with your black-out," I whispered.

He hissed me to silence, then was motioning for me to get behind him. The pencil torch which he ran down the door showed me that in his other hand was a gun. Then I heard him gently opening the door. It opened outwards, and I could see over his bent shoulders, for he was leaning forward at the ready, like a man with his bayonet at the On Guard.

But what I could actually see was nothing at all, except that pin-point of light, and that was as big in the darkness as a sea beacon. Everywhere was an incredible quiet, and I remembered that the Home Guard were all in the lecture-room, listening to Compress's talk on first-aid.

We must have stood there for a good ten minutes, and the sound of my heart was like the thumping of a drum. Then George's hand went back and clutched mine as if to keep me back. Something was happening, but what it was I could neither see nor hear. Then a queer difference became apparent, and in the same second even the difference had gone, and I knew what had happened out there in the dark. Someone had passed in front of that pin-point of light and had obscured it, and had then passed on. Yet, I thought, it had not been as quick as that. It was rather as if someone had stopped in front of the window for a second or two before moving on. Maybe someone had seen the light and had gone to investigate, and was now' tapping at George's door to tell him the black-out was defective. Or perhaps—

There was a shattering roar! So sudden was it that I fell back, and so loud in the silence that it was as if silence itself was shattered. In the same infinitesimal fraction of a second there was a blinding flash. Before I knew it, Wharton was out of the door and his shout came from outside in the blackness of the night.

"Brende! . . . Brende! . . . Get him! GET HIM!!"

Torches were flashing everywhere, but for the life of me I could never have moved. *So it was Brende after all!* That's all I could think, and then suddenly my legs came to life again, and I was trying to run to the light where the torches all seemed congregated.

# Chapter XVII

"Is he hurt?" I heard Wharton saying. I could still X see nothing in spite of that circle of torchlights.

"His leg's badly cut, sir, but I got him with this all right."

It was Brende's voice!

"When you hollered, sir, I saw him dart my way and I just let out. I reckon you heard the crack."

"Tie him up and take no chances," Wharton said, and the light of the torches moved to a something black on the ground. I could not see a face, and then Wharton stopped and was wrenching off what I knew to be a mask. Then I saw the face. It was Ferris's.

"Get him to the police van," Wharton was snapping. "Say I'll be along in half a jiff. Brende, you double back to the lecture-room and say what I told you. Just a bit of routine explosion ready for to-night's stunt. You come with me, Store, and see if there's any mess to clear up in my room."

I followed at their heels. George switched on the light as he went in, and I could see holes in the curtain and more in the ceiling. Some of the plaster was on the ground, but a more curious thing was something like a guy on a chair with its back to the window.

"Get everything cleared up," George was telling Store. "And fill up that hole outside before they get out of the lecture-room."

Then he seemed to see me for the first time.

"Get the car, will you? You'll find it round by the main gate. I'll be along in a minute."

It wasn't as quick as that, but in less than five minutes we were on our way to Peakridge, and George at last was spilling all the beans.

"I had my eye on Master Ferris from the first," he began.

"George," I cut in. "I'm only too anxious to hear your story, but if anybody else made that opening statement I'd call him a liar."

He chuckled. "I didn't want to hurt your feelings. Whenever we begin a case and you start telling me that So-and-so couldn't possibly have done something, he's the one I look out for."

"You're quibbling," I said. "You had inside information before you got down here at all. You knew Ferris beforehand."

"No I didn't," he said. "I knew no more than I told you. You drive this car and let me do the talking."

So I kept my mouth shut and he got going. In Ireland, he said, they knew all about that attack of many years before, when a rebel headquarters had been blown up, though they didn't know the name of the Black and Tan officer who had done it even if they suspected that his detachment had been operating from as far afield as Mallanaghar. What mattered was that the house blown up was a place known as Kildurin Lodge, and it had been officially occupied at the time by a Hernando Ferrova and his wife and two young children. Ferrova was a Spanish engineer who was engaged on irrigation work for the Government. His other son, Manuel, happened to be staying with nearby friends at the time. Ferrova's wife was English, though of Irish extraction, and the whole family perished in the explosion, together with all the Republicans who had made the Lodge their headquarters.

Manuel went to Liverpool to live with his mother's only sister. When she died he went to his father's people in Spain. Later he returned to England and did journalistic work, and also became naturalised. That was his history as far as it could be traced, except, of course, that he had done exceptionally well in the war in Spain, and that after that war the War Office had thought him a useful man to employ. Ferrova changed his name to Ferris, and was apparently willing enough. Probably his aunt had impressed that tragedy of his youth on his mind, but if he had been brought up by her to make revenge his life's ambition, then that ambition must have dulled, for it is hard work maintaining a hatred for a man whose very name you do not know and who might have been dead for years.

"He doubtless still had it in mind though," Wharton said. "You remember how he always laid his hatred of Germans against the door of what they'd done to Spain, not what'd they done to England. You told me you found that curious. Well, perhaps he hated the English far less than he did the Germans, and that was why he was willing to show the English how to kill Germans.

"Then he came down here and found out that Mortar was the one who had wiped out his family. I'd say he made himself even more friendly with Mortar and Feeder, and got the whole story out of them, and when he was plumb sure, he made up his mind to get rid of them. He was going to blow Mortar to hell, just as his own father had been killed. I'd say that Northover affair was his first attempt. Brende swore it was his gun, you remember, and Ferris heard Mortar's boast about throwing away a Mills. When that attempt failed, Ferris covered it up with an attempt on himself. He lifted a Mills from the magazine and fixed the booby-trap overnight. He knew where the string was and you bet he had his eyes on it while he walked and talked."

"I ought to have known that," I had to cut in. "That explanation he gave for the Mills was far too pat. And it was amazing he should throw himself on the ground just at the right fraction of a second.

"Even when I'd worked all that out on my way back from Ireland," George went on, "I still knew I hadn't much of a case, though I had a first-class motive. Everything was deduction and there wasn't a vast amount of circumstantial evidence, even including the fact that Store had missed a Mills. Still, I told the Powers-that-Be just how things were and how I thought it best to lay a trap for Ferris. They gave me a free hand at once.

"Then after I'd left them I got some more news. He must have made up his mind to kill Mortar on the Saturday, and not before. It was Mortar's birthday and Ferris saw how he could make everything fit in, especially if Feeder were out of the way and Mortar were really tight. On the Saturday, then, he had the bomb ready, and he removed his stamps; but he couldn't send them away till the Monday because he daren't run the risk of posting in camp, and he couldn't get away to Peakridge. So he got Feeder to post the parcel for him on the Monday. Feeder, like Mortar, was absolutely under his thumb, and he told them to keep it all very secret. The parcel was actually sent to a friend of Ferris's, now in the Service. This friend has a safe deposit box in town and Ferris asked him to put the parcel in it for him.

"Ferris got Staff to keep in his room partly to incriminate him and also to know just where he was at the vital time. He also had lifted a cordite cartridge which he chucked in the ruins the next morning to bring Staff still more in. He also threw suspicion on Flick, whom you saw carrying something past the hut that night.

"As for Feeder, his number was up as soon as you offered to take him on as batman. Ferris didn't dare have him in your company, where he might spill the beans about that Irish affair. Feeder was money for jam. He wasn't too strong on brains, as you know, and all Ferris had to do was make out he knew who'd killed Mortar, and he could get Feeder to do anything to wipe the killer out. So Ferris got him to lift a gun and spin that yarn to Brende about Mortar having the bomb in his room. Perhaps Ferris hoped we'd abandon the inquiry when Feeder's yarn to Brende made the whole thing out as an accident. Then he got Feeder to meet him at the stack, and that was that, except that he slipped up on too many things."

That was all at the moment, for we were coming into Peakridge. At the police station George nipped out and I parked the car. When I walked in there was no sign of him, but they put me in a room with a fire and I had a half-hour to wait. When he found me he said everything was done and we might as well be getting back.

"How was Ferris?" I asked him.

"Not in very good shape," he said. "Brende gave him a hell of a wallop on the skull with that Indian club. His leg's pretty bad, too, where the blast caught it."

I began putting on my British warm again. "It's funny about Ferris, George? I still can't think for the life of me how he managed to kill Mortar without giving the show away to me. It couldn't have been a time bomb, for I'd have heard the clock or the mechanism ticking. If it'd been a booby-trap, there'd have been a risk of my moving about in Mortar's room and setting it off. And Ferris was as natural as you and I are at this moment."

"You mean to say you don't know how it was done?" he said, peering at me from under his shaggy eyebrows.

"I've just told you so."

He chuckled. "So the Old Gent's one up on you, is he?"

Then he was making free use of the telephone that stood on the side table. It connected apparently with the main office, for he was asking to be put on to the school.

"Yes," he said. "Ask for Quartermaster-Sergeant Store. Say it's urgent."

Then he was telling me to get the car round to the front. It was a palpable excuse to get me out of the room so that I should not hear what he was concocting with Store, not that I minded about that. So I went out to the car, and then as my hand fell on the ice-cold metal of the door handle, something flashed into my mind—that nightmare that had kept me awake for best part of a night. The Yard expert had reported that at the time of the explosion Mortar had been on his back!

As I waited in the car for George I began to put things together. It was a quarter of an hour's wait and long before it was over I thought I knew just how Mortar had been killed. The devilish ingenuity of it was making me wince and I was glad when George at last appeared. He was so obviously pleased with himself at what he had been arranging with Store that not for the world would I have spoiled his fun. When he told me to drive slowly I knew that something was being prepared against my return, and I was also remembering something about which I as yet knew little.

"What was the trap you laid for Ferris?" I asked.

"Oh, that," said George. "The first thing was to connect up with Store by telephone so that Store couldn't have been seen reporting anything to me or Harness. Later on I had to take Brende into my confidence and arrange for him to place a picked lot of men. I got Flick and Staff out of the way with a job of work in the stores, and I induced the Colonel and Collect to attend Compress's lecture. Nurse Wilton would be there in any case. Then I got the camp Quartermaster to make me that metal black-out arrangement. At a suitable time I sent for Ferris, and I don't mind telling you I had my gun handy while he was in the room. As soon as he came in I drew the black-out curtains, and rather carelessly, so as to impress on his mind that there was nothing between us and the outside air but a sheet of glass and a bit of thin, black material. I sat with my back to the window and said I was sorry to trouble him; in fact I wouldn't keep him at all, but there was an official communication I'd like him to read in his own room. He took the envelope, gave me a queer look, and out he went.

"When he read that communication he had a shock. I talked a lot of balderdash about friendship, and my young nephew and so on, and said nobody knew a word but myself, and I shouldn't spill the beans till after dinner that night. Then I told him more or less what I'd discovered, and that gave him two choices—to bolt or to wipe me out before I told what I knew. He did what I expected, that is, he tried to get me.

"No sooner did he leave my room than I slipped the metal sheet under the curtain. The corner was purposely cut off so that anyone could just see in from outside. Then I rigged up a tunic with an arm nicely visible from outside. When Store rang me up to say that Ferris had been to the magazine and gone again in a hurry after being in the neighbourhood of the Millses I slipped into your room, coming round the back way.

"You know what happened. Ferris slipped on a mask—the one he'd probably made for attacking Collect and keeping his mouth shut—and moved out to reconnoitre. A quick peep showed me still at my table, so he stepped back, pulled out the pin, let the lever go and waited two seconds before smashing the bomb through the window. That required some nerve, and he had it. What he didn't know was that the metal sheet made the bomb come back at him. It didn't kill him but it made his leg a nasty mess. Even so he tried to bolt, but unluckily for him he ran slap into Brende with that Indian club."

That was Wharton's story, and it may have read a bit academic, for I haven't told it in his own words. You have also had to imagine the derisive chuckles, the triumphant snortings, and the calculated deprecations. There was more such to follow when we got out of the car and he announced meekly—and as I had anticipated—that there was something he wanted in my room. He wouldn't keep me a minute, he said, for he had endless telephoning to do. He wouldn't even be able to get along to dinner but would have something sent to his room. He kept prattling on till we were at the hut and it was too late for me to do any talking or even interpose a question. Store was waiting there.

"There you are then, Store," he said mildly. "Come along in, will you? Major Travers wants us to show him something."

I realised that I must have left the door unlocked. Store switched on the light and I simulated an enormous surprise.

"What the devil's been happening to my room?"

"Just rigging it up like Captain Mortar's room was that night," Store told me, with a look at Wharton as if to put the blame on him.

It was a good imitation at least. The camp bed was by the partition, the chair just inside the door and my trunk near the end of the bed. Probably there were wires artistically hidden, but I daren't look for fear of giving the game away.

"Remember to keep your mouth shut about this," Wharton said, and wagged a monitory finger at Store. "Now this is what happened. You and Ferris left Mortar on that chair. What he was going to do ultimately was to get into bed, and the time-interval gave Ferris time to get away, and you with him. He didn't want anything to happen to you because you were the sole support of his alibi. Right, then. Mortar did get into bed, and we know by some of the fibres that were in his remains that he must have stripped at once and put on his pyjamas. You get on the bed yourself and lie down just as he did."

"No booby-traps?" I felt compelled to say.

He snorted contemptuously, so I made no more ado but went through the motions of getting into bed, just as I was. I pulled down the blankets, sat down gingerly and then shot out my whole length. The bed creaked and sagged, and at once there was a pop?

"Good Lord!" I said, as I hopped out. "What was that?"

George was chuckling away and digging Store in the ribs. "You ought to thank heaven it wasn't a Mills," he told me. "Remember asking Store to make you a gadget like the one he showed us? This is it. He had it all ready." The gadget was simplicity itself; just a piece of rounded wood like a piece of broomstick, stuck in a tin which exactly fitted it. At its bottom was metal to which wires were soldered, and they were connected with a baby detonator. When Mortar was blown up similar wires had been connected to the detonator of the Blacker bomb. At the bottom of the tin were more wires connected with the power-plug of the electric stove, and all one had to do was leave a good space between the bottom of the wooden stick and the bottom of the tin, and everything was perfectly safe. Ferris put the whole contraption under Mortar's bed, with the top of the stick—which might be called the plunger—in actual contact with the wire mattress of the camp bed, so that everything was held in place.

When Mortar got into bed, then you can see what happened. The wire mattress would creak and sag, and when his full weight was on it, it would press down the plunger and make contact. Off would go the bomb, and, since the home-made plunger was set close up against the bomb, it would be blown to powder and never a trace of it would ever be found.

I pretended to be suitably overcome at the discovery, and Store was thanked and departed with his contraption, Wharton asking him to have it handy in case he wanted to borrow it again.

"That was a hellish cold-blooded business, George," I couldn't help saying.

"He was a hellish cold-blooded chap," Wharton said. "Everything he did was sheer devilish calculation. If he hadn't killed Feeder, or if he'd sacrificed his precious stamps, we'd never have found him out." He shook his head. "He was like Hitler and the Dictators. Couldn't afford to be static. Mind you, I believe he intended to kill both Mortar and Feeder in any case. Both had been concerned in killing his own parents, and Feeder was due to be polished off even before you offered to take him on as batman. Then there was Collect to be wiped out because he knew too much, and then I had to be wiped out. You'd have been too, if I hadn't warned you."

"Maybe I would," I said. "But I think Ferris spared me because I was such an obvious fool. I honestly was a fool," I went on. "I ought to have seen a dozen things that I missed. I don't want to make excuses for myself, except perhaps this. Even my brains aren't what they were. When you spend your time trying to keep up with Army Council amendments and deletions, you suffer from chronic thinkers' cramp. Those three lectures of mine are pretty hard work.

"What's up now?" I asked, for he was staring.

"I just remembered," he said. "That lecture of mine."

"Yes," I said, with as much regret as I could summon. "In the morning I suppose you'll be away and gone. That lecture was down for the afternoon."

"Oh?" he said, and glared at me. "Why should I be away and gone? I'm down for the lecture, aren't I?"

"George," I said. "Don't tell me you're going to waste the taxpayers' money again? Flying about all over the place in aeroplanes, and now clinging on here and taking a holiday and making out it's to do with a lecture." He chuckled, and then his face straightened and he was giving me another stare. "What do you mean, keeping me here talking? Haven't I got enough work to do to keep me up half the night."

Muttering to himself he went off. I reorganised the room to my liking, and before I had half finished the job I could think of several things to which I should like to find answers. But the answers were not to come till the morning.

# Epilogue

IN THE MORNING George was closeted with the Colonel before breakfast and he didn't come in for his meal till I had almost finished mine. After breakfast Harness sent round a chit to be signed by all officers of the staff, as well as Brende and Store: the Colonel's compliments and he would be glad if all the under-mentioned would make it convenient to attend Captain Wharton's lecture at fifteen hours.

Now I knew that George had an exceedingly agile mind, yet I was very much alarmed. Everything in the Army had altered since his day. I had read scores of secret and other documents on Security, as well as A.C.I.s, none of which had been or were now available for him; how on earth he was going to deliver a lecture on Security fairly beat me. If I had to give one myself I calculated I should need all the documents and a week's research.

At what I thought might be a suitable time I went to his room, and there he was, undoubtedly preparing his lecture. He looked, in fact, rather like a backward urchin making his first attempt at a subtraction sum, except that he wasn't actually licking his pencil. "Anything I can do to help, George?" I said.

I had never seen him look so exasperated.

"Anyone'd think there wasn't a war till this one. What do you know about Security in any case?"

"All right, George," I said. "I'll go quietly—if you'll tell me just one thing. Why did you take Maisie to the cinema that night? You needn't glare and you needn't deny it," I went on. "Why did you take her to the pictures?"

Then he pretended he'd just remembered. "Oh, that," he said. "Just thought I'd let her know Flick was married, so as to see how she took it."

"I see," I said. "And you tried to pump her afterwards. You took advantage of her indignation."

"I don't know about that," he said. "I didn't get anything out of her, if that's what you want to know."

"Well, you've queered Flick's pitch," I said, recalling the brief scene at the hospital corner. "I don't think he'll be taking her out to the long grass any more. You're sure I can't help you, George?"

He gave me such a look that I left him hurriedly. In the Mess Shorty made me some coffee; while I was drinking it, who should come in but Collect, all dressed up. Out went his hand.

"Here you are then," he said. "I was looking for you to say good-bye. Just off to the War Office."

I shook hands and wished him the best of luck. As I came out with him, on a very sudden impulse I asked him a question.

"Tell me something, Collect, will you, and in the strictest confidence. You saw Ferris looking for that bomb, didn't you?"

"Yes," he said, looking rather surprised.

"I saw you looking for it," I told him. "Ever since then I've wondered why."

He smiled a bit sheepishly, and was still hesitating. "Well," he said. "I hardly expect you will believe me, but this is why. Everybody said it was dangerous to look for it, so I thought it might be a feather in my cap if I located it. I was getting a bit tired of hearing about fighting soldiers so I wanted to show them what an old veteran could do."

"Splendid," I said. "I wish to heaven you *had* found it."

Off he went to the waiting car and somehow I was feeling far more kindly disposed towards him, and not because he was leaving us. Part was due to a species of shame at my having doubted his word about that attack, and I actually found myself wishing that the War House would find him a snug appointment among the elect, where camouflage was a thing one read about and the presence of a Blacker bomb would have caused a panic. Not a bad sort in his way, old Collect.

There was still another question to be answered, and that answer came towards the end of the morning. Everybody was on the ranges, and when I looked in the lecture-room nobody was there but Flick, tinkering with the cinema projector. He came over to me at once.

"Is it true now, Major," he said, "what everyone's saying, that Ferris bumped off Mortar?"

I frowned heavily and mentioned something about confidential information.

"Ah, now, Major," he told me cajolingly. "You know I'd never be after telling a word."

"Good," I said. "Then I'll swop information with you, for I'll never be after telling a word either, bedad. You tell me first what it was that you were carrying that Saturday night when you left Maisie Wilton and came round by the end of the hut."

He stared. "Carrying something?"

"Yes," I said. "Ferris and I saw you. He tried to make out it was his two books of stamps you'd lifted from his room."

"Did he," he said. "The dirty unmentionable."

He scowled ferociously, shaking his head again. "I'll tell you what it was I was carrying," he said, and picked up two of the Sorbo seats. "Keep that to yourself, Major, or I'm ruined entirely." Then he winked. "The country round here is a bit hard on the backside."

I smiled, for I knew why Maisie Wilton had been so hot and bothered when I asked what Flick had been carrying. "I see. One for you and one for the lady. Sure you took two and not one?"

"Sure it was two," he said, putting them back on their chairs. But he said nothing about hoping there'd only be one some other time. I told him just a little about Ferris and left him with his eyes popping. As I made my way across the parade ground, I couldn't help thinking that Flick, too, was not such a bad chap after all. Besides, wasn't he, with myself, the sole remaining representative of the Not-so-Regulars?

*     *     *     *     *

Well, fifteen hours came at last and there was a full gathering, with the Colonel occupying the front pew, and I at his elbow. Wharton was absolutely in his element. Flick had done something to the lights that made them more concentrated on the platform, and much as I feared for the up-to-dateness and even usefulness of George's matter, I knew that he knew that he was having the chance of his life.

When he did get on his pins, he swindled all of us, as I might have known he would have done. He had donned his antiquated glasses, and he peered at us from over their tops. A pin could have been heard to fall.

"I regret to say, gentlemen, that I have been called away by the War Office on another appointment, and so this will be my first and last lecture. Under the circumstances I thought it best not to deliver one of those official talks I had prepared, all dry as dust and up-to-date, so perhaps you'll forgive me if I try to be interesting instead."

And straightaway he was back at the days when he was an Intelligence Officer on the Western Front. I heard for the umpteenth time the story of the German spy, but the audience lapped it up, as I did the first time I heard it. There were the other spy stories and even glimpses of the Special Branch, and altogether his lecture was a riot. The Colonel told me afterwards that Wharton was just the man the school needed, and I heard Staff say languidly to Flick; "Well, he mayn't be orthodox, but he can certainly spin a damn' good yarn."

At the very end George conformed to precedent and asked his audience if there were any questions. I had a perfect snorter on the tip of my tongue, and one that would have tied even him in the very devil of a knot. But I didn't ask it. I even joined vociferously in the final applause. After all we democrats have to stand by each other.

THE END

9 781912 574155